RISING DARKNESS

Books by Nancy Mehl

From Bethany House Publishers

ROAD TO KINGDOM

Inescapable
Unbreakable
Unforeseeable

FINDING SANCTUARY

Gathering Shadows
Deadly Echoes
Rising Darkness

FINDING SANCTUARY, BOOK 3

RISING DARKNESS

NANCY MEHL

BETHANYHOUSE
a division of Baker Publishing Group
Minneapolis, Minnesota

Published by Bethany House Publishers
11400 Hampshire Avenue South
Bloomington, Minnesota 55438
www.bethanyhouse.com

Bethany House Publishers is a division of
Baker Publishing Group, Grand Rapids, Michigan

Printed in the United States of America

Library of Congress Cataloging-in-Publication Data

Mehl, Nancy.
Rising darkness / Nancy Mehl.
pages ; cm. — (Finding sanctuary ; 3)
Summary: "Years after leaving her Mennonite background, Sophie's newspaper job gives her access to information she can't ignore, and when she travels to Sanctuary, Missouri, for answers and recognizes a man she used to love, her own past gets tangled in the dangerous investigation"— Provided by publisher.
ISBN 978-0-7642-1159-1 (softcover)
1. Mennonites—Fiction. 2. Women journalists—Fiction. 3. Man-woman relationships—Fiction. I. Title. 2015
813′.6—dc23 2015015705

Cover design by Dan Pitts

Nancy Mehl is represented by The Steve Laube Agency.

15 16 17 18 19 20 21 7 6 5 4 3 2 1

To the One who takes away our ashes
and gives us beauty instead.

PROLOGUE

The look on Snake's face when the bullet hit his chest was burned into Terry's mind. No one was supposed to die. They had planned it so carefully. He silently ran over the list in his head: Wait for the guard. Follow him inside. Tie up the guards. Get the money. Get out. It had seemed so easy. One of the guards was working with them, and they'd assumed the other guard would hand over the money without a struggle. But that hadn't happened. Now two guards were dead, and Snake was barely clinging to life.

Terry looked down at his own arm. Thankfully, the bullet had gone right through. It was still bleeding, but he would recover. Snake had caught the worst of it. He couldn't even remember Snake's real name. Did he have a family? He seemed to remember him mentioning a sister, but he had no idea where she was. Did the guards have families? He swore under his breath. Of course they did. Everyone had a family, didn't they? Except for him.

He suddenly noticed his speed. Ten miles over the limit. He slowed down, allowing other cars to whiz past. He couldn't risk being pulled over.

He glanced again at Snake. He was pale and breathing quickly. What could he do to save his partner? Where could he get help? Had the car been reported stolen yet? How much time did he have?

Although it was risky, he decided to take Snake to a doctor he trusted. He'd convince him to help the injured man, if it wasn't too late. He'd seen death before, and Snake was as close to the abyss as anybody could get. He hoped the doc would be quick. He needed to clean up, divide the money, ditch the car, and lie low for a while. Thankfully, he had a friend who'd agreed to hide him until the heat died down. Then he'd buy another car and head to his next destination. A place where he could disappear. A place so safe no one would ever find him.

He had no intention of letting Snake know where he was going. If Snake lived, he couldn't risk giving him too much information. His crimes had graduated beyond theft now. He could face the death penalty.

He ran over everything in his mind once again. Even though he was almost sure he hadn't left anything behind that could lead to his capture, he was smart enough to know that nothing in life was certain. All it took was one slip. One forgotten detail. If he could just get through the next few days while the city of St. Louis buzzed with the story of one of the greatest crimes it had ever seen, his plan would play out. Once he got to Sanctuary, he could fade into the background, disappearing until the world forgot all about him.

CHAPTER ONE

There was something about the smell of a prison that made me feel an almost overwhelming urge to run. It wasn't the high fences that surrounded the facility in El Dorado, Kansas, or the dour-faced security guards, or even the electronic doors that slid shut behind me as I made my way to the room where visitors met with inmates. For some reason, it was the sharp aroma of bleach and disinfectant that made me feel as if something dark lurked beneath the unpleasant smell.

I glanced around the large room at the other visitors who had come to meet with prisoners. Although most of the conversations seemed relaxed, even friendly, there was something about the men who wouldn't be walking out the front door when their visit was over. The panic in their eyes that came from the reality of knowing there was no way out. I shivered involuntarily and stared down at the cold, white tabletop. Even though it was only March, the air-conditioning in the room was turned up high. I pulled my jacket tighter around me, trying not to shake.

The door to the room opened, and a guard led a man in. I almost didn't recognize him. Tom Ford had changed. His dark, greasy hair was cut short, and his acne-scarred face had cleared. He was still small, but his matchstick-thin arms now had muscles. It seemed bizarre to think he was actually healthier now than he had been as a free man. He didn't meet my gaze as he approached the table where I waited for him. When he sat down, the chains around his ankles rattled.

"He needs to be back in his cell in thirty minutes," the guard said brusquely before he turned and walked over to stand next to another guard who leaned against the wall. I smiled at them but was rewarded with blank stares. I had the distinct feeling they felt the friends and family of prisoners were as guilty as their charges—as if they were somehow responsible for their criminal behavior.

The guard who had led Tom into the visitors' room watched me with narrowed eyes, his expression bordering on antagonism. His attention made me uncomfortable, so I swung my gaze back to Tom, who appeared to be ignoring me. I began to feel claustrophobic and extremely uncomfortable.

Finally, Tom looked up and frowned at me. "You're that reporter from the newspaper in St. Louis, right? When you called here, I told you not to come. That I changed my mind."

I nodded and swallowed several times, trying to calm my ragged nerves.

"Why didn't you listen? It's not like anyone's beatin' down the doors to talk to me. No one else even bothered to answer my letters."

I took a deep breath. "I want to hear what you have to say." My voice was nearly a whisper, and I forced myself to breathe in and out slowly. I had an important task to accomplish. I needed to focus and finish what I came to do.

"I was wrong to write to your paper," Tom said gruffly. "Terrance Chase is dead."

"Did your letter have anything to do with that special on TV?" I asked.

He didn't respond, just stared down at the table.

"That show brought a lot of attention to the robbery—and Chase. What did you see that prompted you to write to us?"

Still no answer. Just a cold glare, probably designed to make me back off.

"Over six million dollars stolen. Two guards dead, along with Chase's partner."

No reaction. I met his gaze head-on.

"You don't recognize me, do you?" I said finally.

"I ain't never met you. I'd remember."

I managed a small smile. "The name Sophie Bauer didn't help?"

He shook his head. "Still don't know you."

"I'm Sophie. Sophie Wittenbauer."

He still looked confused, and I wanted to slap him.

"From Kingdom?" Bringing up the small Mennonite town in Kansas where I'd grown up made my stomach clench. Breaking free from that place had been the best thing I'd ever done, and I was certain everyone in Kingdom felt the same way.

This time his jaw dropped, and recognition chased away his perplexity. "You look totally different. Your hair's different. And you're not . . ." He colored and pursed his lips.

"Fat?"

I'd had my ugly, dishwater-blond hair cut short and streaked. Now I wore it in a cute bob I felt looked good on me. Of course, losing so much weight had changed me more than anything else. And trading my one simple, faded, dirty black dress for attractive modern clothes made a world of difference, too. Thinking about the dress I'd worn in Kingdom—two sizes too small and with a hem that reached to my ankles—made my stomach turn over. I would never be that person again. Gone was the unkempt teenager I had once been. And good riddance.

"You look different, too," I said.

He nodded. "Prison will do that to you."

"So will changing your life." I clasped my hands together on top of the table because I didn't know what else to do with them. "After I left Kingdom, I got my GED. I'm working my way through college and will earn a degree in a little over a year. Right now I'm working for the *St. Louis Times*." I neglected to tell him my current assignment was obituaries and the occasional restaurant review. But hopefully, Tom Ford would be my ticket to writing bigger stories. Stories that mattered.

He stared off into the distance. "Yeah, I understand. I'm hopin' to get another chance someday, too. But right now I'm lookin' at a long stretch." His eyes locked on mine. "That's why I wrote those letters. Thought maybe my information about Terrance Chase might get me a deal. But nobody believed me. Nobody even got back to me. Until you, that is."

"There have been a lot of rumors about Terrance Chase. Especially after that TV special. But most of the information has been bogus. Just people wanting to insert themselves into the investigation. The overwhelming belief is that Chase is dead. An old friend of his swears to it. Says Chase was ambushed and killed. The money taken."

Tom shrugged. "Maybe I was wrong. Wouldn't be the first time."

I sighed. "Look, Tom. I saw a copy of your letter. You sounded convinced that Chase is alive, and that you know where he is. Then suddenly you change your mind? It doesn't make sense. Are you afraid of something?"

Tom grunted. "In here?" His gaze darted around the room and then came back to settle on me. The bold, cocky expression he'd been exhibiting slipped a notch. His voice was so soft, I could barely hear him say, "Of course I'm afraid."

A chill ran through me. I wanted this story. Even if I had to lie. "You don't have to worry," I said, ignoring a brief twinge of conscience. "Talk to me off the record. I won't print anything you don't want me to. But if you give me something I can use to find Chase, I could go to bat for you. You know, try to get you a reduced sentence."

His eyes narrowed. "I'll need more than that. You gotta get me outta here, Sophie. Less time and a new prison. Someplace where no one knows me. I . . . I feel like I'm being watched all the time. Ever since I sent those letters."

Part of me wanted to tell him the truth. That I had no ability to help him. That I was just a peon at the paper. But what came out of my mouth was fueled by my determination to be *somebody.* To prove I wasn't the worthless human being my father had told me I was. An image of his leering face floated through my mind, and I felt ill. "You have my word. I'll do everything I can to protect you. My paper has a lot of contacts. With people who can help you."

He appeared to consider my offer. Once again his eyes scanned the room. The tension in his expression tugged at my emotions, but I couldn't back down now.

"Tell me why you changed your mind about sharing what you know," I said. "And tell me the truth."

He took a deep breath and let it out slowly. "I got a note. Found it stuck under my breakfast plate."

"What did it say?"

"Snitches get stitches."

I raised my eyebrows. "No mention of Terrance Chase? How do you know the note was about him?"

He scowled at me. "Believe me, I know. This isn't summer camp, Sophie. When you get warned, you gotta take it serious. You ain't never been in prison. You don't understand."

"Did you talk to anyone about your suspicions?"

Tom shook his head. "There's only one guy here I trust. A guard. He's been helpin' me get my mail out. After I sent the letter to your newspaper, he came and warned me that I shouldn't let my mail go through the warden's office anymore. I could bring lots of trouble on myself. He smuggled all my other letters out of here himself."

I frowned at him. "I'm glad you have someone you can trust, but I still don't understand how you know that note was about Chase."

He sighed dramatically. "It's the only thing I been sayin' that someone would get upset about. Maybe I was overheard. Or someone snatched a letter. I don't know. If one of these guys got wind Chase was alive, they'd be all over it. For the money."

"Okay. Let's put that aside for a moment. I have some other questions."

"Off the record. Like you said."

I nodded. "Off the record."

"Go on."

"The only reason I put any stock in your letter was because I remembered a guy named Terry I saw you talking to once. If my memory is correct, he looked a lot like Terrance Chase. If it *was* him, maybe you really do know something the authorities don't."

"It was him all right."

I couldn't keep the skepticism out of my voice. "Why would a guy who got away with over six million dollars be hanging out with you?"

Tom smiled. "You mean why would he waste time with a lowlife punk like me?"

I wouldn't have put it that way, but I didn't correct him. It was exactly what I'd been thinking.

"First of all, I didn't know who he was back then. He called himself Terry Martin." Tom shrugged. "I used to make some money selling license plates I knew weren't gonna be missed for a while. Terry was in the area for some reason. Don't know why. When he heard about my services, he asked for help. That's all there is to it."

"I don't understand," I said. "Who wouldn't miss their license plates?"

He began to pick at a piece of loose skin next to one of his fingernails. "Lots of folks in the country near Kingdom only drive to nearby small towns and back and forth to church. They don't pay no attention to the numbers on their plates. And some of the Mennies have trucks they don't use that much. I switched out their tags with those of the guys my dad arrested. Most of them wasn't gonna be drivin' for a while so they wouldn't realize their plate was gone. If it was a newer plate, I could guarantee almost a year of safe driving."

Tom sounded almost proud of his ingenuity. When I frowned at him, his expression changed.

"I'm not saying it was right. Back then, all I cared about was makin' money. And gettin' somethin' over on my dad."

Tom's father had been the sheriff assigned to the county where I used to live. His son's illegal activities had cost him his job.

"How is your father?"

Tom shook his head. "He died last year. Heart attack." He bit off the piece of dead skin and picked it off his tongue. Then he flicked it on the floor.

"Oh, Tom. I'm so sorry." And I was. Saul Ford had been a terrible sheriff, but in the end, he'd tried to do the right thing. Even though it had meant his son would spend years of his life locked up in prison.

"Me too. But we made up, you know. He stood by me. Came to see me every week." Tom quickly wiped away a tear that snaked down his cheek. He sniffed several times and then fought to regain the tough-guy bravado he'd obviously created to make it through life in prison.

"I'm glad. I know he loved you, Tom."

"Don't wanna talk about that no more," he said in a raspy voice.

"Okay." I actually felt sorry for him. Something I'd never expected to experience when it came to Tom Ford. "Then let's get back to Terrance Chase. When you saw him, it was . . .

what . . . a few years after the robbery? Why would he wait so long to get new tags?"

Tom shrugged. "It's easy to fake stickers, you know, for different years. But the metal tag is different. His was shot. He needed new Missouri plates. Two of 'em. I happened to know about an old farmer who died while visiting his family in a small town not far from Kingdom. I took his plates. His truck was just sittin' in a field. No one cared about those plates. Then I told Terry about another guy who could make new stickers. That way you don't have to steal 'em. They can tear if you're not careful. After that, he was set for a while."

"Did you ever see Terrance again?"

"No. There wasn't a chance. I got arrested for . . . well, you know."

Yes, I knew. For some reason, neither of us seemed willing to talk about that. "When did you realize who he really was?" I asked.

"That special on TV. Just like you guessed."

The guard who'd led Tom into the room glanced in our direction, so I checked my watch. We still had time left. Hopefully, he wasn't going to pull the plug early.

"If Chase *is* alive, why do you think you know where he is?"

"Because I heard somethin' I wasn't supposed to," Tom said. "When I met Terry at a local diner to give him his plates, he was on the phone. I heard him talkin' to someone. At first I didn't pay no attention, but after seein' that show, I got to thinkin' about it. Then I read a story about a kidnapping case. Some Mennie . . ." He flushed. "Sorry. Some Mennonite boy turned out to be a stolen kid. He was being hidden away in a small town in Missouri. The name of the town was the same as the name I heard Terry say on the phone."

"I'm not Mennonite anymore, Tom. You don't have to apologize to me."

He blushed. "I shouldn't use that word anyway. My dad used it all the time, and now I don't even realize when I say it." He stared into my eyes. "I'm sorry, Sophie. For everything. I used you, and it was wrong. I know that now. I've had a lot of time to think in here, and I'm not proud of the things I done back then—when I knew you."

I was shocked to hear him apologize. This wasn't the same Tom Ford I'd known when I'd lived in Kingdom. But even though he seemed sincere, I wasn't ready to absolve him.

"Are you sure Terry was talking about a town?" I asked, ignoring his apology.

Tom shook his head. "Not at first. But after I saw the story about the kidnapped kid, I put two and two together."

"Do you know who he was talking to?"

"No. It was kind of a weird conversation."

The guard who'd been watching us took a step forward. We certainly hadn't been talking for thirty minutes. Why did he seem so concerned about our conversation?

"Tom, don't talk to anyone about Chase," I said quickly. "Not even the guard you trust, okay? And stop writing letters. In fact, get rid of any notes or letters you have that mention him."

Tom frowned. "Okay. But my friend won't say nothin'."

"What if he accidentally slips? Or someone overhears you talking to him? Please don't take any chances. Shut this down. I don't want you to get hurt." Although I sounded concerned for his safety, in my heart I knew my main goal was to protect my story. I felt guilty, but I quickly dismissed it. Investigative reporters lie all the time. It's part of the job.

"Okay," he said softly. "I'll get rid of everything. And I'll keep quiet." He leaned in a little closer. "Anything you can do would help, Sophie. Find Terry Chase and then get me a deal for sending you in the right direction."

"I'll do my best. Don't worry," I said. "You just be careful. If I find anything helpful, I'll keep your name out of it. Except with the district attorney who prosecuted you. He's the one who can get your sentence reduced. Of course, I can't guarantee anything, Tom. All I can do is try. Do you understand?"

He nodded. "Just do what you said. Don't tell nobody about me until you can get me outta here. Write down this number. Use it if you want to get a message to me. They listen in on prisoners' phone calls."

I took a notepad and a pen from my purse. "All right."

Tom quickly rattled off some numbers, which I wrote down. Then I put my pen and notebook back in my purse.

I noticed the guard say something to his buddy, who frowned. He began walking toward us. "Tom, where is this place? The place you think Chase might be hiding?"

Tom saw the guard, too, and he blinked quickly, fear shining in his eyes. "It's called Sanctuary," he said in a whisper. "Sanctuary, Missouri. It's a Mennie . . . I mean, a Mennonite town."

I felt as if my heart had turned to lead and dropped all the way to my toes. "A . . . a Mennonite town?"

He nodded. "You should understand that. Great place to hide, huh?"

If I still believed in God, I'd have found this information funny. God's way of messing with me. The last thing I ever wanted to do was set foot in a town that reminded me of Kingdom. But my desire for a job as a crime reporter outweighed my revulsion toward my Mennonite background.

"Do you know anything else?" I asked quickly. "Anything that could help me find Chase?"

"I don't think so. But there was a strange thing he said that didn't make no sense."

"Can you repeat it? Exactly?"

He nodded, his eyes locked on the guard who was definitely headed our way. "He said, 'It's safe. It's protected by an angel.'" Tom shook his head. "Terry wasn't religious. I'm sure about that. I never could figure it out."

"Time's over." The guard stood next to our table, glowering at us.

"It hasn't been thirty minutes," I said, looking at my watch. "You can't . . ."

"It's all right," Tom said brusquely. "I ain't got nothin' to say to you, lady. I told you that. Don't bother me no more. I mean it." He looked up at the guard. "Get me outta here."

The guard motioned for Tom to stand up. Before he led him away, Tom's eyes met mine. The panic I saw there shook me to my core.

The other guard came over and stood next to my table. "I'll walk you out, ma'am," he said.

His hawklike features were accented by a crew cut that began with a sharp V at the top of his forehead. His dark-brown eyes glared a hole through me.

I got up and walked toward the exit, the guard close on

my heels. When we reached the first door, he unlocked it, and we headed toward the last exit. There was no sound in this part of the prison except the *tap, tap, tap* of my heels and the slight squeak of his shoes. They blended together in an odd and disturbing song. For some reason, the peculiar symphony made beads of sweat break out on my forehead. When we reached the final exit, the guard's arm shot past me and held the door shut. I turned and found myself staring up into his face. His expression made me take a quick breath.

"I'd advise you not to take your friend too seriously," he said in a low voice. "It could cause you both some trouble you don't want."

With that, he unlocked the door and held it open. I hurried out of the prison, the guard's words and the final expression on Tom's face fighting for the right to claim the fear that made my heart beat so hard I wondered if the people who walked past me could hear it.

CHAPTER TWO

After finishing up a couple projects with looming deadlines and arranging for two weeks away from work, I got in my car and headed to Sanctuary, Missouri. It had been easy to get the time off since no one else wanted to take their vacation in March.

I'd been at the paper for a couple of years. One year as a college intern, then, after being hired, I'd spent another year writing about death and food. My editor had been hinting at moving me away from the obits to a better spot in the Entertainment department. Bigger stories. Covering restaurants, movies, concerts, plays, etc. For a twenty-one-year-old who was still wet behind the ears, it was a real honor, especially since I didn't officially have my degree yet. And even though the position was one some of my colleagues would probably have killed for, more than anything I wanted to be a crime writer. It had been my goal ever since I'd started school. I couldn't explain my interest. It was a far cry from my Conservative Mennonite background. Maybe it was the fascination of seeing people act out in anger and passion—something that wasn't allowed in the community I'd been brought up in. Or maybe it was a desire to see justice. And right now I had a chance to get everything I wanted by covering a story that would leave most Kingdom residents horrified.

As I drove, I went over the details of the robbery in my head. A St. Louis armored car company had been robbed in May of 2008. Supposedly, the robbers overpowered one of the firm's employees as he arrived for work. The employee was forced to let the masked gunmen inside, where they proceeded to kill him and another guard. Because the robbers seemed to know the guards' routines, and there was an unusual amount of gold and unmarked cash on the premises that day, the police suspected someone on the inside was involved. Most of the suspicion was directed toward a guard named Charles Abbott, the man who'd let the robbers into the building. However, that theory was never proven. Before they died, the guards got off some shots of their own. Both of the robbers were hit by gunfire, but they still got away.

Terrance Chase had been connected to the theft through an anonymous tip not long after the robbery. A couple who'd once rented him a room turned over some notes they'd found behind a dresser in the room he'd vacated. The notes had details of the robbery that only someone directly involved would know.

After researching Chase's friends and associates, the investigators concluded that Chase's badly injured accomplice was Richard Osborne, nicknamed Snake. Osborne also disappeared around the time of the theft, and his family had no idea what had happened to him. His sister told the investigators that if Rick were alive, he would have contacted them, thus leading to the belief that he had died of his wounds. It was assumed that Chase had disposed of the body, since Osborne was never found.

Local police and the FBI scoured the country, looking for the elusive robber, but they never caught him. The money disappeared without a trace. After a few years, the case grew cold and was virtually dropped.

Then, two months ago, a cable television station aired a special about the robbery. The station had hired three investigators to work together to solve the cold case of Terrance Chase and the 6.6 million dollars he'd gotten away with. Although it was more a publicity stunt than a true investigation, one of the participants, a retired police detective, interviewed an old friend of Chase's who swore the robber was dead. The man said he'd heard someone had killed him and taken all the money a couple of years after the theft. The investigators appeared to believe him. The show ended with the assumption that Chase really was deceased. The other two detectives, a retired FBI agent and a private investigator, concurred with the theory. However, I knew they were wrong because Chase's supposed death occurred before I saw him with Tom.

"But if Chase made a clean break, why go to someone like Tom for car tags?" I said to myself. Tom had said Chase was in the area for a completely different reason. Maybe so. Maybe the car tags were an afterthought. But still, it seemed risky. Of course, Tom and his redneck buddies were probably pretty safe to work with. They weren't the kind of people who would be knowledgeable about old crimes. And it was easier to hide in rural areas than in large cities. After thinking about it, it began to make more sense than I'd believed at first.

I turned these new insights over in my head for a while. I was only about ten miles away from my turnoff when I realized I needed gas. I saw a sign for an upcoming exit that had a gas station, so I took the turn and found the station, thankful for the opportunity to fill my tank. If Sanctuary was anything like Kingdom, this could be one of my last chances to buy gas for a while.

I turned off my engine and grabbed my purse. As I looked for my wallet and my debit card, I realized I'd accidentally stuck several bill payments in my purse instead of putting them in my box before I'd left. I'd been so preoccupied with getting out of town I'd forgotten to mail them. I decided to take care of them when I got to Sanctuary. As I put them back in my purse, I saw the photograph of Terrance Chase I'd brought with me. I picked it up and looked at it closely. I'd stared at the man's face so many times it was burned into my mind. Not completely trusting my memory, however, I'd wanted an actual picture I could compare to anyone I thought might be him. I put the photo back in my purse and then got out of the car and quickly filled my tank. Feeling thirsty, I grabbed my purse and went into the small gas station and bought a drink.

Once I was back in my car, I felt both excited and worried about being so close to my destination. I reminded myself that Sanctuary wasn't completely Mennonite. Research had told me that although the town was founded by Mennonites, now they were in the minority.

"It's not Kingdom," I said out loud. "Get yourself together. You can do this."

I got back on the highway, and before I knew it, I was on the final road leading to Sanctuary. Once again, I felt my tension level rise. Ghosts from my past seemed to taunt me. Was I really the confident reporter I pretended to be? Or the scared little girl who always felt she was on the outside looking in? Could I really pull this off, or would it be a complete disaster? Would the specter of my father fill me with so much trepidation I'd run away from Sanctuary the way I'd fled Kingdom?

Although Sanctuary appeared to be a rather isolated community, searching through old obituaries had led me to the name of a woman from the small town who'd passed away about six months earlier. She'd had two sisters who had died before her and no other living relatives. After concocting a story about my mother being the illegitimate daughter of one of the sisters, I'd contacted the pastor of the Mennonite church in Sanctuary. Although he'd seemed rather reticent at first, I finally convinced him I was who I said I was. Once I'd put him at ease, he'd been kind and accommodating, even offering to help me piece together what I could about my supposed grandmother, Clara Byler. I felt some remorse about using him for my own purposes, but too many years of betrayal and pain had shown me I was the only person I could trust to do what was best for me. And finding Terrance Chase was definitely in my best interest.

It was almost four in the afternoon when I finally pulled into Sanctuary. It was pretty much what I'd expected. A small town with dirt streets, wide sidewalks, full of old buildings and a smattering of houses. Settled by Mennonites in the 1800s and called New Zion, eventually the town welcomed people with different beliefs.

I wondered if Pastor Troyer's initial reluctance to talk to me had been due to all the unwelcome media attention Sanctuary had received a couple of years ago. Even so, it seemed to be the perfect place to hide for a criminal running from justice.

I drove past several businesses on Main Street, as well as a large gray church with blue and white trim and a huge white cross on a tall spire. I could tell by looking at the building that it wasn't Mennonite. Too decorative.

As I drove farther into town, I spotted several buggies tied up in front of a hardware store. A conservatively dressed Mennonite couple walked toward one of them. When I saw them, that old feeling of dread came over me, and my father's face flashed in front of me again.

I tried to calm my jangled nerves as I drove to the other side of town, easily finding the plain white building that housed Sanctuary Mennonite Church. Staring at the building, I felt a tickle of dread wriggle around inside my stomach. I took a deep, cleansing breath and began to repeat the positive affirmations I'd learned from reading a book about creative visualization.

"I am calm and relaxed in every situation. I can control my thoughts. No one can dominate me. I am in charge of my life. I am a winner. I am successful in everything I do."

I repeated the affirmations several times, until I felt myself begin to settle down. These affirmations had helped me immensely. I'd even recorded myself saying them, and I played the CD when driving in my car. Visualization had given me the courage to step out and walk toward the life I wanted and deserved. Sometimes I would sit alone, close my eyes, and see myself as a successful crime reporter with money, respect, and power. Now, I turned on the CD player and let my own words give me the courage to face my past.

As I sat in front of the church, a girl came out. A blue dress peeked out from beneath a black cloak, and a white prayer covering sat atop her head. Unwelcome emotions threatened to overwhelm me. Once again, I whispered the words designed to make me stronger. When I felt ready, I got out of the car and approached the girl.

"Excuse me," I said. "I'm looking for Pastor Troyer."

The young girl, blond with rather sturdy features, smiled. "Pastor Troyer is my father. If you will follow me, I will take you to his office."

I nodded at her, and she turned back toward the simple, unadorned structure. Once we stepped through the door, my insides knotted again. It looked so similar to the church in Kingdom—before the fire that destroyed it. I suddenly felt faint and grasped a nearby chair, trying to steady myself.

"Are you all right, miss?" the girl said. Her eyebrows knit together with concern.

I smiled to put her at ease. "I'm fine. Sorry. Driving all day wore me out, I guess."

"Do you need help?"

I shook my head. "No. I'm fine now. Just lead the way."

She looked as if she didn't believe me. That was good since I didn't believe me either. But I did everything I could to control myself as I followed her down a long hall to what I assumed was the pastor's office.

When we stepped inside, a thin man with the obligatory Conservative Mennonite beard and plain clothing smiled up at us. As he stood, I noticed that his daughter seemed comfortable in his presence. I'd never felt that way with my father. I suddenly wanted to run back to my car. Back to the safety of my positive affirmations and the life I'd built away from Kingdom. Summoning every bit of courage I had, I addressed the Mennonite pastor who represented everything I hated.

"Pastor Troyer?"

"Yes, can I help you?"

I walked toward him and held out my hand. "I'm Emily McClure. I talked to you about my grandmother, Clara Byler?"

"Oh yes, Miss McClure. We've been expecting you." After shaking my hand, he pointed toward one of the chairs sitting in front of his desk. "Please, have a seat."

"I really appreciate your help in learning more about Clara," I said as I sat down.

"Excuse me a moment, Miss McClure." He turned his attention to his daughter. "You can go on to the clinic, Ruth. Thank you for your help."

"Okay, Papa," Ruth said. She waved at me. "I am happy to have met you."

"I'm happy to have met you, too, Ruth."

I watched as the girl left her father's office. "I'm sorry,

Pastor, but I noticed you said something about Ruth going to a clinic. Is she okay?"

His smile widened. "Yes, thank you for your concern. She is helping out at our veterinary clinic. Ruth loves animals, and her work there is very important to her."

"How nice that she does something she enjoys."

"Yes, it is." He came around and took a seat in the chair next to me. "Now, let's talk about your grandmother. I hope I can be of help to you. As I told you on the phone, Clara didn't live in Sanctuary as an adult, but her sister, Miriam, was a resident all of her life. I knew her about as well as a pastor can know one of his church members. She was a sweet lady who loved the Lord and enjoyed helping people. A wonderful cook, she was always available to new mothers and the ill in our congregation. I also knew your grandmother, Clara. She visited Miriam frequently before she passed away." His forehead wrinkled in thought. "The third sister, Martha, died when she was young, I believe."

"Yes, Martha passed away when she was in her thirties." Thanks to online ancestry sites, at least I had some facts about my pretend family.

"To be honest, I was surprised by your call. Miriam never mentioned that her sister had a daughter. I would've thought she'd want to be involved in her great-niece's life."

I nodded. "Well, back in those days, and especially in the church, having a child out of wedlock was something a woman would probably keep to herself."

"Yes, you may be right." He shrugged. "Over the years I have found that many people have secrets. Some they never share."

"I suppose that's true. Thankfully, after my mother discovered she was adopted, she decided to search for her birth mother. And here I am."

"Your mother didn't want to join you on your search?"

"Yes, she did. But she and my father live overseas now, so it really wasn't possible." I was pretty comfortable with this cover story. I would have said my mother was dead, but with all the sisters deceased, it felt like there were too many bodies piling up.

He studied me for a moment. Then he nodded slowly. "Well, we can talk more later. I will take you to my friend's house. Esther Lapp has graciously offered you a room in her home while you are here."

"That's very kind."

He chuckled. "Esther enjoys company. Her children live in other states, so life can be lonely. A young woman lived with her for a while, but she recently married, and Esther is alone again. You will be a very welcome guest."

"I hope she will allow me to pay her."

Pastor Troyer shook his head. "She will not. Spending time with you is all the payment Esther needs. And since she knew Miriam and Clara better than anyone, she will be the best source for answers to your questions. I hope by the time you leave us, you will have the information you're seeking. Now, allow me to show you the way to Esther's house. It is almost time for me to go home, and I live very close to her. If you could drive us, I can just walk from her house. This way my wife will not have to come for me."

He stood up and walked to the door, and I followed him out. My journey in Sanctuary was beginning. When I'd first decided to track down Terrance Chase, I'd thought I'd be excited at this moment. I was going undercover, just like a real crime reporter. But instead of anticipation, I felt apprehension. Why did I have to revisit my nightmares to achieve my dreams?

CHAPTER THREE

Pastor Troyer walked around to the passenger-side door of my car and got in. Back in Kingdom, some of the residents refused to ride in cars. It seemed that things were a little more relaxed here in Sanctuary. Even though I'd turned my back on my Mennonite roots, I had to admit I sometimes missed the quiet of a small town. Sometimes the noisiness of the city got on my nerves.

When I started the car, my affirmations CD began to play. After I turned the car around and started back toward town, I reached over and switched it off.

"Sorry," I said.

Pastor Troyer looked over at me. "You find these statements helpful?"

Sure that New Age affirmations weren't something the Mennonite pastor agreed with, I shrugged. "I'm not sure. A friend gave me the CD. It seems to help her."

He looked away. "The Bible is full of positive proclamations. Many times I remind myself that I am the righteousness of God through Christ Jesus. That I can do all things through Him. That I am His beloved and that no man can snatch me out of His hand. That nothing can separate me from His love."

"Wow. That's surprising coming from a Mennonite pastor. I thought you believed it was a sin to point to yourself. That everything must point to God."

After telling me to take a right turn, the pastor chuckled. "When I say who I am through Christ, am I not pointing to Him? It is easy to believe that God is too great to care about a worm like me. It is harder to believe that the Master of the Universe is personally interested in my life. That He loves me so much the very hairs on my head are numbered. Don't you agree?"

When I turned to look at him, the car swerved, and I had to refocus on the road. A family in a buggy looked over at us, concern written on their faces.

"Sorry," I said. "I guess I need to pay more attention to my driving." Although I didn't answer his question, it left me feeling a little flustered. Our pastor in Kingdom had said the same thing, but I'd forgotten about it until now. My father and mother hadn't believed in a merciful God. To them, righteousness was something you had to earn. Something I could never achieve. After leaving Kingdom, I'd decided to reject the concept of God completely, and for the first time in my life, I'd finally felt free. Now I only believed in one thing: me.

The pastor didn't pursue an answer to his inquiry; he just directed me down another street until we pulled up in front of a large white house. An elderly Mennonite woman sat in a rocking chair on the big front porch. Wearing a long green dress and a black prayer covering over her gray hair, she looked exactly the way I'd expected. Except for the joyous smile on her face. Some of the older women in Kingdom looked like they'd just eaten lemons, including my mother. Of course, not everyone had been that way. In fact, the faces of several women I'd known popped into my thoughts. Funny that I'd forgotten about some of the good people from my old hometown.

I parked the car, and the pastor and I got out.

"Good afternoon, Esther," Pastor Troyer called out. "I am delivering your new houseguest."

Esther stood up from her rocking chair and hobbled over to the edge of the porch. "I am so glad you have come to stay, Emily. Believe it or not, the young woman who just left was named Emily, as well."

I smiled at the friendly woman. "I really appreciate your graciousness. I hope I won't be a poor substitute for your previous guest."

Esther waved her hand at me as I pulled my suitcases out of the trunk. Pastor Troyer picked up two of them and headed toward the house.

"Leave the rest, Emily," he said. "I will fetch them."

I shook my head. "Thank you, but I can easily get these." I pulled out my laptop and a large, soft tote bag. I walked up to the porch and stood in front of Esther. "Lead the way."

She patted my arm. "I wish I could help you with your bags, but alas, I am afraid my strength is not what it once was." She pulled open the screen door, and I stepped into a large living room with comfortable furniture. I was thrilled to see there was electricity. Although I knew how to live without it, that wasn't something I ever wanted to endure again.

"Your room is upstairs. It is the last room on the left. Please go ahead of me. I am afraid it takes me some time to climb the stairs."

Pastor Troyer waited for me to go first, so I hiked up the narrow stairs while he followed behind me. When I reached the top, I headed toward the end of the hall and the room Esther had indicated. I heard the elderly woman's voice behind us.

"You will stay in my daughter Rebecca's room. The first room you passed belonged to my son, Benjamin. I keep it ready for a friend from St. Louis who comes to visit me from time to time. Maybe you will meet Zac while you are here."

"Esther should run a bed and breakfast." Pastor Troyer's voice was full of humor. "She is a wonderful hostess and generously shares her gift of hospitality."

I stopped in front of the door Esther had indicated and waited for her to catch up. She came up the hall, a little winded by the climb.

"Oh, pshaw." She grinned at the pastor. "The gift is not one I give. It is one I receive. I love company." She walked up next to me. "We have so much to talk about. I hope I will be able to share something with you about your family."

"I hear you're the expert," I replied. "I look forward to learning more about my grandmother. It seems my mother's birth was kept a secret since having a baby out of wedlock was considered shameful."

Esther, who was several inches shorter than I, peered up at me. "Your great-aunt was not a judgmental woman. And her sister did not seem like someone who would turn her back on family. I must confess I am having a difficult time merging your story with the women I knew."

I just nodded at her. Was she saying she didn't believe me? Had I picked the wrong family to borrow for my purposes? I'd assumed that Mennonite values would make my story believable.

Esther finally quit studying me and opened the door to my room. It wasn't what I'd expected. Rather than being stark and plain, it was lovely. The carved mahogany bed was covered with a beautiful maroon quilt, and a side table held an antique glass lamp that reminded me of a Tiffany lamp I'd seen in an antique store. A matching dresser sat against one wall, and a couch covered with maroon brocade had been placed along the other wall.

"I don't believe I've ever seen a couch like this," I commented, walking over to the odd-shaped piece of furniture.

"It is a fainting couch," Esther said. "Years ago, women were seen to be delicate creatures who needed a place to rest from the trials of life. But I was told that their fainting may have had more to do with the tight corsets they wore than weakness of spirit or flesh." She put her hand over her mouth and giggled, almost sounding like a child.

I laughed, too. "I don't think I'll be doing any fainting, and I certainly don't wear a corset, but it looks like the perfect place to relax and read a book."

Esther nodded. "There are many books in Benjamin's room. If you find yourself short of reading material, please help yourself to his library." She walked over and pulled open the drawer in the side table. "And here is a Bible you are welcome to read."

"Th—thank you," I replied, although I had no intention of taking her up on her offer.

"Well, I must get home," Pastor Troyer said. "Again, welcome to Sanctuary, Emily. Please call me any time. I will do whatever I can to help you. There are some written records in the church basement you might be interested in. Down through the decades, the church has tried to keep track of the families and individuals who have lived in Sanctuary. They started out as property records, but many years ago, a church member decided to use them as a way to preserve our history. We usually do not open them to anyone outside of the town, but since you are related to one of our residents, we will let you go through them, if you wish. I would just request that you keep your research limited to Miriam's family. Even though we do not add any personal information to our notes, we still do not wish to invade anyone's privacy. Let me know if you would like to avail yourself of these records, and I will unlock the room for you."

"I may take you up on that," I told him. "Thank you so much for all your help." I held out my hand.

"You are very welcome." The pastor shook my hand and left the room. In his place, a gray-striped cat sauntered in.

"This is Clyde," Esther said. "I have four cats. I hope you are not allergic?"

I shook my head. "I love cats."

As if he understood me, Clyde jumped up on the bed and began sniffing one of my suitcases.

"You mind your own business, young man." Esther gently pushed him away. "Get down from there."

"Please, Esther, unless you don't want him in here, let him stay."

The old woman smiled at me. "Again you remind me of

the other Emily. She loved my cats, too. You might find them a bit clingy. They are missing their friend." She pointed at Clyde and shook her finger. "You must be careful with this silly feline. Lately, he has developed a tendency to get tangled up in my feet. I have tried to break him of this habit, but so far, he has been very rebellious and unwilling to change."

A loud meow from the hallway signaled another feline visitor. This gray-striped cat was much larger than Clyde and had white on his face. I noticed a slight limp.

"This is Sam. He has a little touch of arthritis. Although he would love to jump up on your bed, he cannot safely do it. It is too high."

As if he understood his owner's words, Sam walked over to the fainting couch and scooted underneath it. Then he curled up on the floor.

"I noticed the bed is higher than anything I've seen before."

Esther pointed to a small stepstool next to the dresser. "Using this stool will help you to safely get up and down from the bed. Beds were made higher many years ago. I should probably replace this one, but it was Rebecca's, and I am . . . sentimental."

"Thank you. The stool may save me some bumps and bruises."

"This is true." She turned to leave the room. "Why don't you unpack and rest a bit? Dinner will be at six o'clock."

"Oh, Esther. I don't expect you to cook for me. I noticed a couple of restaurants when I drove into town. I'll just get something there."

"I think you will enjoy them, but this first night, why don't you eat with me? I would like to get to know you better."

"If you're sure it's not too much trouble, that would be lovely. Thank you. I'll be down by six."

"Good. I look forward to it." A smile made the corners of her eyes crinkle. "I do not like cooking for myself. When I prepare food for someone else, it gives me an excuse to eat the foods I really like."

"I'm sure whatever you make will be delicious."

"I hope so, dear." She sighed. "Well, I had better get downstairs and leave you to unpack. Please, if you need anything, just let me know."

"I can't thank you enough, Esther." I was grateful to her, but right now I wanted to be alone. Memories of home were coming from every direction, and I needed time to regroup.

She nodded and left the room, closing the door behind her.

I sat down on the fainting couch and tried to quell the butterflies doing jumping jacks in my stomach. I was happy to have made it to Sanctuary so I could look for Chase, but why did it have to be a Mennonite town? Why did he decide to hide out here? I guess it could have been worse. He could have ended up in Kingdom. The thought made me laugh lightly to myself.

Thinking about my hometown caused another face to float into my mind. One I'd been pushing away for a long time. Jonathon Wiese. The only man I'd ever loved. A man who could never be mine. His incredible blue eyes seemed to be looking at me from somewhere far away, but I could still see him clearly. The longish dark hair he was always pushing out of his eyes, the curve of his cheek, his strong arms. I also remembered the kindness that had caused him to reach out to an awkward and unloved teenager, trying to let her know that she was important to God—and to him. But the truth was, I'd been nothing more than a disturbed child who'd earned his pity. Despite his compassion, I'd betrayed him—and everyone in Kingdom. The pain of remembrance was too deep. I shoved it back into the dark place where I kept the hurt I couldn't face.

Once again, I began to recite my affirmations, trying to find an inner peace. For some reason, it wasn't working, so I switched my attention to the present, forcing myself to concentrate on what really mattered now—finding Terrance Chase. I'd come here without a real plan except to question residents about single men who had moved here after 2008—and compare my picture of Chase with anyone who could possibly be my target. I realized that my passion was stronger than my strategy, but now that I was here, Pastor Troyer had presented another possibility. Although I wasn't sure how helpful the information in the town's records would be, at least they gave me a place to start. If there were actual dates, they would help me build a list of men who moved here after the robbery. Being able to narrow it down would help me find Chase faster. With the records and the picture together, I might make some progress.

Even though I felt encouraged, the more I thought about the task in front of me, the more I began to wonder if this was a fool's errand. I could understand Chase hiding out for a while in a small town, but with the money from the robbery, why would he stay? He couldn't spend very much of his ill-gotten gains in Sanctuary. It was possible he'd left town years ago. If so, my only hope would be to track him from here. Try to figure out where he went after leaving Sanctuary. Hopefully, the records not only recorded new residents but also made note of the people who'd moved away. If they didn't, my job would be a little tougher.

I glanced at the clock on a small table near the door. Five-twenty. I only had forty minutes until dinner. From here on out, I'd have to stay in character. I was Emily McClure—illegitimate granddaughter of Clara Byler. Would it be difficult to concentrate on one false story while trying to investigate something entirely different? I'd picked Clara because she didn't actually live in Sanctuary as an adult. I'd figured it would be easier to fool people with someone not so connected to the town, but after meeting Esther, I was a little nervous. Would I really be able to pull this off?

I was just starting to unpack when my phone rang. I grabbed it out of my purse and looked at the number. Kansas. When I answered, I received a recording that an inmate from El Dorado was trying to reach me. I accepted the call. After a few seconds, I heard Tom's voice on the line.

"Sophie, are you there?" he asked.

"I'm here, Tom. What's going on?"

He spoke in such hushed tones, I could barely hear him. "You've got to help me, Sophie."

I could hear the anxiousness in his voice. "Has something happened?"

"Yeah. Someone seems very interested in your visit. I think I'm in real trouble here."

Had I actually put Tom in danger? How could that be? "Tom, are you sure?"

"It's not my imagination. Please help me before things . . . get out of hand."

"Isn't there someone there you can go to for help? What about your guard friend?"

"No, he can't help me, and I can't get to the warden."

"Okay. Maybe I should call the warden's office. See what I can do to get you some protection."

There was silence for a moment. "Maybe they'll listen to you since you work for a newspaper."

Or maybe not. Either way, I felt I had to try to help him. "Look, you stay safe, and I'll see what I can do."

"Sophie, whatever you do, don't—"

There was a sudden *click*, and I realized we'd been disconnected. I put my phone away and wondered what to do next. What if he was just overreacting? It wasn't as if Chase was locked up in El Dorado. The robbery had occurred so long ago, there wasn't any reason to think Chase had friends who were concerned about protecting him. Tom had mentioned people wanting the money from the robbery. But that was a long shot after all these years.

After thinking it through, I came to the conclusion that whatever was going on probably had nothing to do with Terrance Chase. Regardless, I'd promised Tom I'd try to help him, and I would. Since it was after five, I'd call the prison in the morning. At least I could ask someone in the warden's office to keep an eye on Tom. I probably wouldn't mention the paper since I didn't want to get in trouble for misrepresenting them—or me. But I'd feel better knowing someone in a position of authority was aware one of their inmates felt concerned for his safety.

I finished putting away my clothes, and then I brushed my hair, checked my makeup, and headed downstairs. As I walked down, an odd feeling of unrest washed over me. Probably due to this town and Tom's call. But I couldn't shake the sensation that something was wrong. It was as if an alarm bell were ringing somewhere inside me, but I couldn't figure out what the warning meant.

CHAPTER FOUR

"More chicken?"

Esther's fried chicken was a temptation, but after losing almost eighty pounds, I was very careful about what I ate. "Thanks, but I'm full." I patted my stomach. "It's wonderful, though. The best I've had since . . ." I'd almost mentioned Kingdom. Lizzie Housler, who ran a restaurant in the small town, made the best fried chicken I'd ever tasted. However, Esther's was a close second.

"Since when, dear?" Esther asked.

"Since my mother's," I lied. My mother had been a terrible cook. When she prepared a meal, it was usually something from a can. And it tasted like it.

"Would you tell me more about your mother? And how you found out about your grandmother?"

I'd prepared myself to handle questions like that, but reciting my false story to Esther was more difficult than I'd anticipated. Esther was a kind woman, and lying to her made me feel ashamed. I quickly ran through the rehearsed narrative—

my mother had no idea she was adopted until her mother died and her father went into a nursing home. As she was cleaning out their house, she found the adoption papers in a small safe in her parents' closet. Although she wasn't in a position to search for her birth mother, she gave me the information. And now I'd come here to learn more about my biological family.

"Don't get me wrong," I said. "I had a very happy childhood, and I'm not judging Clara—or her family. I'd just like to know more about them. I wonder if I have any other relatives somewhere."

Esther shook her head. "No. The sisters were the only remaining members of their family. Both parents were only children, and it seems your mother was the only child born to any of the sisters. I'm sorry."

"That's too bad," I answered, even though I'd already known those things. "But as I said, I feel blessed to have been raised by a wonderful mother and father."

Esther handed me a bowl of green beans, and even though I'd declared I was full, I helped myself to another small serving. They were delicious, cooked with bacon and onions.

"And where are your parents?" she asked.

"They're doctors, working in Africa."

Actually, I felt rather proud of my concocted tale. No way to contact my supposed parents. No way to confirm my birth through other Byler family members. I felt pretty confident no one could poke a hole in my story.

"A noble cause," Esther said. "And what is it you want to know about Miriam? And Clara, your grandmother?"

I put down my fork and took a deep breath. "I guess I just want to know what kind of people they were."

Esther nodded. "Well, Miriam was a dear friend. Very kind. She loved people, and she would have loved you. She was also a very honest person. As I told you, I am very surprised she never mentioned you. Even if there was some shame associated with having a baby and not being married, I am surprised Miriam felt embarrassed to tell me about it."

"Perhaps Clara asked her sister to keep her secret. Was Miriam the kind of woman who would take a promise to her sister very seriously?"

Esther appeared to turn this over in her mind. Finally, she said, "Yes, I guess most sisters would protect each other's secrets. That might explain it."

She smiled at me, and I breathed an inward sigh of relief. It looked as if my cover story would hold up just fine.

"Thank you, Emily," she said. "Miriam's friendship meant a great deal to me. If I really believed she could not trust me with something so important in her life, it would cause me pain. But as you say, a promise to a sister is sacred."

"I'm sorry, Esther. My intent isn't to hurt you."

"It is not you, my child. You appear to be the innocent one in this situation."

My tenacity took a serious hit as guilt coursed through me. Suddenly, Esther's delicious dinner felt like rocks in my stomach. Here she'd opened her home to me, offered me her food, and I was using her for my own advantage. I quickly corrected my thinking. If I wanted to be an investigative reporter and write stories about crime, I had to have some backbone. Be willing to deceive people for the information I needed. It was part of the job. I pushed away any feelings of remorse. It was time to steer the conversation toward my real interests. I wanted to learn more about Sanctuary.

"Esther, I'd really like to know more about you—and this town. It's such a lovely place."

She took a sip from her glass of tea and nodded at me. "Of course. Why don't we do that over coffee and cake?"

"That would be wonderful. Thank you."

As I helped her carry the dishes from the table, I was able to see her kitchen. All in all, it was an average kitchen. It could have used a little updating, but it was warm and inviting. There were wooden cabinets painted a faded cornflower blue and old linoleum counters that testified to a lot of use over the years. A colorful rag rug lay in front of the sink. The most striking thing in the room was the old stove. It was huge—gas burners on top and two big doors on the front. It looked well used and had probably watched generations of Esther's family come and go. On one side of the room was a wooden table with four chairs. It appeared to be handmade and had been painted the same blue as the cabinets. It was covered with a navy-blue-and-white-checked vinyl tablecloth. A wooden napkin holder with a rooster painted on one side sat next to two old jadeite salt and pepper shakers. Esther opened her cabinet door and took out two jadeite coffee cups. Once I left Kingdom, I'd been surprised to find out that jadeite was highly collectible. It was common in my old hometown. I wondered if Esther knew or cared about the value of her dishes. Probably not.

Once the food was put away, she cut two large pieces of chocolate cake and carried them into her comfortable living room. She was almost to the coffee table when Clyde suddenly jumped out from under the couch and ran between her feet.

Esther scolded him. "See what I mean? You must be careful. Especially on the stairs. That bad, bad cat."

Clyde dashed across the room and bounded up the stairs. To him this was obviously a fun game, and it amused him that his antics got so much attention.

"I will fetch the coffee. Cake cannot be eaten without coffee."

"Sounds great. Let me help you—"

She shook her head. "No. You stay here. You look weary. How do you like your coffee?"

For some reason, the words *from Starbucks* jumped into my mind, making me want to laugh, but I kept a straight face and said, "Black is fine."

Ever since moving to St. Louis, I'd worked to purge Kingdom from my life. Even in regard to my coffee. Most Kingdom residents would be horrified to hear that anyone would buy flavored coffee at prices they would consider extravagant. But every day before work, my first stop was the Starbucks next door to the newspaper office. I really missed my morning Cinnamon Dolce Latte.

While Esther went to get our coffee, I looked around her simple but cozy living room. The furniture was old but made with care. The couch had large, carved wooden legs shaped like balls. Although I was certain it had been re-covered many times, the couch was currently encased in a navy brocade with light white and gold flowers. It was easy to see that blue was Esther's favorite color. Her coffee table was mahogany with claw-foot legs and carvings around the sides. The windows were covered with sheer white curtains, and on the floor was a gorgeous azure and white Victorian hooked rug. It was obviously old, and a little faded, but its beauty was still evident.

The rug covered polished parquet floors. Nothing in the room was new, but everything was clean and neat.

It was so different from our dirty, unkempt house in Kingdom. I'd tried to keep it clean, but my parents were so messy, eventually I gave up. I shuddered as I remembered old food, dirty dishes, sticky floors, filthy clothes, and stacks of papers piled up in every corner, a monument to my parents' lack of respect for themselves—or me. The church had tried to help them more than once, sending people by to clean and repair our dilapidated house, but my parents didn't appreciate it. They expected charity and got angry if someone didn't come over every week to assist them in some way. Finally, frustrated with all their excuses, the church backed off. For my sake, however, every once in a while a group of church women would come by and clean. And if our neighbors noticed a serious problem with the house, they would stop by and take care of it, often without asking for permission. I never heard my parents thank anyone. It was true they weren't in the best health, but they were capable of keeping themselves and their home tidy. They just didn't want to. Since I'd left Kingdom, I'd become almost obsessed with cleanliness. I couldn't relax unless my apartment was spotless. I'd suffered through a severe case of the flu a few months ago, but even then, I couldn't sleep unless the dishes were done and everything was clean and in its place.

"Here we are." Esther toddled into the room with two cups and saucers in her hands. I jumped up and took one from her.

"Thank you." Even though I missed my usual latte, I had to admit that Esther's coffee smelled great. A small sip confirmed it. Rich and robust, it was delicious. It reminded me of the only thing my mother had ever made that wasn't a disaster. Coffee. She'd known how to make great coffee. However, finding a clean cup to put it in was another thing.

"So you want to know more about Sanctuary," Esther said after she sank down onto her couch. I sat across from her in a comfortable overstuffed chair. The coffee table was between us, and I put my cup down on a coaster, next to my cake plate.

"Yes. How long have you lived here, Esther?"

Her eyes took on a faraway look as she considered my question. "I came here as a small child. My parents and I lived on a farm just a little ways outside of town. They died a long time ago. When I married, my husband bought this house. We raised our children, Rebecca and Benjamin, right here. My husband is gone now, too, and my children have moved away. They have their own lives. Unfortunately, I don't get to see them very often."

"I suppose most of the people who live in Kingdom now were born here?"

"Most of them, yes. But we also have some residents who moved here more recently." She smiled at me. "We do not try to keep people out, Emily."

"The town seems . . . peaceful. What if someone wanted to, I don't know, open a liquor store in Sanctuary?"

"Again you remind me so much of my Emily. She once asked the same question." Her expression became more serious. "They would not find a place to put their business. There are not many vacant buildings in Sanctuary, and any that exist are either owned by a resident or by one of the churches."

That told me that even though this wasn't Kingdom, where people needed permission to join the town, in Sanctuary prospective residents were probably checked out rather carefully. If Chase had been here, he must not have raised any red flags.

"Pastor Troyer told me there are records at the church that track the people who have lived in Sanctuary. Surely they don't include everyone. That would be quite a task."

Esther took a sip of her coffee. "It is not that difficult in a town this size. Tell me, are you thinking about Miriam or someone else?"

I almost choked on Esther's chocolate cake. Before I could come up with an answer, there was a knock on the front door, giving me time to regroup. I was moving too fast. If I didn't backtrack, I might make Esther suspicious. And I needed her on my side.

She excused herself and went to the front door. I heard her ask someone to come inside. A middle-aged woman stepped through the door. She was dressed in black slacks and a deep purple blouse. Obviously not a Conservative Mennonite.

"Emily, this is my friend Janet Dowell," Esther said. "She lives next door."

As I stood up, Janet walked over and extended her hand. "I'm so glad to meet you," she said. "Esther adores company. I'm sure she's thrilled you're staying with her."

I shook her hand. "I hope so. I'll do my best not to be a bother."

Janet was a lovely woman with blond hair, blue eyes, and a joyful smile. She instantly seemed like someone I'd like to know better. Unfortunately, I wasn't here to make friends.

"Esther isn't bothered by people," she said. "She loves everyone."

Esther laughed. "You are embarrassing me, dear friend. I am afraid I cannot live up to your wonderful words."

Janet grinned at her. "You more than live up to them." She looked over at me. "I'm so sorry to interrupt, but we're planning a church supper Saturday, and we need Esther to bring a couple of her incredible pies." She swung her gaze back to the elderly woman. "Do you have time to do a little baking for us?"

Esther's eyes sparkled. "I would love to. I also have some apple butter I put up last season, and it needs to be eaten. May I bring that, as well?"

"Absolutely. Nothing tastes better than your homemade apple butter."

Esther nodded. "Will Sarah be there?"

"She wouldn't miss it. She's asked Paul, so he'll be joining us, too."

Esther clapped her hands together. "I am so glad to hear this. How are things progressing with them?"

Janet beamed. "Very well. I tend to think they might have an announcement before long." She seemed to suddenly remember I was there. "I'm sorry, Emily. I don't want to intrude any longer. I'd better get going."

"It was so nice to meet you," I said. "May I ask a question? I'm surprised you attend church with Esther. I mean, you don't look Mennonite."

"Actually the supper is being held at my church, Agape Fellowship. In Sanctuary, the two churches do many things together. We have some different traditions, but our main belief is the same: Jesus and His redemptive power."

"The other Emily told me that many churches do not get

along in the world," Esther said. "But that is not the case in this town. Our pastors are close friends, and the members of the churches like to spend time together. We have all kinds of events. Including church suppers. One of my very favorite things."

"We'd love to have you join us, Emily," Janet said.

"Thank you so much. I'd like that."

"Good." She reached over and hugged Esther. "I need to get going, but I'll pick you both up around five o'clock Saturday afternoon. The supper doesn't start until six, but I offered to help set up."

"I look forward to it," Esther said. "See you then, my friend."

Janet left, and Esther and I sat down again. Determined to steer our conversation in a safer direction, I asked her more about the churches. "I'm a little surprised to hear the two churches work together so well. Don't Mennonites frown on some of the practices in other churches? I mean, about women not wearing prayer coverings? Or the men and women mixing together in church?"

Esther, who had picked up her coffee cup again, set it down and looked at me through squinted eyes. "I find it odd that you know so much about my church. Were you raised Mennonite?"

I took a quick breath. I was handling this badly. I thought quickly. "N-no. I did some research before coming here. I wanted to know what a Mennonite town was like."

This seemed to satisfy her, and she nodded. "Actually, this is not a Mennonite town now. When it was originally founded, it was certainly Mennonite. But now we are only a part of the population."

"But you said something about being careful with who is allowed to live in Sanctuary. What did you mean?"

"You asked if someone might be allowed to open a liquor store here. They would not find anyone to sell them space because folks in Sanctuary cherish this town." She stared down at her hands for a moment, appearing to be a little uneasy about my question. "Sanctuary has an appropriate name," she said slowly. "There are people here who have come because they seek a new life. A fresh start. This is a good place for starting over. We protect each other's privacy. Suffice it to say, this is a very special place. One that its citizens appreciate and value."

I raised an eyebrow as I looked at her. Was that some kind of warning? Looking at the elderly Mennonite lady, I quickly dismissed the thought. My own paranoia was getting the best of me.

"Well, it's lovely," I said. "You're very blessed to live in such a nice place."

She nodded. "I love the people in this town. They are my friends." She covered her mouth as she yawned. "I am sorry, Emily, but I am rather tired. I know people your age can go all day without wearing out, but I am not so fortunate. Would you mind if we brought our conversation to a close tonight? We can talk again tomorrow."

"Of course not," I said quickly. "I'm sorry. I should have realized . . ."

"That I'm an old woman and need my rest?" Esther laughed. "I do not expect you to know ahead of time when I am weary."

I smiled at her. "Tomorrow I plan to spend some time

going through the church records. Can we talk again in the afternoon?"

"That would be fine."

"Now, let me help you clean up."

"Thank you," she said. "But if we can just rinse the dishes, I will wash them in the morning."

"Nonsense," I said gently. "Please, Esther. Let me do it. I promise I'll be careful. I won't break anything."

Esther's eyes widened as she looked at me. "All right, child. If you really want to do that, it would be appreciated."

"Thank you. You won't take any payment for putting me up. At least let me help out some."

She nodded and got to her feet. Together we carried our plates and cups into the kitchen. After getting a glass of water to take to her room, Esther said good night. Her bedroom was on the first floor, not too far from the kitchen. I'd noticed that Janet had spoken rather loudly when in her presence. Obviously, Esther was a little hard of hearing, so I doubted I'd need to be too careful about making noise after she went to bed.

I washed the dishes by hand and put them in the drainer to dry. Although I loved the dishwasher in my small apartment in St. Louis, there was something almost therapeutic about doing things the old-fashioned way. There was a window over the sink that looked out over the backyard. Although it was dark outside, a light on the back of the house illuminated the yard with a soft golden glow. Esther's house backed up to a row of trees, and to my surprise a deer stepped through the foliage and walked slowly into the small clearing. She stopped several times and looked around. I stood still, afraid to move, afraid she would see me and run. Finally she dipped her head and began to eat, and I realized Esther had put out food for her. I watched, transported back in time to Kingdom. There had been a family of deer that occasionally came into our yard. I put food out whenever I could sneak something out of the house. Carrots, corn, sweet potatoes, apples, regular potatoes, and lettuce. Whatever I could get my hands on when my parents weren't looking. I loved to watch the deer feed through my bedroom window while I lay in bed at night. Until my father caught me taking food outside. He threatened to kill the deer and eat them if he ever saw them again. I stopped feeding them, and eventually they quit coming. At the time I felt as if I had betrayed them and lost the only friends I'd ever had.

It wasn't until the deer finished her meal and disappeared back through the trees that I realized tears coursed down my cheeks. I'd promised myself my father would never hurt me again, and it made me angry to allow him and his cruelty back into my mind. I wiped my face with the back of my hand and eventually managed to harness the raw feelings I'd spent years trying to ignore. I finished the dishes while whispering my affirmations until my emotions were back under control.

After I dried everything and put the dishes away, I walked through the quiet house to the front door. I'd noticed some rocking chairs when I'd come in, so I went outside and sat down in one of them. Then I rocked back and forth as I watched the lights turn off in the houses that lined both sides of the street. Suddenly, a clear vision of Jonathon floated in front of me again. The tears I thought I'd conquered earlier once again spilled over and wet my neck. I dabbed at them with my fingers, frustrated with myself for allowing this town to stir up old memories and pain. If I wanted to achieve my goals, I'd have to find a way to defeat the voices that whispered from a dark and distant past. I couldn't allow them to wrap their tentacles around me again.

I continued rocking while the air around me cooled. The sounds of nature created a symphony that finally brought a strange peace to my troubled mind. I'd forgotten the cacophony of noises that serenaded the nights in Kingdom. But as I listened to the old familiar sounds, instead of the resentment I'd felt earlier, something else filled my thoughts. A longing for something I couldn't quite explain or understand.

CHAPTER FIVE

I came downstairs the next morning and found Esther had prepared scrambled eggs, bacon, and pancakes. Since my usual breakfast consisted of yogurt and coffee, I was overwhelmed. Not wanting to hurt her feelings, I ate a little bit of everything and then called Pastor Troyer. He told me I could come by the church and go through the records any time that day. After a couple cups of coffee, I said good-bye to Esther and took off for the church. I listened to my affirmations all the way there, but for some reason, they didn't give me the same sense of peace they usually did.

"This stupid town is doing something to me," I muttered as I drove down the dirt streets to the church. I'd begun to remember more and more about Kingdom. Things I'd forgotten. Some good memories about kind people. But unfortunately, I also recalled what I'd done. How I'd hurt the town. I was certain no one in Kingdom still had any spark of compassion for me, and I didn't blame them.

I pulled up in front of the church and parked. If anyone

had told me a month ago that I'd be walking into a Conservative Mennonite church, I'd have told them they'd lost their mind. But here I was.

When I entered the church office, Pastor Troyer was talking to a woman. When he saw me, he greeted me, and the woman turned her head to see who was behind her.

"Emily, may I introduce you to my wife, Dorcas?"

The shock of hearing my own mother's name rendered me temporarily speechless. All I could do was nod at the woman. Dorcas Troyer looked nothing like my mom. She was a slight woman with graying chestnut hair and large brown eyes. For some reason, in that moment, she reminded me of the doe I'd seen in Esther's yard the night before.

"It is so nice to meet you, Emily," she said in a light, lyrical voice. "Jacob told me you arrived yesterday."

Thankfully, I was finally able to speak. "It's nice to meet you, too," I said. "I appreciate all the help your husband has extended to me."

"That is his job"—she patted her husband's arm—"but I am happy he is a blessing to you. I understand you wish to go through the records we keep of Sanctuary residents?"

"Yes, if it would be all right. I'd like to know when my grandmother's family first came to live in Sanctuary."

Dorcas nodded. "A good idea. Actually, her family may have been among our earliest settlers. I believe they came here when we were called New Zion. I hope your search will give you the information you seek." She stepped toward the door. "I will take you downstairs and show you where the records are kept."

"Thank you. I really appreciate that."

"Dorcas has taken over the maintenance of our records," Pastor Troyer said, sending his wife a smile. "And she does a wonderful job."

"And the work began when the town was founded?"

He nodded. "At first it had more to do with land ownership. Then it became about church membership. Eventually, as others moved here, the goal changed to keeping an account of everyone who has lived in Sanctuary. It was in the early nineteen hundreds when the church began to chronicle all the residents. Since then, we have kept up the custom. Having a history of our small town is helpful—and interesting. You will see notes about births, deaths, families, and even jobs and contributions to the community. It is a wonderful way to learn more about our town."

I could see the pastor's Bible on the desk in front of him, and a notepad next to it. He was probably working on his sermon. Even though I had more questions, I decided to save them for later and let the pastor get back to his work.

"Thank you so much, Pastor Troyer. Again, I appreciate your help."

He nodded and smiled.

"If you will come with me," Dorcas said gently, "I will take you to the basement."

I trailed along behind her as she walked down a long hall and turned the corner. The church was larger on the inside than I'd guessed. We passed several empty classrooms until we ended up at the stairs. As we descended, I realized for the first time that, just like Esther's house, the church had electricity. I'd heard that many Conservative Mennonite communities had accepted electricity and phones, and some members even drove cars, had electrical appliances, and surfed the Internet. But the one thing that hadn't changed was the acceptance of television. It was still seen as an instrument of worldliness and discouraged from finding a place in a Mennonite home.

"The records room is here," Dorcas said, bringing my attention back to the matter at hand.

She opened an old wooden door that creaked in the dark. Then she reached around to the wall inside the room and flicked on the light. Although it helped illuminate our surroundings, it also cast a strange yellow glow over everything. It was a little eerie.

I followed her to a sturdy-looking but ancient desk in the corner of the room. "This is where I work on the town records," she told me. Just as I was wondering how in the world I was going to see anything in the poorly lit room, she turned on a small desk lamp. Thankfully, it gave off much better light. The top of the desk glowed brightly, but somehow, the small lamp made the room around us seem even darker.

"There aren't any windows?" I asked.

"They are painted, so no light comes in. I'm sorry. It was done years ago when the room was given a new coat of paint. I would like to see this changed, but we have not found the time to scrape the paint off. I know it makes the room very dark." She turned and pointed at several old wooden filing cabinets behind us. "The files are here."

I was surprised by the number of drawers. How many people had lived in this small town over the years?

She pulled open a drawer in the cabinet nearest us. "The files are in date order," she said. "If your grandmother's relations were among the founding families, the information will be here. As my husband said, first you will see land records. Over the years, the church has tried to go back over all the old records and correlate them with the population files, but I cannot guarantee that all of the names have been transferred. Your search may take some time."

I smiled at her. "That's fine. I'm not in a hurry."

"I would be happy to stay and help, if you want."

That was the last thing I wanted. "Thank you so much, but it's not necessary. As you said, it might take some time." I reached into my purse and pulled out a notebook and a pen and put them on the desk.

"As you wish." She turned to go but swung back around before she stepped out of the lamp's circle of light. "You are welcome to come here any time, but if you would let my husband know when you are here and when you leave, it would be helpful."

"I will. And thank you again, D-Dorcas." I had a hard time saying my mother's name, but the pastor's wife didn't seem to notice. She just smiled and slipped into the darkness that encircled me.

When I heard the door close, I slumped down onto the desk chair. One thing after another kept reminding me of my past. Now the pastor's wife had the same name as my mother? The whole thing was ridiculous.

"I am calm and relaxed in every situation. I can control my thoughts. No one can dominate me. I am in charge of my life. I am a winner. I am successful in everything I do." My whispers disappeared into the murky surroundings. With a sigh, I got up, went to the nearest filing cabinet, and took out two large record books. They would sit on the desk, so if anyone came in, it would look like I really was trying to find information about my birth family.

I checked my watch to see what time it was. A little after nine. That gave me almost three hours before lunch. I suddenly thought about the call from Tom. I'd meant to call the warden's office before I came to the church, but I'd been so focused on going through the records, I'd forgotten. The more I'd thought about it, though, the more certain I became that Tom's concerns were groundless. Why would anyone in the prison care about a robbery that happened so long ago? It was silly. Tom was safe, surrounded by guards and cameras. No one could get to him. He was safer in that prison than anywhere else he could be.

However, I'd made a promise, so I pulled out my phone. It would only take a few minutes to call the prison. I just hoped they wouldn't think I was nuts. I pulled up the number Tom had called me from the night before and tried to return the call, but it wouldn't connect. It was probably because I was in the basement. I just couldn't get a good signal, so I put the phone back in my purse. Tom would have to wait until I left for lunch.

I pulled a small flashlight that I kept for emergencies out of my purse. Then I began to search through the cabinets, looking for records kept after 2008. Eventually I found a book with a label on the front that indicated it was from 2008 to 2009. Glancing toward the door first, I pulled out the book and carried it over to the table. As I opened it, I considered what I would tell Dorcas or Pastor Troyer if they came to check on me. How would I explain why I was looking at this particular volume? In the end, all I could do was hope they didn't show up.

I scoured the entries recorded after May of 2008, the month the robbery occurred. There weren't any new residents added in May. Only one in June, and it was a woman. July had three new residents. Two of them were a married couple. The other was a single man. I wrote down his name and went to the next month. This time I found two single men. I slowly worked my way through to the end of the book and ended up with only one more single man. When I checked my watch and realized it was almost noon, I decided to switch over to the older books and research the Bylers. I needed to have something to show for my time should anyone ask.

I ignored the land information since I cared more about the names of the first citizens. As I scanned the first book, I was surprised by how interested I became. As Dorcas had said, the town was called New Zion back then, and the names were German and Dutch. It occurred to me that the Byler family might have come here under a different last name. If that were true, it could take some time for me to find the information I needed. But thankfully, I found a Joseph Byler and his wife, Elizabeth. The records were divided by arrival, addresses, births, and then deaths. Joseph and Elizabeth's address was on a county road, so I assumed they were farmers. They had five children: Jeremiah, Isaac, Sarah, Rachel, and Mary. As I followed their story, I found out that Mary died when she was three years old. I kept going down the list until I saw that Jeremiah married in 1898. His wife was Katherine. Sarah married a man named William Hoffman in 1900. A year later, they welcomed a daughter named Margaret.

I wrote down all these details and kept looking, not finding any more entries for the family until 1910, when Isaac married and moved away. I stuck a piece of notebook paper between the pages where I'd stopped and put all the books away. Then I turned off the lights and left the room. When I stopped by Pastor Troyer's office, the door was closed. I knocked lightly, but there was no answer, so I wrote him a quick note and slid it under the door.

As I walked out into a mild, springlike afternoon, I should have felt relieved to be free from the dark, dank basement. But the truth was, I'd enjoyed looking through the books and reading about the people who had started this town so long ago. I got in my car and drove toward downtown Sanctuary. I'd seen two restaurants on my way through town yesterday and wanted to check them out. There was no better way to get to know people than to spend time in their local cafés.

As I drove down Main Street, I looked at the small businesses that lined the road. One large building housed a school, a library, and a post office. I hadn't expected the post office and realized I could mail the bills I'd accidentally stuck in my purse. I'd thought about sending them out from Esther's, but I was afraid she might see the envelopes and wonder about the return address. Even though I'd only used my initials, the fact that they didn't match up with Emily McClure would seem suspicious.

I pulled up in front of the post office and went inside. My plan was to drop my envelopes into a mail box, but as I headed toward the large metal container in the corner, an elderly woman waiting in line at the counter caught my attention.

"Mail's already been picked up for the day," she said. "If you want it to go out now, you gotta give it to the postmaster."

I thought about dumping it in anyway, but handing it to a real person seemed safer. I took my place in line behind the helpful woman. There was only one other person in line ahead of us. I caught sight of the man handling the counter and had to choke back a laugh. If I were casting a television show set in a small town, I'd have picked him to be the postmaster. Short, balding, and timid-looking, he wore round, wire-rimmed glasses, a long-sleeved white shirt, and sported a red bow tie and matching suspenders. I watched as he processed two packages for the man and sold stamps to the woman in front of me. The clerk seemed personable and friendly, and people appeared to like him.

When it was my turn, I read his name tag. *Evan Bakker*. He smiled as I stepped up to the counter.

"May I help you?"

I nodded. "I just need to mail out some envelopes. They already have stamps." I opened my purse and handed him my stack of mail.

"No problem." He took it from me. "Are you visiting someone?"

"I'm in town doing some research about a relative who recently passed away. Miriam Byler."

"Miriam?" He shook his head. "Lovely, lovely woman. She will be missed." He smiled. "I can see the resemblance. Around the eyes."

Well, that was new. He must really need those glasses he wore. "She was my great-aunt."

A man came in the door, and Mr. Bakker greeted him. I thanked the postmaster for his help and had started to leave when he said, "Miss?"

I turned around and saw him holding up the picture of Terrance Chase.

"This must have gotten mixed up with your mail."

I hurried back and took it from him. "I'm sorry. Thank you for finding it." I smiled at him. "A relative." Thankfully, there wasn't anything with Chase's name on it or any way for the clerk to know he was looking at the face of a missing murderer. The man standing at the counter glanced at the picture, but he didn't seem interested.

I took the picture and quickly left the building. When I got in my car, I stuck Chase's photo inside my wallet. What I should have done in the first place. Neither man seemed to recognize Chase, but I wondered if I should have asked them if he seemed familiar. Had I missed a chance? After thinking about it, I decided showing his picture around wasn't the best way to find him. First I needed to narrow down my suspect list. Tipping my hand too early could backfire. It might alert Chase that I was looking for him. Besides, if he really was in Sanctuary, he'd probably changed his appearance drastically.

It occurred to me as I sat in my car that the postmaster might be someone who could help me if the church records led nowhere. If anyone knew who came to town and when, it would be the postmaster. I filed that option away in the back of my mind where I could pull it up if I needed it later.

I did feel some relief knowing my payments were finally on their way. Paying my bills on time—even early—was almost an obsession with me. My parents hadn't taken responsibility for their debts, and I had no intention of following in their footsteps. I could still remember being sent to different stores, trying to return used items and asking for the money back. The memory still caused me acute embarrassment.

I drove farther down the street and checked out the two

restaurants in Sanctuary. Between The Oil Lamp Restaurant and The Whistle Stop Café, I chose the latter because it seemed a little more crowded. Although it was a long shot that Chase would be sitting at a table just waiting for me to spot him, I needed to start my search. I laughed to myself at the thought that it could be that easy. I just hoped it wouldn't take too long. I didn't want to hang around this town any longer than I had to.

As I picked up my purse, I couldn't help thinking about Cora's Corner Café, the only restaurant in Kingdom. At first, the Mennonite crowd had shunned it, believing food should be prepared by wives and served at home. But as single farmers began to drift in for breakfast, word spread. By the time I left Kingdom, it was almost always packed. Even the most stubborn member of the church eventually broke down and joined his friends around a table at Cora's. After Cora moved away, Lizzie took it over. It was just as popular under her leadership.

I got out of the car and headed for the front door of The Whistle Stop. As I reached for the handle, a man's hand came from behind me and pulled the door open.

"Here, let me," he said.

I turned to thank him and found myself looking straight into the striking blue eyes of Jonathon Wiese.

CHAPTER SIX

I froze, unable to accept what I could clearly see. For a split second, I wondered if I'd lost my mind. Was this a hallucination? Was I seeing Jonathon because I'd been thinking about him? But it wasn't a dream. Somehow, Jonathon Wiese was standing next to me. He was so close I could smell the soap he'd bathed with. I felt dizzy, but I quickly gathered myself together as much as I could under the circumstances.

"Thank you," I said softly. As I walked into the restaurant, my legs felt like rubber.

A pretty young woman walked up to me. "Just one person?" she asked with a smile.

I nodded, not able to think clearly about anything except the knowledge that Jonathon was right behind me. More than anything, I wanted to turn and run out the door. Get as far away from this place as I could. But that would only draw attention to me, and there hadn't been any sign of recognition from Jonathon. I was fairly confident he wouldn't recognize me. Tom hadn't known me, so I had to hope Jonathon wouldn't either. I looked nothing like the dirty child I'd once been.

The waitress's eyes swept across the room. "We only have one table clear right now." To my horror, I heard her say, "Jonathon, would you mind sitting with this lady? At least until we have another table cleaned off?"

"I'd be happy to. Thanks, Rosey." That wonderful voice. The one I'd been trying to erase from my memory for so long. I felt a touch on my shoulder. "I hope you don't mind, ma'am."

All I could do was shake my head. Once again, a feeling of unreality enveloped me. How could Jonathon Wiese be in Sanctuary?

I followed the waitress to the table she indicated. As we made our way across the room, people called out to Jonathon, greeting him with enthusiasm and confirming that I hadn't been mistaken. It was definitely Jonathon.

When we reached our table, he held out my chair, and I sat down. As he slid into his seat, I scanned his face again. As impossible as it seemed, I was sitting across from a man I'd never planned to see again in this lifetime.

I suddenly noticed a hand in front of my face. I turned to look up at the young woman who'd seated us.

"I'm Rosey," she said. "My mom and I own this restaurant."

I took her hand and shook it. "I—I'm Emily McClure. Just visiting. Trying to find out something about a family member who used to live here."

She frowned and let go of my hand. "Oh? Do you mind if I ask who?"

"Miriam Byler. Turns out she was my great-aunt. Her sister, Clara, was my grandmother. My mother just found out she was adopted and that she was Clara's daughter." I was babbling, but frankly, I was just happy I could get any words out at all.

Rosey's eyebrows shot up. "I knew Miriam pretty well. Met Clara, too. She came to town quite often before she passed away. When she came to visit, she and Miriam would come here to eat." She smiled. "They were both wonderful women. You should be proud to be related to them."

"Thank you," I said, trying to smile back. "I really appreciate that."

She nodded. "What can I get you two to drink?"

"I think I'd like a cup of coffee."

Rosey smiled at me. "You're stronger than I am. If I had coffee in the afternoon, I'd be up all night." She swung her attention to Jonathon. "And for you, Pastor?"

Pastor? My mouth almost dropped open. Jonathon was wearing contemporary clothing, not the usual Mennonite uniform. I noticed his hair was shorter than I remembered it. He'd always worn it a little long back home. But as a pastor, he probably felt the need for a more conservative hairstyle. Suddenly, I remembered the other church I'd passed as I came into town. Jonathon must be that church's pastor.

"I think I'll join the young lady," he said with a glance at me. "I'll have coffee, too."

"Two brave souls," Rosey said. "Here are your menus. I'll be back in a minute."

I took the menu from her hand, but Jonathon waved his away. Obviously, he'd been here before.

As Rosey went to help someone else, I quickly scanned the room. I'd come here hoping to spot Terrance Chase, but at the moment I couldn't think about anything except Jonathon. Unwillingly, I met my dinner companion's eyes.

"I'm Jonathon Wiese," he said with a smile. "Welcome to Sanctuary. If I can do anything to help you, please let me know. Miriam and I were friends."

I steeled myself the best I could, running my affirmations through my head. I was no longer Sophie Wittenbauer, a wayward, pitiful child. I was Sophie Bauer, educated, sophisticated, and strong.

"I appreciate that," I said, trying to sound more confident than I felt. "Right now I'm working with her pastor." Though I tried to maintain some degree of control, my voice shook slightly.

He nodded. "Pastor Troyer. Good man."

I decided to try again. This time my voice sounded stronger. "May I ask how you knew my great-aunt?"

Jonathon shrugged. "In a town this small, it's hard not to know everyone. Miriam was a lovely lady who enjoyed company. I spent a lot of time visiting with her. I pastor the other church in town, Agape Fellowship."

Before I could say anything else, Rosey came up to the table with our coffee. "Do you know what you want?" she asked. "Or do you need more time?"

"I—I'm sorry. I haven't even looked at my menu yet." I nodded toward Jonathon. "You go ahead. And please, don't feel you need to sit with me. If another table opens up . . ."

"Unless you mind, I'd like to stay," he said. "But maybe you'd prefer to eat alone?"

Yes, I want to eat alone! Go away! But I couldn't say that. I looked very different from the girl he'd known, but I still needed to keep up my façade so he didn't become suspicious.

"No, please stay. I enjoy meeting new people."

Liar! I really didn't like meeting people. I didn't like people, period. People had baggage, and most of them loved to dump it off in your life. I had no time for that.

"Thank you. Why don't you come back in a few minutes, Rosey?" he said. "Do you mind?"

"Of course not. You take your time, honey." She touched my shoulder, and I jumped involuntarily.

"I'm so sorry." She chuckled. "I didn't mean to scare you. I'm kind of a touchy-feely person."

"Well, I'm not," I snapped. I was instantly sorry for my sharp remark. I sighed and shook my head. "Now it's my turn to apologize. Please forgive me. I'm just tired from my trip here." I gave her my best smile, designed to charm. "And obviously cranky."

The hurt look on her face vanished. "That's okay, honey. I understand completely. After being on my feet all day, I usually feel like knocking a few heads together."

Jonathon laughed. "Oh, Rosey. You and your mother are the nicest people I know. If you raised your voice, I'd pass out."

"We have our buttons. I don't have to remind you about what happened in Farmington last summer."

He grinned. "No, you don't. That story circulated through town for quite a while."

She leaned toward him conspiratorially. "Now you hush, Jonathon. Don't tell our visitor my family secrets." She winked at me. "I'll be back in a few."

"So what happened in Farmington?" I asked when she walked away.

"Rosey and her mother, Mary, went there to buy some supplies for the restaurant. On the way into the store, they discovered a dog locked in a hot car. The poor thing was already half dead. After trying the doors, Mary got a rock and broke open a window. They got the dog out, gave it some water, and called the police. When the owner finally got back to his car, he was greeted by Rosey, Mary, a crowd of concerned bystanders, and the cops. Believe it or not, his main concern was his car window. He started yelling, and Mary got up in his face. Told the guy off big-time." Jonathon motioned toward the restaurant's kitchen. "When you meet Mary, you'll understand. She's one of the sweetest, most mild-mannered people you'll ever run across. But hurt a child or an animal, and something explodes in that little woman. Something fierce."

"So what finally happened?" I asked.

"Well, let's just say the guy ended up with a citation and a broken window no one had any intention of replacing. And Mary and Rosey walked away with a new dog."

"They got the man's dog?"

Jonathon nodded. "Mary told him they were taking her, and he was too afraid to say no. Livy is a very happy beagle, being loved and pampered by Mary and Rosey."

"The dog stays alone all day while the restaurant is open?"

Jonathon chuckled. "Another animal lover, I see. You don't need to worry. First of all, The Whistle Stop isn't open in the evening. But even so, Livy isn't alone. At last count, she lives with six cats and four other dogs—Pogo, Maggie, Candy, and Teddy. They have a doggy door that opens into a fenced backyard so they can come and go as they please."

"Six cats and five dogs? Wow. That's a lot of mouths to feed."

"That doesn't include the horses, cows, and chickens. I love animals, but Mary and Rosey seem to have a heart for them that only God could provide."

I didn't respond. Sure, God loved animals. Too bad His great love didn't extend to abused children.

I picked up my menu and perused the offerings. When I finally settled on something, I put the menu back down on the table.

"So what do you do, Emily?" Jonathon asked.

I pulled out my rehearsed answer. "I work for an accounting firm in St. Louis." Since it sounded like the most boring job in the world, I figured it would stop further questions cold in their tracks.

"Oh?" He stared at me for a moment. "You don't look like an accountant."

"Really? And just what kind of person do I look like?"

Before he could answer, a pretty woman with long blond hair stepped up to the table. "Are you ready to order?" she asked.

"Emily, this is Mary Gessner. The woman I was telling you about."

Mary's eyebrows arched in surprise. "What have you been saying about me, Jonathon Wiese? It had better be good."

"It was. I promise." He nodded toward me. "Mary, this is Emily McClure. She's visiting our fine town for a while. She's related to Miriam Byler."

"No kidding? Nice to meet you, Emily. Where are you staying?"

"With Esther Lapp. It seems to be the place strangers end up when they come to Sanctuary."

"You're right about that." She pulled a notepad out of her apron pocket. "What can I get you two?"

"You know what I want, Mary. My usual."

"Let's see." Mary pursed her lips and looked off into the distance to show she was thinking. "It's Wednesday, and the special is chicken fried steak. So I'm guessing you want meat loaf?"

Jonathon's wide grin made it clear Mary was pulling his leg.

"Chicken fried steak for you. And what about you, Emily?"

I ordered a small side salad and a bowl of soup.

"This is why this lady is so trim and you're . . . not," Mary teased Jonathon.

"I'll have you know I'm still at my high school weight," Jonathon said with an exaggerated pout.

"Yes. But that was muscle."

Mary flipped her long hair and walked away, leaving Jonathon laughing softly.

"I don't get it," I said when she was out of earshot. "You're not the least bit overweight."

He smiled. "I know. We're just teasing each other because we like to. It doesn't mean anything."

"I'm surprised to hear someone treat a minister so lightly."

"Oh really? May I ask what kind of church you attend?"

I felt myself blush. "I don't anymore. I'm sorry to sound so judgmental. Old habits, I guess. In the church I used to go to, married pastors didn't joke around much with other women."

"I'm not married."

I noticed for the first time that he wasn't wearing a ring, although in the Conservative Mennonite church, married couples didn't wear wedding rings. I'd been so certain he'd married Hope Kauffman, the woman he'd loved in Kingdom, that I had simply assumed she was here with him.

"You look surprised. I know it's unusual for a pastor to be single, but I couldn't marry someone just because I wanted to pastor a church. Wouldn't be fair to her. Or to me."

Surprised wasn't the word for how I felt. *Shocked* was a better description. I tried to find a way to cover my reaction. "I'm sorry. I didn't mean to get personal."

"It's okay. I'm not offended. The truth is, I was in love once. But she picked someone else. If I ever find a woman who makes me feel the way she did, I'll consider marriage again. But so far that hasn't happened."

So he wasn't with Hope. She must have married Ebbie Miller instead. I felt a twinge of pity for Jonathon. He'd been head over heels for Hope. But even though I had compassion for him, something inside me leapt with pleasure. Just as quickly as the feeling came, I squashed it. I couldn't go down this road again. I'd been madly in love with Jonathon once. So in love it hurt. But he didn't love me back. Didn't see me that way. To him I was only a troubled teenager. A child. Even now that I was an adult, he would never be interested. A man of God wouldn't want anything to do with a woman who'd turned her back on Him. A woman too damaged to be worth anything to any man.

"What about you?" he asked suddenly. "Is there a Mr. McClure?"

I shook my head. "No. My job comes first. There's no time for anything else."

He looked at me strangely, and I immediately realized how odd my comment sounded. Most people wouldn't be so passionate about accounting.

"I want to own my own firm someday." I spewed the first thing that popped into my head. "It's my dream."

"Oh."

I watched him study me, and I felt myself melting under the power of those astonishing eyes. Was there any chance he'd recognize me? Was my goal of tracking down Terrance Chase in jeopardy already?

When he finally spoke, his voice was low and soft. "I don't know, Emily. It's like I'm seeing one person, but I sense someone else hiding inside. Someone who seems so familiar." His eyes suddenly widened, and he laughed. "Wow. Where did that come from? Sounded rather ominous. Sorry. I must be feeling a little melodramatic today."

"We all wear masks, Pastor," I said. "The person we present to the world is rarely the person we really are."

"You're right." He took a deep breath. "Let's see if I can peer beneath the mask of an accountant." He stared down at his coffee cup for a moment, and then he looked up and gazed at me through narrowed eyes. "I think you're a successful woman who knows what she wants. You were strong enough to come to a town full of people you don't know, to track down a family that never claimed you. This shows a real sense of curiosity and determination." He grinned. "Maybe you should be a writer or a reporter. Or even a detective."

I laughed nervously at his evaluation, which was way too close to the mark. My anxiety had reached a peak, and warning bells were going off in my mind. If I wanted to find Chase, I needed to stay as far away from Jonathon as possible. He was dangerous. Not only to my mission—but also to my heart.

"Well, I'm sorry to disappoint you, but I'm not very adventurous. It's true that coming here might seem . . . brave, but it has more to do with creating a family tree." I shrugged. "It's like accounting. I'm just filling in the gaps. Making sure everything balances correctly."

Jonathon didn't say anything. Just kept looking at me.

"So tell me about your church," I blurted out, trying to find something to distract him.

The preoccupied look left his features, and he launched into a long story about his church and the people who attended Agape. His excitement was evident, and I could tell he was passionate about being a pastor. He seemed happy and fulfilled. I couldn't help but wonder if accomplishing my dream of becoming a crime reporter would bring me the joy I saw on his face. It was a goal I'd wanted to achieve for a long time, but as I listened to him, I realized I had lost track of why.

As he talked, my mind wandered back to the past. I could see Jonathon standing next to me on the road to Kingdom. His azure eyes mirrored the flowers that grew wild in and around our town. I could feel the sun beating down on us and my heart racing at his nearness. The memory caused an ache inside me. Something I didn't understand. I hated

Kingdom and was glad to be away from it. So why did I suddenly yearn to stand on that road again, with Jonathon by my side?

Mary stepped up to the table with our food, breaking me out of my reminiscing. Jonathon stopped talking while she placed our dishes in front of us. We both thanked her, and then she left to take care of other customers. I gazed around the crowded restaurant, remembering I'd picked The Whistle Stop because I wanted to see as many people as possible, hoping to spot someone who looked like Chase. A quick examination didn't reveal a single person who could have been the notorious robber.

"Did you hear me, Emily?"

Jonathon's question got my attention. "I—I'm sorry. What did you say?"

"I've bored you, talking so much about my church. I'm sorry."

"No, I found it very interesting. I just remembered a call I need to make." That much was true. I really should contact the prison. I couldn't keep putting it off.

"Do you have time to finish your lunch?" Jonathon asked.

I shook my head. "Maybe Mary could pack it up for me, and I can take it back to Esther's. I'm sorry. I should have made this call earlier. It just slipped my mind." Although it was the last thing I really wanted, I had to get away from Jonathon.

"I understand. I just hope you're not leaving because I dominated the conversation."

"Of course not. I didn't mean to give that impression."

Jonathon offered me a wide smile, and my heart flip-flopped inside my chest. He was so handsome. I wanted to reach out and touch his face, but I couldn't. And I never would. It was time to accept that fact and get on with my search.

"Good," he said. "If you're still in town, maybe you'd like to come to my church Sunday morning?"

I quickly shook my head. "Sorry. I'm not the church type anymore. I quit believing in God a long time ago."

His eyebrows arched, but the smile didn't leave his face. "It's not a prerequisite for attendance. Just come. I'm sure some of our members would love to meet you."

My ears perked up at this. It was Wednesday. If I hadn't found Chase by Sunday, it might be a good idea to go where a lot of Sanctuary's citizens gathered. There was no way I'd set foot in the Mennonite service, which was okay since I was pretty confident Chase wouldn't go that far to cover his identity. "Okay," I said finally, "I may take you up on that."

Jonathon's smile grew bigger. "Great. Service starts at nine-thirty."

Returning his smile, I signaled for Mary. "I'll do my best."

"I really hope you do," Jonathon said slowly. "It would be nice to see you again."

"Thank you." I wasn't sure what he meant by that, but I dismissed it as good manners.

"Did you need something, honey?" I looked up and found Mary already standing next to me.

"I need to get my food to go. I forgot about an important phone call I have to make."

"Okay," she said. "But you can call from in here, you know. Do you have a cell phone?"

"Yes, but it's a rather private call."

"I understand," Mary said. "I'll get you some carryout containers."

"Are you feeling okay?" Jonathon asked after Mary left. "You look a little pale."

I wasn't surprised. Seeing Jonathon again was an incredible shock. But I reassured him quickly. "Yes. Sorry. A slight blood sugar problem. When it drops, sometimes I don't feel very well."

"Is there anything I can do?"

I braced my hands on the tabletop in front of me. "No, I just need to lie down for a while."

"One of my friends has the same problem. Drinking orange juice helps. I'll be right back." He jumped up and walked back toward the counter. He said something to Rosey, who was ringing up a customer's bill. She nodded at him, finished with the man, and then hurried to the kitchen. Seconds later, she emerged with a glass of orange juice. Jonathon took it and came back to our table.

"Here," he said, handing me the glass. "Drink this."

Obediently, I took the glass, downed the juice, and thanked him. Other customers were watching us, probably wondering what all the fuss was about. Now, instead of feeling faint, my face grew hot. I'd always had rather rosy cheeks, never needing makeup to enhance them. I was pretty sure by now they were beyond red.

Thankfully, Mary showed up right after that with two foam containers. She scooped my salad into the larger box and poured my soup into a round container with a lid. "Here you go, honey," she said, putting everything in a plastic bag. She also added some crackers, some plastic ware, and a small foam cup containing dressing to the bag.

"Thank you so much," I said. "Do I pay you here or up front at the cash register?"

Mary patted my shoulder. "You don't pay me at all. It's on me. A welcome-to-Sanctuary gift."

"Thank you. That's very kind." I took the bag from her and then headed for the front of the restaurant. More than anything else, I wanted out of that place. Away from Jonathon. Away from the powerful feelings that tried to overwhelm me. I'd just reached the exit when Jonathon stepped in front of me and opened the door. He followed me out onto the big wooden porch outside the restaurant.

"I wanted to tell you how much I enjoyed meeting you. I really hope we get another chance to talk."

Again I had that strong urge to reach out and touch his face. Jonathon had never worn a beard, but he wasn't clean shaven either. Some men might have looked scruffy with a light growth of hair on their face—but not Jonathon. It only added to his handsome features.

"Thanks. Me too. Maybe some other time?" What was I saying? Why hadn't I simply told him I was going to be too busy to spend time with him—or anyone?

"Sure. I'll hold you to that."

I practically ran to my car, got in, and quickly drove away. The bag of food I'd put on the seat next to me fell over, but I didn't stop to check it until I reached Esther's. When I turned off the engine, I sat there for several minutes, watching Sanctuary cloaked in afternoon sunlight, wondering what to do. Should I stay or should I take my shattered heart and run away?

CHAPTER SEVEN

By the time I was ready to climb out of my car, the sun was already getting low in the sky. Daylight Savings Time was still a couple of weeks away, so the sun still set early. I glanced at my watch. Just a few minutes after five. I'd done it again. Missed calling the warden's office. I suddenly remembered the number Tom had given me and wondered if I should try it instead.

I grabbed the bag from The Whistle Stop and carried it to the front porch. Then I collapsed into one of the rocking chairs, feeling drained and confused. I put the sack down and opened my purse, finding my notebook and pulling it out. After flipping a few pages, I found the rapidly scrawled number Tom had given me. I punched it in and waited.

A male voice came on the line.

"Hello?"

I told him I was calling to check on Tom. "I just want to make sure he's doing okay," I said. "And I'd appreciate it if you'd tell him I called."

There was a long silence. "Can you hold on a moment please?"

"Sure." While I waited, I picked up my bag from the restaurant and checked it out. The container with the salad dressing was on its side, but it was still closed. Thankfully, the soup was still secure, as was the salad.

I sat in the gathering dusk, waiting for the man who'd answered to return to the phone. I hadn't been hungry at the restaurant, but now my stomach growled. I began to grow impatient and was thinking about hanging up when suddenly he came back on the line.

"Can I ask who's calling?" he asked abruptly.

"A friend. I'm not asking for any personal information. I just want to know if he's all right. He called me yesterday and seemed upset."

More silence. "Is this Sophie?"

My mouth dropped open. "I'm sorry. What did you say?" How could this guy know who I was? What should I say?

"Tom told me about you," he said softly. "I'm Donnie Matthews. I'm a guard here and a friend of his."

This had to be the guard Tom trusted. The one who'd gotten his letters out of the prison. "Yes, I'm Sophie. I didn't realize this was your phone number. Is Tom all right, Donnie? He called me yesterday. Wanted me to help him."

"Tom was attacked last night, Sophie," he said in hushed tones. "He was beaten up pretty bad. He's going to be okay, but he's lost all phone privileges. You won't be able to talk to him for a while."

I instantly felt guilty. He'd called me for help, and I'd ignored him. Had my visit gotten Tom hurt?

As if he could read my thoughts, Donnie said, "It's not your fault. You couldn't have prevented this. Trust me."

"I—I'd like to see him, but I'm out of town. In Sanctuary, Missouri. It would take me almost nine hours to get there."

"Tom told me you were there, trying to find Terrance Chase. You might as well stay where you are. I'm pretty sure he'll be denied visitors for quite a while. It happens sometimes when inmates fight. To be honest, finding Chase might be the only thing that can really help him. Right now he's in isolation, so he's safe. I can't guarantee anything when he's put back into the general population. Frankly, I'm wondering if someone here knows Chase and is trying to keep Tom quiet."

"But how could that be? Tom said you were the only one who knew what was going on."

"I believed that, too. Except for the letter he sent you, I snuck all his other mail out of the prison so no one would find out what he was up to. I can't figure it out. Maybe he left something in his cell and the wrong person saw it."

For some reason, the guard with the sharp features popped into my mind. He'd seemed especially interested in Tom and me. Could he have been in Tom's cell when he was out in the yard? It certainly explained the way he'd acted. I told Donnie about him and his demeanor while Tom and I visited.

"I know exactly who you mean. His name is Harry Rand." He paused for a moment. "He might be behind this. He could have found out what Tom was doing and passed the information on to someone else. Harry's a mean son of a gun. I think he brings contraband into the prison for some of the inmates. I've never caught him at it, but I've certainly had my suspicions."

"Maybe you should stay away from him, Donnie."

"I will. The best thing I can do right now is act like I have no idea why Tom was beaten. Keep my head down."

"What about the prisoner who attacked Tom? Who is he?"

Donnie sighed. "Just a troublemaker. Basically, he's an attack dog. Not someone who would be looking for Chase. The kind of guy who could be manipulated by someone else to start a fight."

"Like Harry Rand?"

"Exactly."

I thought quickly. "I'll work as fast as I can to find Chase. It's particularly important you keep me out of this, Donnie. I made up a story so I could come here and search for Chase. I don't want anyone to find out what I'm up to. Especially Chase."

"I understand that. I would never tell anyone about you. Or Tom."

"Will you keep me updated? Let me know how Tom is doing?"

"Sure."

"Did my number show up on your phone?"

"Yes. I've got it, Sophie. Let's hope Sanctuary lives up to its name. I don't like knowing Harry saw you talking to Tom . . ."

"He has no idea where I am," I said. "As long as he doesn't find out, I'll be fine."

Another long silence. I began to feel nervous.

"Sophie, I don't want to think this . . ."

"What, Donnie?"

"I'm wondering if whoever beat Tom was looking for information. If someone connected to Chase is behind this, more than anything, they'd want to know who you are and . . ."

"Where I am," I finished for him.

"Right. Remember, there's still a lot of money missing. The idea of finding Chase and the money could drive someone to do something . . . violent."

As I thought about Donnie's conjecture, it made more sense than anything else. At first I'd thought Tom's warning could have come from one of Chase's cronies trying to protect him. Yet the crime had happened so long ago, that idea seemed far-fetched. But what if it had been someone looking for the money? There could be a lot of candidates. It was not only a much more likely scenario, but it also meant I could be in some trouble if my location was revealed.

"Have you talked to Tom?"

"I can't. I'm not assigned to the part of the prison where he's being held. It would look really suspicious if I asked to visit him." There was a brief silence before Donnie said, "Please be careful, Sophie. What if Tom told someone about you?"

"I don't believe he'd do that." Even as I said the words, I wasn't sure they were true. I didn't really know Tom Ford anymore. There wasn't any reason for me to believe he'd protect me if he was threatened.

"I hope you're right. But we can't be sure of that."

"Let's wait until we have some solid answers. Whoever hurt Tom might have had a completely different motivation. I understand fights in prison aren't all that rare."

"Well, that's true, but I still think you should be cautious." He hesitated for a moment. "Sophie, do you need any help? I could come to Sanctuary."

"And what would you do here?"

"I'll help you search. And protect you. It's what Tom would want."

I was touched by this man who'd tried to look after Tom and now wanted to defend me. "That's nice, really. But I'll be fine. Sanctuary is a very small town. Anyone new would stick out like a sore thumb. Kind of like me. You have my word that I'll be careful."

"Okay," he said slowly. "But I wish you'd consider it. What if something happens and you need help? Who could you turn to?"

Jonathon's face popped into my mind, but I dismissed it. There was no way I was going to tell Jonathon who I really was. I was too embarrassed. Besides, he probably still hated me. Just like everyone else in Kingdom.

"I don't know. Don't worry, Donnie. If anything weird happens, I'll call you." A chilly breeze drifted over me, and I shivered. "I've got to go. But thank you so much. For helping Tom, and for being here for me. It makes me feel better—having someone else who knows what's going on."

"Well, I'm glad, but I still wish you'd let me come."

"Thanks again, but I'd much rather have you keep an eye on Tom. Call me if anything changes with him, okay? And if you can possibly find a way to let him know I called, I'd appreciate it."

"I'll do my best. Good-bye, Sophie."

"'Bye, Donnie."

I hung up and gathered my food. Esther's front door was unlocked, and when I went inside, I didn't see her anywhere. It wasn't very late. Had she already gone to bed? Not sure, I went to the kitchen, poured myself a glass of iced tea, and took my soup and salad out of the bag. The soup was cold. A quick look around the kitchen didn't reveal a microwave, which didn't surprise me. But I found a pan, poured the soup into it, and started heating it up on Esther's ancient stove. While my soup warmed, I took the plastic fork, spoon, and knife out of the cellophane wrapper and put them down on the kitchen table. After pouring the dressing on my salad, I started eating. The vegetables were still crisp and fresh, and the dressing was incredible. Homemade. After the soup was hot, I poured it back into its foam container and tasted it. It was delicious. Almost three years of fast food and my own cooking, which was pitiful at best, made me think once again about Lizzie's restaurant in Kingdom. There was nothing better than food cooked by someone who knew what they were doing.

I realized with a start that Kingdom had drifted back into my thoughts again. Ever since I'd set foot in Sanctuary, my old hometown had been pushing its way back into my consciousness. After all the years of trying to forget, why couldn't I stop thinking about the past? Seeing Jonathon was a shock, but I'd put him out of my mind before, so surely I could do it again. The truth was, being so near him again had shaken me to the core.

"Stop it, Sophie," I said to myself. "You're not going down this road again." I tried to recite my affirmations, but for some reason, they felt like dirt in my mouth. Positive words weren't going to help me this time. Either I had to make up my mind and ignore him—and the past—or I'd have to give up and leave Sanctuary.

No. I'd run away from myself once, and I just couldn't do

it again. *Wouldn't* do it again. Terrance Chase could actually be here—or at least *was* here at some point—and this was my only chance to find him. To write the story of a lifetime. To become everything I wanted to be. I couldn't fail. I had to stay the course.

I finished my meal, cleaned up, and headed upstairs. When I opened the door to my room, I saw a piece of paper on the bed. It was a note from Esther.

> *Feeling a little tired tonight. Went to bed early. Will see you in the morning, honey. Maybe we can talk then. Please help yourself to anything you need. I put clean towels in the bathroom for you.*
>
> *Esther*

I'd completely forgotten we were supposed to visit this afternoon. I'd been so focused on the books in the church basement that I'd blown Esther off. Her kindness touched me and made me feel guilty all at the same time. I tossed her note in the trash and slumped down on the fainting couch. Frankly, everything in this town made me feel guilty. Pretending to be someone else was exhausting. I couldn't help but be concerned about Tom, but the thing foremost on my mind was being forced to face Jonathon again. What were the chances something like this could even happen? Some people in Kingdom would tell me this was God's hand. That He'd brought me here for a reason. That He had some kind of plan for my life. But I wouldn't buy into that. His supposed love had placed me in a family that hated me and abused me. He'd let me get involved with Tom and mess up my life so badly

I'd had to run away at eighteen. Everything I had now was because of one person. Me. I had no intention of ever letting the delusion of a loving God back in my life. I knew better.

"You hear that?" I said softly. "If I don't believe in You—if I don't hope You love me or that You want to help me—I'll never be disappointed again. I can make my own way. I don't need You. I don't need anyone."

I gathered my pajamas and headed to the bathroom. After soaking in a hot bath for a while, I walked down the hall to Benjamin's room. I found an old novel that looked interesting and went back to my room. When I walked in, I found two of Esther's cats curled up on my bed. Clyde and Frances, a pretty calico, were settled in for the night. Seeing them made me smile. Animals had a way of seeing the best in people. If only people could do the same.

Being careful not to disturb the cats, I climbed into the large bed. I opened the book and tried to read, but a voice kept whispering to me, asking why I felt it necessary to explain my lack of faith to a God I didn't believe existed.

I forced myself to read until I grew tired and turned off the light. It took a long time to drift off to sleep because that voice just wouldn't be stilled.

CHAPTER EIGHT

After a restless night, I finally rolled out of bed around six in the morning. I got dressed and made a visit to the bathroom. Figuring Esther wouldn't be up yet, I was surprised to hear sounds coming from the first floor. When I went downstairs, I found her in the kitchen.

"Well, good morning, honey," she said when she saw me. "I figured you would sleep in today."

I shook my head. "That would have been nice, but I'm afraid my body wasn't in agreement."

She laughed and motioned toward the kitchen table. "I understand that all too well. The older I get, the more my body bosses me around."

She poured a cup of coffee from the enamel percolator on the stove. "I will start breakfast in a minute, but if you are like me, coffee comes first."

I grinned at her. "We're very much alike. Thank you."

She handed me the cup, and I took a sip, hoping the caffeine would chase away the weariness that seemed to fill my mind and body this morning.

Esther poured herself a cup and then sat down at the table next to me. "When you arrived here, you told me why you were in Sanctuary, but I still do not know much about you, Emily. I would like to know you better."

As I gazed into the elderly woman's eyes, the idea of telling her more lies made me feel sick to my stomach. Maybe I could wrap my lies in a little truth. "I was born and raised in Kansas," I said. "I don't have any brothers or sisters." I shrugged. "I told you how I found out about Miriam."

Esther reached over and touched my hand. "But tell me about *you*. What do you do? What do you like? What do you want to do in life?"

I told her the lie about working for an accounting firm. And that I wanted to own my own firm someday.

She frowned at me. "You do not seem to be the type of person who would be happy with a job like that."

I almost spit out my coffee. Jonathon had said the same thing. What was it these people thought they saw in me that made them think I couldn't be an accountant? Suddenly, I wished I'd come up with some other story.

"I—I guess it's a job."

She nodded. "Yes, it is a job, and there is nothing wrong with it. But isn't there something else you really want to do, Emily? Besides accounting, I mean? You are so smart and personable. I believe you could be successful at anything you put your mind to."

Without warning, my eyes filled with tears. I tried to quickly blink them away, but I wasn't fast enough.

"Oh, my dear girl." Compassion filled Esther's face. "Surely others in your life have told you the same thing."

I took a napkin from the wooden holder on the table and wiped my face. "No," I said softly. "I'm afraid there aren't many people who see me in a positive light. And rightly so. I've made many, many mistakes."

Esther stared at me for a moment and then looked away. When she spoke again, her voice was so quiet, I could barely hear her. "Everyone makes mistakes, dear. My husband and I raised our children in the nurture and admonition of the Lord. But after he died and I was all they had, they turned their backs on God. And me. Somehow I failed them. I have seen Rebecca and my grandchildren twice since she moved away. And I haven't seen my son in years." When she looked back at me, she had tears in her own eyes. "I used to go over and over in my mind all the things I said and did that were wrong. The times I was too busy for them. The times I was too short with them. If I could go back and do it over, be a better mother, I would. But I cannot fix the past. And neither can you. If God does not hold our mistakes against us, then we should not do it either. It is time you let go of the past, Emily. Give it to God. His shoulders are much larger than yours."

I felt a rush of anger rise up inside me. "God doesn't care about me, Esther. I used to pray and pray, asking Him for help. Things just got worse. I'm on my own now, and I like it that way."

As soon as I let those words out of my mouth, I knew they were wrong. I needed a place to stay in Sanctuary, and now I'd ruined my chances of remaining in this house. I should have just agreed with her.

To my surprise, Esther didn't look angry. Instead, she got up and came over to me. When she wrapped her arms around me, I couldn't hold back the tears of grief and hurt that poured out. I fought to restrain my unruly emotions, but it took everything I had to finally stop crying. Throughout it all, Esther held me, something I wasn't used to. Finally, once I'd grown quiet, she squeezed me and let me go. Then she went back to her chair and turned it toward me, taking both of my hands in hers.

"I know this may not make sense to you now, Emily, but God has answered your prayers. He brought you here. To Sanctuary. To me. You are here for a reason. He has always been with you, and by the time you leave this town, you will know that, too."

I seriously doubted that would happen, but Esther's expression of concern meant more than I could say. I'd been shown very little compassion in my life. But as soon as that thought came into my head, I realized it wasn't true. There had been many kind people in Kingdom. Jonathon and Lizzie. The pastor of our church. And a few other women in Kingdom, like Hope Kauffman. She was probably Hope Miller by now. I was certain they no longer cared much about me. In fact, they probably hated me. Everyone except Lizzie, that is. I'd told her the truth about the terrible thing I'd done, and she'd helped me anyway. I could still remember her words. *"God is in the business of giving second chances, Sophie. Even third and fourth chances. His mercy is endless. Just don't give up. He has a great plan for your life, and He'll never leave you."* She'd given me enough money to get out of town and start a new life. I would be indebted to her forever.

"Thank you, Esther," I said. "You're very kind. I appreciate it. I'm sorry about what I said. I hope it didn't upset you."

"No, honey. It didn't upset me. God can handle your feelings and your hurt." She gently squeezed my shoulder. "He has heard worse, I am certain. But I will tell you this." She looked into my eyes, and I could swear she was peering into my soul. "God definitely led you here. You watch for His footprints."

I nodded dumbly. What was she talking about? Why did everyone seem to think God had a plan for my life? God clearly didn't care about me. And footprints? So far, the only footprints I could see were the ones He left when He walked away.

"Now, let us get some food in our stomachs." Esther moved her chair back to its previous position. "Then we can spend some time talking about your grandmother."

"That sounds great." But it didn't. I wasn't sure what to ask her about a woman I didn't really know. I'd wanted to get back to the church and go through the records today, yet I couldn't ignore Esther again. I decided to go to the church in the afternoon.

After turning down my offer to help her, Esther sent me to the living room, where I sat down and sipped my coffee while I waited. Eventually, I carried my cup out to the front porch and took my place in the rocking chair again. It was such a quiet, peaceful morning. I watched as Janet Dowell came out of her house. When she saw me, she started walking my way.

"Good morning, Emily," she called when she reached the porch. "How are you?"

"Just fine. Enjoying a cup of Esther's delicious coffee."

She laughed. "She certainly does make good coffee. In fact, everything she makes is great. She's a wonderful cook."

I patted my stomach. "I've discovered that. It's going to take a lot of time in the gym to work off her cooking, I'm afraid."

Her blue eyes twinkled. "I totally understand. Well, I just wanted to say hi, but I'd better get going. I'm running a little late for work today."

"Can I ask what you do?" Trying to categorize Sanctuary's residents might help me find Chase. I intended to question everyone I could.

"Sure. I run the veterinary clinic. Ever since our last vet went . . . away."

I remembered the story about the TV reporter who came here to find her brother. If my memory was right, the town's veterinarian had tried to kill her.

"Sounds like a wonderful job," I said. "I love animals."

She grinned. "Me too. Some days more than others. Well, I'm off. Nice to see you again."

"You too."

She walked back toward her house, got into her car, and drove down the street.

A few minutes later, a lovely red-haired woman came out of the house with a young girl who looked very similar to her. They walked down the porch steps and headed toward town. I watched them until I couldn't see them anymore, then I went back into the house. Esther was just coming into the living room as I walked through the door.

"Breakfast is ready," she said.

"You really didn't need to make me anything. I usually don't even eat breakfast."

Esther shook her head. "You young people. Don't you realize that breakfast gives you energy for the rest of the day?"

"I guess we don't. I'm usually up and on my way to work early in the morning. There's just not time."

"Well, while you are here, you will eat breakfast. That way, I know you have enough fuel to keep you going."

I laughed. "Yes, ma'am."

I followed her into the dining room, where I saw she'd loaded my plate with bacon, scrambled eggs, and fried potatoes. A smaller plate of toast sat next to it.

"Oh, Esther. I just don't think I can eat this much. If I do, I won't be able to fit into my clothes."

She pointed to the vacant chair in front of the huge plate of food. "You sit down and do your best. If you cannot eat it all, I will not complain."

"I'll certainly do what I can. It all looks delicious."

When we were both seated, Esther asked if it was all right for her to say a prayer. I nodded but kept my eyes open as the small elderly woman spoke to her God.

"Lord, I thank You so much for sending Emily here. It is such a blessing to me. Help her to see herself as You do, dearest God. Thank You for providing this food and blessing it to our bodies. In Jesus' precious name, amen."

Esther was sincere in her faith, I could see that. Yet her husband was dead, and her children had deserted her. Still, here she was, thanking God. I couldn't understand it. She was obviously living in denial. But that was her business, not mine.

I reached for the coffeepot, which was sitting on a hot pad, and poured another cup of coffee. I wasn't looking forward to spending the next couple of hours hearing more about some woman I didn't know—and never would. Maybe I could work in some questions about newer residents. Men who'd moved here after 2008.

But that plan quickly died.

"Now, honey," Esther said, looking straight at me, "I would like you to tell me the real reason you've come to Sanctuary."

CHAPTER NINE

I stared back at her for several seconds, not sure I'd heard her right. Finally, I said, "I'm sorry. I don't understand . . ."

Esther smiled. "Honey, I knew Miriam really well. I also know that her sister Clara could not bear children." She held up one hand. "And before you try to argue with me about this, I must tell you that, due to a medical condition, Clara had a hysterectomy when she was still very young. She could not possibly be your grandmother."

I tried to think of an excuse to keep my story intact, but nothing came to mind. "Why didn't you say something earlier?" I asked finally. "You let me come into your house and listened to me, even though you knew I was lying. And you've been so nice."

"That is an easy question to answer. I like you. And as I told you, I believe God sent you here." She smiled. "Before you panic and run away, you need to know that I have no intention of telling anyone that you are here under . . . false pretenses."

I peered at her through narrowed eyes. "And why is that? If you know I've been deceitful, why don't you tell me to clear out?"

"I will not thwart God's plan. Besides, I believe you have a good heart, even though you also have a lot of pain inside. I do not believe you are here to hurt anyone."

"I'm not," I responded quickly. "Except maybe for a very bad man. A man who killed two innocent people."

Esther took a quick breath. "Sanctuary is a place where some people have come looking for refuge from the past. We respect their privacy. But we do not want our town to be a hiding place for people who have done such terrible evil."

"Wasn't it just a couple of years ago when you were overrun by the media? Had to do with a boy being kidnapped?"

She nodded. "Our peace was shattered for a while. Some people even left town for a while. But people in the world have short memories. When the story disappeared, so did the news people. We are safe once again." She paused for a moment and appeared to study me. "Now, while we eat, I want you to tell me the truth. All of it."

"I don't know . . ."

"My silence is given only on the condition that you do not lie to me again." She picked up a piece of bacon and took a bite.

I waited while she chewed and swallowed, my mind racing as I tried to think of how best to handle the situation. In the end, I decided to come clean. With most of it, anyway. There were some things I had to keep to myself. No one could know about Kingdom—or about Jonathon.

"What do you want to know?" I asked slowly.

Esther fastened her blue eyes on mine. "First of all, who are you really?"

"My name is Sophie Bauer. I work for the *St. Louis Times*. I'm looking for a man named Terrance Chase. In 2008, he and another man robbed an armored car company, killing two guards. They got away. The rumors are that both men are dead, but I don't believe that. I think Terrance Chase changed his name and identity and came here. I'm not sure he's still here, but if he is, I want to find him. Not just for my story, but mainly because he should be brought to justice for what he did." I met her intense gaze. "And if you tell anyone what I just told you, he might get away . . . again. Those guards had families. Children. I know that as a Mennonite you don't believe in retribution, but you do believe in justice. That's all I'm looking for." Of course, that wasn't really true. For me, the story was first, justice was second. But Esther didn't need to know that.

The elderly woman didn't say anything for several seconds. Finally, she pointed at my plate. "Eat your food before it gets cold. I will keep your secret. For now. But if I find out that you have lied to me—or if I feel you are doing something to hurt this town or anyone in it, I will have no choice but to seek help."

"I understand, but I promise you, my story won't hurt Sanctuary."

"Unfortunately, that may not be in your power. If this man—this Terrance Chase—is found here, what will happen to us?"

"I—I can't answer that question, Esther. But we can't allow

him to get away with what he did, can we? Isn't finding him more important than protecting Sanctuary's anonymity?"

She didn't answer. It was obvious she was really worried.

"All I can do is promise you I'll try to keep Sanctuary out of the story." Of course, there was no way to really do that. A twinge of conscience made me feel uncomfortable, but I couldn't afford to be swayed. I had to do this. It was my only chance at the life I wanted. The life I *needed*.

"You must try, Emily," Esther pleaded. "This town is very special. To all of us."

"I understand. Just remember, he may not even be here. Or if he was ever in Sanctuary, he may have already left by now. Worrying about this before I find out the truth is a waste of time. That's the real reason I'm going through the town's books in the church basement. I'm tracking all the men who arrived after the robbery. Chase may be one of them. If that turns out to be the case and he's already gone, I'll leave and look for him somewhere else."

Esther sighed. "I believe we should finish eating our breakfast, Emily. Then you must go forward with your search, but I would appreciate it if you would keep me updated on your efforts. Maybe I can help you. If you share the names you find, I can tell you about them. I'm old and have lived here a long time."

"That would be incredibly helpful. Thank you." I hesitated a moment. "You're still calling me Emily. May I ask why?"

Esther chuckled. "Again, I am an old woman. If I am not careful, I could blurt out your real name. If I continue to see you as Emily, the chances of this happening are lessened. Besides, if I see you as *my* Emily, it will help me. I trust her, and I want to trust you."

But you can't trust me. The truth struck some part of me. A softer part that still existed inside the hard shell I'd wrapped around my heart.

"The funny thing is, my Emily has another name, too. She came here under false pretenses. Like you."

"Where is this . . . Emily?"

"She lives on a farm outside of town with her husband, Reuben. She usually comes by two or three times a week. You'll meet her. She used to work for a television station. She goes by the name Wynter. Such a pretty name, but I still call her Emily."

A small alarm sounded in my mind. This must be the reporter who found her kidnapped brother in Sanctuary. "You can't tell her the truth about me, Esther. Okay?"

The old woman nodded. "I understand. I will not tell her. As long as you keep our bargain." She offered me a small smile. "I still believe you are here for reasons you do not yet understand, Emily. You think you are searching for this Terrance Chase person, but in the end, you will find something much more important."

Her constant insistence that there was some kind of larger plan was starting to get on my nerves. But Esther had a good heart, and I didn't want to hurt her. I just smiled and kept my mouth shut.

It took me a few minutes to eat most of the food on my plate. By now it was barely warm, but I didn't care. I needed to get to the church and do more research. I thanked Esther for the breakfast, carried my dishes into the kitchen, and rinsed them. Then, after grabbing my purse and my jacket, I left.

As I got into my car and started it, my affirmations CD

began to play. For some reason it irritated me, and I clicked it off. I was focused on finding Chase, and I wasn't in the mood for reciting the same old words over and over. I wasn't calm and relaxed and was failing miserably at controlling my thoughts.

"But I am in charge of my life," I said out loud. "No one is going to make me do anything I don't want to do. No one." For some reason, my words sounded hollow.

By the time I got to the church, my irritation had turned into anger. I parked in front of the building, turned off the engine, and tried to figure out why I was upset. Was it that Esther had seen through me? That I'd lost the upper hand? Did I feel I was at her mercy now?

I checked my makeup in the rearview mirror. "No one tells me what to do," I said to my image. "I'm in control. I'm in control." But if that were true, why did I feel so out of control this morning?

Trying to quiet the emotions raging inside, I got out of the car and headed into the building. I found Pastor Troyer in his office. After telling him I was going downstairs again, I quickly made my way to the dark, dank basement. I went over to the old, beat-up desk and turned on the lamp. Once again, I started removing books, searching for single men who might be Terrance Chase. When one of them left town, I wrote that on another page. I'd compare the records later. I worked through lunch and into the afternoon. I was up to 2010 when the door to the room swung open and Dorcas Troyer came in.

"I am sorry to interrupt, but I was worried about you. I brought you something to eat and drink."

I quickly closed the book I was working on and put my notebook on top of it so she wouldn't notice the year on the front. Since she'd mentioned that Miriam and Clara's family might have been among the town's earliest settlers, looking through the 2010 book wouldn't make much sense.

"Thank you, but you didn't need to do that."

As she came out of the shadows and into the circle of light offered by the lamp, I noticed she had a tray in her hands. "I hope you like chicken salad," she said. "And I thought you might like a bottle of root beer."

Although I hadn't thought about eating until that moment, I realized I was actually very hungry, which was strange because of the large breakfast I'd had at Esther's. "That's very kind of you."

"I work down here a lot," she said with a smile. "There is something about this room that makes me feel . . . so alone. As if there is no one else in the world."

"I know what you mean. It's a little . . . creepy down here."

"Creepy. Yes. The perfect word." She put the tray down on the edge of the desk. "Do not worry about bringing this back upstairs. Just leave it here, and I will get it later."

I thanked her again as she turned to leave. She might have my mother's name, but she certainly didn't act like my mother. She was kind and gentle. She disappeared into the shadows, and I pulled the tray closer. After taking a few bites of Dorcas's delicious sandwich, I went back to the book I'd been looking at before she came in. Page after page, person after person. I began to see patterns. People who moved here. People who died here. Children who left, and children who came back. For the most part, residents stayed in Sanctuary. I stopped a few times to eat and eventually finished my lunch.

I made it halfway through 2011 and suddenly felt tired. I checked my watch. Four-thirty. Time to go. I didn't want Pastor Troyer to wait for me, so I packed up everything, turned off the desk light, and headed for the door.

When I got upstairs, I knocked on Pastor Troyer's door to tell him I was headed out. I heard him call out, "Come in," so I opened the door. I was shocked to see Jonathon sitting in a chair in front of the pastor's desk.

"I—I'm sorry," I said. "I didn't mean to interrupt."

Pastor Troyer waved at me. "You are not interrupting. I am afraid my friend and I have moved from spiritual things to debating the best place to fish. You have saved me from losing the argument."

Jonathon shook his head vigorously. "There's only one way to settle this. Next time we go out, we'll fish your spot, but after that, we'll go to mine. If we catch more fish in my spot, you have to provide bait for the next three trips. If you win, I'll bring the bait."

Pastor Troyer rubbed his beard several times while his eyes twinkled with humor. "I will take that challenge. But you must bring something besides those old, tired worms you tried to pass off as bait last summer."

Jonathon's expression was comical as he looked over at me. "I'm wounded. How can a man who calls himself a pastor accuse me of such a terrible thing?"

I managed a weak smile. "I have no idea." Wanting to get away as quickly as possible, I mumbled something to Pastor Troyer about being finished downstairs, and without waiting for a response, I closed the door and practically sprinted out of the church. Why did I keep running into Jonathon? Though I doubted he would ever figure out who I was, every time I was near him, it felt as if that dirty ragamuffin I had once been was trying to break out. I dreaded being seen as that person even more than I feared losing my chance of locating Terrance Chase.

I was almost to my car when I heard someone call my name. I turned around to see Jonathon bounding down the stairs of the church, headed right for me.

"Going to a fire?" he called out.

I shook my head as I put one hand on the car door. "Sorry. I didn't want to intrude."

"To be honest, I was waiting for you. I'd stopped by to talk to Jacob about something, and he told me you were working in the basement. I'd started to wonder if you were ever coming upstairs."

"Waiting for me? Why?"

He cleared his throat. "I wanted to ask you to dinner. I mean, unless Esther is expecting you."

The word *no* was in my mind and on the tip of my tongue. But for some reason, "That sounds nice," came tumbling out. *Have I lost my mind?* Unfortunately, my mouth seemed to have a will of its own. As did something inside me that went haywire every time I saw Jonathon.

"Great. How about The Oil Lamp? The Whistle Stop closes at four."

"All right."

"Good. Why don't we both drive over there? That way, we can each go straight home after dinner."

"Sure. That makes sense." I got into my car, trying to calm my trembling body.

Jonathon stood there for a moment, staring at me. I looked away and waited. Finally, he got in his truck and began to drive down the street. I started my car and followed him, beating myself up for allowing this to happen. I turned on my affirmations CD and began to echo the words that felt so false to me now. What had happened to me from the time I'd entered this stupid town until now? Why was I falling apart? Was it because it reminded me of Kingdom? Or was it because of Jonathon? I felt as if I might be losing myself somehow, yet I didn't know how to stop it.

At the restaurant, I parked next to Jonathon's truck and got out, still feeling overwhelmed and unsure. I followed him inside and was met by an attractive woman in jeans, a bright red sweater, and a colorful apron.

"Hey, Jonathon," she said with a smile. "Who's your friend?"

Jonathon introduced me to Randi Lindquist, the owner of The Oil Lamp. Unlike Mary and Rosey, who were soft-spoken, Randi was much more assertive.

"Good to meet you," she said loudly. "Got a table in the corner, if that will work for you."

"Sounds great," Jonathon said. He motioned for me to go ahead of him, and I walked past several crowded tables, people greeting Jonathon just like they had at The Whistle Stop. He seemed very popular in Sanctuary.

We'd just sat down when I noticed Janet walking toward us with the pretty red-haired woman I'd seen leaving the house this morning and the same little girl following behind her.

"Just had to say hello," Janet said to Jonathon.

"Hi, Janet." He stood to greet her. "This is my new friend, Emily McClure."

"We've met. Hello again." She turned to the redhead standing next to her. "Emily, this is Sarah Miller and her niece, Cicely."

"I'm happy to meet you."

"Esther tells me you're doing some research about your family," Sarah said.

"Yes, my grandmother, Clara, was Miriam Byler's sister."

"Oh?" She smiled. "Miriam was a lovely lady. I met Clara a few times when she came to visit. She was very nice. I'm sorry you never got to meet them."

"I am, too."

"Just wanted to check about Saturday, Pastor," Janet said. "What time do you want the food delivered to the community room? Same as always?"

He nodded. "I'll open the doors at four. We'll eat at six. As you know, there's not a lot of refrigerator space, so tell everyone who is bringing food that needs to be kept cold not to bring it any earlier than five. We'll have the warming trays ready for hot food."

Janet moved her purse to her other shoulder. "As hard as we plan for these dinners, we still get surprised. The women in this town love to cook." She smiled at Jonathon. "But we'll get it figured out. We always do."

Sarah laughed. "It's not just the women. I hear Evan Bakker is smoking a turkey and Abner Ingalls plans to bring his fabulous barbequed brisket."

"Oh goodness," Jonathon said. "My mouth is already watering."

Sarah looked at me. "Sanctuary is full of great cooks. I hope you'll be joining us on Saturday."

"Janet already asked me. I'm looking forward to it."

"Good," Jonathon said. "I was going to ask you myself."

Janet raised an eyebrow and looked back and forth between Jonathon and me. I felt my face get hot. Small towns. Everyone had to stick their noses in everyone else's business. By the end of the day, people would probably be gossiping about Jonathon and me. Not only would that be unfair to Jonathon, I didn't need the attention.

"We're going to grab a table," Janet said. "It was nice to see you again, Emily."

"And it was nice to meet you," Sarah added. She turned to look at her niece, who smiled shyly at me.

"Nice to meet you," the girl said softly.

"Nice to meet you, too." When they walked away, I frowned at Jonathon. "I hope my having dinner with you hasn't put you in an uncomfortable position."

His eyebrows shot up. "I don't understand."

"I—I'm sure you don't want people in your congregation thinking we're on a date or something."

His bright blue eyes seemed to see inside me. "I'm not asking you to marry me, Emily. We're just getting to know each other. I hope that's okay with you."

"Of course. I—I just didn't want to give anyone the wrong impression."

He smiled. "I appreciate your concern, but don't worry about it. Besides, it wouldn't bother me too much for people to think we're on a date. I'm sure every man in this restaurant would be jealous of me."

I opened my mouth to respond, but nothing came out.

Jonathon's eyebrows arched again. "Have I embarrassed you? I'm sorry. It wasn't my intention."

At that moment, I had no idea what to do or what to say. The man I'd loved since I was a child was flirting with me. But of course it wasn't really me. It was someone else. Someone I was pretending to be. If it wasn't so sad, it would be funny. What could I possibly do? What could I possibly say?

"It—it's okay," I choked out. "You just . . . surprised me."

He shook his head. "I probably shouldn't have teased you. I hope you're not offended. It's just . . ." He looked at me strangely. "Ever since I met you, I've had the weirdest feeling. Like I've met you before. I haven't been able to shake it. I know it's not possible because I'd certainly remember."

Fear made me pull myself together quickly. "I've never been to Sanctuary before this. We've never met. I must just remind you of someone."

At that moment, Randi walked up to our table and slapped down a couple of menus. "What do you two want to drink?"

"Coffee," we said at the same time.

Jonathon grinned. "Great minds think alike, I guess."

"Either that or you're both bored," Randi said wryly.

"Definitely not bored." Jonathon snuck a look at me.

Randi chuckled. "Wow. You're sure full of surprises, Pastor." She stared at me a moment before turning to leave.

Things were spiraling out of control. I had to find a way to stop it. "Jonathon," I said after Randi was out of earshot, "I—I may have misled you in some way. I have a boyfriend. And as I said, I'm not a . . . church person."

Jonathon's expression stayed the same, but I noticed a

spot of color on each cheek. The old Sophie was screaming at me, wondering if I'd gone crazy, but the new Sophie wasn't ready to be hurt again. And I knew that was exactly what would happen unless I pulled in the reins and stopped this from going any further.

"I'm sorry," he said quickly. "Please forgive me if I've made you uncomfortable in any way."

"Nothing to forgive," I said. "If things were different, I'd be very interested. But we're just not a good match. You need someone who believes in God."

"Actually, I find that almost everyone believes in God. They just don't think He believes in them." His eyes sought mine. "But He does."

As he watched me, his eyes suddenly widened. I felt as if my heart actually skipped a beat.

"I just realized who you look like. I should have figured it out sooner. I've only known one other person with amber eyes. A girl from my hometown. Her name was Sophie Wittenbauer."

CHAPTER TEN

I couldn't seem to swallow past the huge lump in my throat. All I could do was stare at Jonathon and hope he wouldn't realize who I really was.

"She's someone I knew a long time ago," he told me. "You remind me of her."

My lips felt numb, but I managed to ask, "A past girlfriend?"

He quickly shook his head. "No. She was just a child. A lost child." He picked up his menu and squinted at it. "I tried to help her, but I failed. I think about her a lot, wondering what happened to her."

Feeling as if he'd convinced himself I couldn't possibly be the person he remembered, I found it a little easier to breathe. I picked up my menu, too, and began to look over the dinner offerings. "Maybe she turned out okay. You never know."

He nodded. "You're right." He lowered his menu so he could meet my gaze again. "I hope I haven't ruined our chance at being friends."

I smiled at him. "Of course not. It's nice to have someone to talk to besides Esther. Not that she isn't a wonderful person, but . . ."

"She's quite a bit older than you . . . and Mennonite?" Jonathon filled in. "I understand. I'm glad you're coming to the supper on Saturday. You'll get to meet a lot of Sanctuary folks. I'm sure you'll like them."

"Sounds like Sanctuary's best cooks will be showing off. How can I miss that?"

He laughed. "No one in their right mind would stay away."

A woman with brown curly hair and a kind face showed up at our table with coffee.

"Hi, Maxie," Jonathon said. "How's the job working out?"

"I love it, Pastor. Thanks for recommending me. Randi's a great boss, and I love spending time with people. It gets me out of the house."

"Emily, this is Maxie Anderson. This wonderful lady attends my church. I'm very fortunate to be her pastor."

"Nice to meet you, Maxie." I shook her hand. "You must be very special."

She colored and looked at the floor. "I don't know about that, but I'm certainly blessed to have a pastor who saw I needed help and went out of his way to change my life." She set the coffeepot on the table near me. "You see, I lost my husband last year. Being alone started to make me sad . . . and a little bitter. When Randi decided to hire a waitress, Pastor Jonathon almost forced me to take the job. I was pretty mad at him for a while. But now . . ." She blinked away tears. "Well, I look forward to getting up in the morning again. These people are not only my friends, they're my family."

Her eyes seemed to lock on to mine. "I've found that being alone isn't good. It shrinks your soul."

Startled, all I could do was nod. The woman didn't even know me. So why did her words feel as if they were directed toward me?

She took our orders, picked up the coffeepot, and scurried off.

I looked at Jonathon. "Wow, I'm impressed."

"Don't be," he said. "Anyone could have figured it out. Randi's the one who took a chance on her. Maxie had never waitressed before. Randi hired her anyway, and now she's glad she did. Maxie does a great job, and everyone loves her."

"Well, still. You helped her get out of the house and into a new life. Good for you."

"Thanks."

The restaurant was very busy, and I watched the people as much as I could. There were a lot of men seated around the room. Some were around the same age as Terrance Chase, but none of them looked like his picture. I was aware he could have changed his appearance, but there were some things he couldn't change. The shape of his face and his height would remain, no matter what else he altered. From my research, I'd learned that Terrance Chase was five foot, ten inches. Back when he'd robbed the armored car company, he'd had brownish-red hair and hazel eyes. Stocky and muscular, he could have easily slimmed down by now, dyed his hair, and started wearing contacts. I'd studied his face so many times, I was hopeful I'd recognize him no matter what he did to disguise himself.

"Emily? Did you hear me?" Jonathon asked.

I turned my head to stare at him. "I'm sorry. I was just scoping out the room. This is such a great restaurant. I love the retro look."

He nodded. "It's certainly got atmosphere. Reminds me of a restaurant back in my hometown."

I took a quick breath. "And where is that?"

"A little town called Kingdom, Kansas. A lot like Sanctuary, except it's almost entirely Mennonite. Conservative Mennonite."

"Really? You don't seem like someone who grew up in a Mennonite town."

"My whole family is Mennonite. For some reason, I just never seemed to fit. After . . ." He sighed. "Well, after something happened, I decided to leave. See if I could fit in better somewhere else. Not that I don't love my family or my friends. I do. I go back to visit quite often. But I believe we all have a destiny, and mine wasn't in Kingdom. I think that's why I always felt different."

"I understand," I said. "We all feel like outsiders sometimes."

After some small talk, Maxie brought our food. I'd ordered grilled chicken and wild rice. It was absolutely delicious. While I ate, Jonathon told me about his life in Sanctuary, and I just listened. He'd really fallen in love with this town and its people. When we finished eating, I was ready to leave. I just couldn't take being this close to him any longer. My feelings were still so strong, I felt my resolve to stay away from him slipping.

"I need to get back to Esther's." I grabbed my purse. "I hate to run off, but unfortunately, I brought some work with me from the firm, and I need to catch up on it."

"Last time we ate together, you had to leave to make a phone call. Now you have to work. Don't you ever just relax?"

"When I can. Unfortunately, that doesn't happen very often."

"I understand what that's like, but we all need to take some time for ourselves once in a while."

"I'm sure you're right."

He started to reach for my ticket, but I grabbed it before he could.

"Thanks, but I'll get it. After all, we established that this wasn't a date."

He carefully pulled it out of my hand. "But I asked you to dinner. Date or not, it's my treat."

Rather than argue and make a scene, I relented. I went outside and stood on the front porch while Jonathon paid our tab. When he came outside, he seemed ill at ease. I felt the same way.

"Again, I apologize if I said anything that embarrassed you," he said quietly as he walked me to my car.

I frowned at him. "One thing I don't understand. Why would you be attracted to someone who told you they don't believe in God? I mean, isn't that some kind of rule or something? That you're not supposed to be . . . what is it . . . unequally yoked?"

He chuckled. "Yeah, I guess it's a rule. It's really not in my nature to be so . . . flippant. But like I said, for some strange reason, I feel like I know you already." He shook his head. "Never mind. It doesn't make any sense." He stuck out his hand. "If you'll give me another chance, I'd like us to be friends. Deal?"

"Deal." When I took his hand, I felt something like an electric shock go through me. Not trusting myself to look at him, I quickly slipped my hand out of his and opened my car door.

I got in my car, backed up, and pulled out into the street. As I drove away, I saw him in my rearview mirror, staring at me. Was there a part of him that recognized me? I still loved him desperately, but my life was clothed in a lie. One that I couldn't get away from. If I allowed him to get too close, either he'd finally figure out who I really was or I'd have to tell him the truth. And then he would hate me. Hate me because of what I did in Kingdom, and hate me for lying to him.

"If You're real, God," I said out loud, "You've made it clear You don't care anything about me. You didn't help me when I was a child, and now You throw Jonathon in my face, showing me once again that I can never have him. What kind of God are You?"

When I pulled up in front of Esther's, I took a few minutes to dry the tears on my face. As I picked up my purse, I realized there was an envelope lying on the passenger seat. I must have missed it when I'd tossed my purse down. I picked it up. There wasn't any name on the outside. I tore it open and removed a folded piece of white paper. I gasped as I read it.

I know why you're here. Leave town, or you'll be sorry.

I stared down at the plain, nondescript letters. How could anyone know the truth? I felt anger wash through me. There was only one person who could have let the cat out of the bag. I grabbed my purse and the note and hurried into the house. Esther looked up at me from where she sat on the couch.

I walked over and handed her the note. "Can you explain this?" I didn't even try to keep the irritation out of my voice. I'd trusted one person. Just one. And look at what it got me.

Esther read the note then handed it back to me. "I have no idea who wrote this," she said slowly. "I have not talked to anyone about you."

I wanted to believe her. Mennonites took telling the truth very seriously, yet I'd watched my father and mother lie on a regular basis.

"If you didn't tell anyone, what does this mean?"

"I have no idea, Emily. What are you going to do?"

I pondered her question. How could someone else know my reasons for being in Sanctuary? It certainly couldn't be Chase. There wasn't any way for him to know who I was and why I was here. Not yet, anyway.

"Well, I'm not leaving. Frankly, this only proves I'm on to something."

"I don't want you to put yourself in danger."

I studied her for a moment before saying, "It's hard for me to believe you care anything about me. I lied to you. I accepted a room in your house under false pretenses. So why are you being nice to me? Is it because you're still convinced God has some kind of magical plan and you don't want to ruin it?"

Esther smiled serenely. "No, it is not just that. You remind me so much of my son, Benjamin. He convinced himself that I could not love him because of the mistakes he made."

"But he's your son. I'm no one to you."

Esther's eyes widened. "That is not true, Emily. You are precious to God, and you are precious to me. Love is not something to be earned. Love is a gift that is given without strings attached."

"Not in my experience. I've never had love without conditions."

"I have no conditions, child. All I ask is that you tell me the truth from here on out. I may not be your family by blood, but I would like to be someone you can trust. Someone you know cares for you."

For some reason, her words, which I was certain were spoken from a kind heart, upset me even more. "It's late," I snapped. "I'm sure you'd like to get to bed."

She nodded. "Yes, it is past my bedtime, but if you would like to talk a while, I will stay with you."

I started toward the stairs. "No, thank you. I have some work to do and need to go to my room."

Esther stood up. Before I realized what she was doing, she came over and put her arms around me. I wasn't used to being hugged, and I stiffened at her touch.

"You are someone in need of love, Emily. I hope you will allow me into your life." She let me go and stepped back, looking up into my eyes. "There is not much an old woman can do for others. I can pray and cook for church meetings, but that is about it. Old bodies cannot keep up with young ones, I'm afraid. But my mind is not old. And the love in my heart is not old. When God sends someone my way, I take that very seriously."

"I don't think God sent me to you, Esther. I made the decision to come here. For reasons that God probably doesn't approve of. I appreciate the invitation to stay in your home, and your kindness toward me, but if you think you're going to save me or something, I'm afraid you'll be very disappointed."

"Perhaps," she said. "We will see. But you are wrong if you do not believe God brought you here. By the time you leave, you will see this."

"Whatever you say. I'm going to bed." I left her standing there, staring at me. I knew it was rude, but I was exhausted and confused. This wasn't going the way I'd planned. My search had to go into overdrive. I needed to find Chase, write my story, and get out of this town before I was found out—or before I lost my mind.

When I got to my room, I found Sam and Clyde waiting in the hall. I opened the door and let them in. Clyde went for the bed, and Sam took up his usual place on the floor. I wondered where Frances and Maizie were. Probably in Esther's room.

I pulled the list of names from my purse, found my laptop, and began researching. I'd only been at it about thirty minutes when there was a knock at the door. Now what? I swung open the door and found Esther standing there with a small tray.

"Hot chocolate and cookies." She held up the tray to show me. "Rebecca used to love this at night when she had to do homework. I thought it might help you pass the time more pleasantly."

I stared at the elderly woman in surprise. The stairs were difficult for her, and she'd climbed them with this tray in her hands? After the way I'd spoken to her?

"Esther, what if you'd tripped and fallen?"

"Pshaw." She handed me the tray. "As you see, I did not fall."

I noticed she was breathing a little heavily and pointed it out.

She smiled. "Perhaps next time I will call you and you can come and get the tray." She patted my arm. "But tonight I wanted you to be comfortable. I pray you get all your work done and still have a restful sleep. Good night, dear."

As she walked away, I just watched her. When I heard her reach the bottom of the stairs, I closed the door to my room. Then I set the tray on top of the nightstand next to the bed and stared at it. I couldn't remember one time in my entire life when my mother had brought me cookies or hot chocolate while I studied. My parents had seen school as nothing more than a bother. Something that was a waste of time for me. The minute I came through the door after school, I'd had to go to work. Clean the house. Do laundry. Make dinner. Any homework I did was done on the bus ride home. And sometimes late at night after they went to bed. Since we didn't have electricity, I'd studied by candlelight. But even finding candles was difficult. Once I stole some from the hardware store and got caught. Harold Eberly, the owner, asked me why I needed them, and I told him. After that, he started giving me candles whenever I asked. Somehow, Cora Menlo, the owner of the restaurant before Lizzie, found out about my situation. She gave me a battery-operated lamp that was much better than the candles. And she kept me supplied with batteries. For a while, my grades got better, but then my father found the lamp. When he took it from me, he yelled, "We're not charity cases. We don't need nothin' from Cora Menlo." I'd found his protestations odd since my parents lived on charity.

Once again, I surprised myself by remembering kindnesses extended to me from different people in Kingdom. Why had I betrayed them? I rubbed my eyes, trying to push specters back into the dark, but they wouldn't be quieted so easily. A flood of memories filled my head until it felt so full I wanted to scream.

After my father took the lamp away, it was back to studying by candlelight. Eventually, my eyes grew strained, and it became difficult to see. A teacher at school sent a letter home to my parents, telling them I needed glasses. Wanting to get the teacher off their backs, my mother gave me an old pair of my father's. When I'd tried to tell her they didn't fit, she'd slapped me in the face. "They were good enough for your father, and they're good enough for you. You wear them or else." One of the lenses actually helped me some, so when I read, I'd close the other eye and read through the lens that worked. They were big and ugly, but I wore them anyway. It was better than nothing.

After a while, it became too hard to study, and I gave up. My parents pulled me out of school when I turned sixteen anyway, so my ordeal with school ended. But my desire to learn had continued to smolder. Once I got away from Kingdom, I got a job as a waitress, bought glasses that were made for me, and began to study for my GED. After that, I enrolled in a community college, working three jobs and studying most nights with only a few hours of sleep. It was difficult, but I was close to earning my degree a year early. The internship at the paper, arranged by my school, had opened the door to the job I had now. I wanted to show my parents what I'd achieved. Not because I thought they would be proud, but because I wanted to prove to them that I had succeeded in spite of them. That I was worth something, after all. But that didn't happen. I stumbled across an online version of a local paper from Washington, Kansas, a town not far from Kingdom. I could still feel the shock I'd experienced on the day I found my father's name in the obituaries. Even in death, his rejection had been clear. There were no survivors mentioned except my mother.

I climbed up on the bed and went back to work on my research. Thankfully, I didn't have to worry about not being able to see anymore. I'd discovered laser eye surgery and now had 20/20 vision. I drank Esther's hot chocolate and ate the delicious cookies she'd brought while I transferred the names I'd written down in my notebook to my computer. Clyde scooted closer to me, but I wasn't certain if he wanted me to pet him or if he was just interested in my cookie.

After I typed up the names of men who'd moved to town after the robbery, I made another list of the men who'd moved away before June of 2011. There were nine single men on the first list and only two who'd left town. Of course, just because they'd left didn't mean they weren't Terrance Chase. Nine names so far. And I wasn't finished. I still had to go through all the records up to now. I sighed. This was going to be harder than I'd imagined. I would need some help to whittle down the list some.

I checked my watch. It was only a little after ten. It wasn't unusual for me to stay up until midnight during the week. Even later on the weekends, though I usually spent the time watching old movies on TV or reading a book. I'd just decided to look for something online when my phone rang. Surprised, I picked it up and said, "Hello?"

"Sophie, it's Donnie."

"Is Tom all right?"

"Yes, he's fine. Still in isolation."

"That's a relief."

"I didn't mean to scare you. I just wanted to see how you were doing."

"Not as good as I'd hoped. My cover is blown with the lady I'm staying with. I didn't know the woman I picked to be my grandmother couldn't have children. Thankfully, she says she'll keep my secret. I've been doing some research and have some possibilities, but it's going to take a while, and I'm not sure how much time I have."

"What do you mean?"

I told him about the note I found in my car.

"I don't like that, Sophie. What if Terrance Chase knows what you're up to?"

"I doubt seriously it could be Chase, Donnie. I mean, who knows I'm here besides an elderly Mennonite lady? I'm wondering if it's someone who thinks I'm here for some other reason. I had lunch with a nice-looking single pastor. Maybe some eager spinster has it out for me." Although I'd meant it as a joke, Donnie didn't laugh.

"Maybe," he said slowly, "but I don't think so. I found out something you need to know."

"What do you mean?"

After a brief silence, Donnie said, "You know I used to sneak Tom's mail out of the prison so no one here would read it?"

"Sure."

"I thought he'd given me everything. Except the letter to your newspaper. Were you aware that your paper responded to that letter?"

"No," I said slowly. "They acted like they were just going to ignore it."

"I was careful to check any mail that came here for Tom. You know, in case someone wrote back about Terrance Chase. The only things I ever found were a few letters from a couple of his friends and the response from you. I intercepted your letter and took it to him. But today I found something in the guards' office. A letter from your newspaper, thanking Tom for contacting them and telling him they would let him know if they felt his concerns were worth looking into. Stapled to it was a copy of the letter Tom mailed to them. It mentioned Terrance Chase and the robbery. It also contained Tom's claim that he knew where Chase was."

It had never occurred to me that the paper would respond to the letter. They were so dismissive, I'd assumed they'd just trashed it. Obviously, I was wrong. "I don't understand, Donnie. Are you saying someone else intercepted that letter?"

"That's exactly what I'm saying. Someone definitely knows about Tom's claims, and I have no idea who it is. It must be one of the other guards since that's where I found the letter, but who he is and who he told about the letter is anyone's guess."

My mind raced over this new information. "So someone read the letter from the paper, knew about Tom's claims concerning Chase, and probably got an inmate to try to get the location from Tom by beating it out of him?"

"That's my guess."

I tried to figure out just what this meant. It was clear that the ramifications of this discovery were huge.

"If Tom said anything about you, you could be in danger, Sophie."

The words from the note flashed in front of me. *I know why you're here. Leave town, or you'll be sorry.*

"I—I can't leave, Donnie. I've barely begun. Tomorrow I should have my list finished. Then I can start eliminating people. I'm getting closer, and I won't stop now."

There was a long silence. Finally, he said, "Okay. But be careful. Obviously, you've hit a nerve. I'm beginning to think you're on to something. Maybe Chase really is in Sanctuary."

"I hope you're right." Donnie's words bolstered my determination. "Thanks for calling. I appreciate your willingness to help me. I'd better get going. I've got a lot to do tonight, and it's getting late."

"All right. Good night, Sophie."

"Good night."

After I hung up, I tried to concentrate on the task at hand, but my mind was unsettled. Actually, Donnie's information was encouraging. Someone certainly was interested in what I was doing. Was it because of Chase? Were they interested in the missing money? Or was it because I was getting too close to the long-wanted fugitive? The possibility thrilled me. I'd keep going, no matter what.

I sighed deeply, and Clyde looked up at me. "Sorry," I said. He put his head back down, as if absolving me of disturbing his sleep.

Even though I felt I was on the right track, I had to face the fact that my initial strategy was spiraling out of control. I couldn't figure out what upset me most: Tom being attacked, Esther knowing the truth, the threatening note, or the realization that Jonathon was back in my life.

Although I didn't want to admit it, I knew the thing I feared most was Jonathon finding out who I really was. Seeing rejection in his eyes frightened me more than anything else.

CHAPTER ELEVEN

The next morning, I slipped out of the house without telling Esther. She was already up, but I waited until she was in the back part of the house before I quietly snuck out the front door. I drove to The Whistle Stop and bought a large cup of coffee to go, hoping Jonathon ate breakfast at home. Mary stuck an apple fritter, hot out of the oven, into a paper bag and sent it with me, as well.

"You can't start the day off without something in your stomach," she said as she handed me the sack.

When I tried to pay for it, she refused.

"Forget it. If my customers don't eat them, they're liable to find their way to my hips. You're actually doing me a favor."

I laughed and took her gift. By the time I got to the church, I couldn't wait to eat it. The smell was driving me crazy.

I stopped by the office and found Pastor Troyer bent over his desk. "Thank you for letting me go through your records," I told him when he looked up. "It's so helpful."

He smiled. "I am happy to hear that. Maybe when you are

finished, you can share what you have discovered. I would love to research our history. I just never seem to find the time."

I said I'd be happy to tell him what I found out about the Byler family. As I walked toward the stairs, I was grateful I'd been taking notes on the Bylers all the way through my research. Now I knew where the family had come from originally, when they arrived in Sanctuary, and the names of many of their relatives, even though I hadn't made it to Miriam and her sisters yet. At least it was enough to make Pastor Troyer think my time in his basement hadn't been wasted.

I entered the basement room, went to the desk, and got situated. Before I went to work, I drank some coffee and ate the apple fritter. It was hot, crispy, and delicious. If these were available near my apartment in St. Louis, I'd eat them every day. My waistline would certainly pay the price.

After downing enough coffee to finally feel awake, I got the last of the books out and set them on the edge of the desk. I'd stopped halfway through 2011, so I started where I'd left off. By lunchtime, I'd made good headway. I thought about running over to one of the restaurants and picking up a sandwich, but I was afraid I'd bump into Jonathon again. I finally decided to drive over to Esther's, get something to eat, and then come back and finish. I left the books out and hurried upstairs, not bothering to stop by Pastor Troyer's office.

When I pulled up to Esther's, I found another car parked in front of her house. A red Mini Cooper. For some reason, it seemed a strange choice for someone who was a friend of the elderly Mennonite woman. I went inside, hoping to pop in and out without having to talk to anyone. Those hopes were dashed when I found Esther sitting in her living room, a man sprawled out on the couch next to her.

"Oh, Emily. I'm so glad you are here," Esther said when I walked in. "I want you to meet my friend, Zac Weikel."

The man stood up and stuck out his hand. He looked to be in his twenties, tall and thin, brown hair in a ponytail. "Nice to meet you, Emily."

"You too," I said. "Esther told me you might pop in."

"Zac works for a television station in St. Louis." Esther's pride in this fact was evident on her face.

"I'm a photog with KDSM. And I do some reporting when they let me."

I felt the smile freeze on my face. A reporter? Esther hadn't told me her friend was a reporter. "Sounds like a great job," I said, trying to sound casual.

"Sometimes it is. Last week I spent two days taking shots of crappie *not* spawning yet in Missouri. Very exciting."

I laughed. "Sounds like it."

"Esther tells me you're here doing some research into your family."

"That's right. In fact, I've been going through some old records at the Mennonite church. I just came back to make a quick sandwich and head back to work. I don't want to interfere with your visit."

"Oh, Zac's staying the weekend," Esther announced. "You'll get plenty of time to get to know him."

"Oh . . . great." The entire weekend? That was the last thing I needed. I'd wanted to go over my list of names with Esther. There was no way to do that with Zac hanging around.

"Can I prepare your lunch?" Esther asked.

I shook my head. "Is it okay if I make something myself and take it back to the church?"

"Of course, dear. Help yourself to whatever you want." She smiled at me. "Why don't we plan on the three of us having dinner together tonight?"

"That would be nice." I really had no other choice. I couldn't eat dinner in town because of Jonathon.

I excused myself and ran upstairs. After using the bathroom, I stopped by my room and removed the new pages of names from my notebook. I'd accidentally torn one of the pages that morning and was afraid it might fall out. If that happened and someone found it, they'd probably wonder why the notes had nothing to do with the Byler family. For now, I felt better hiding what I was doing from prying eyes. After securing the new pages under my mattress, I felt much more relaxed. It was important to keep them someplace where Zac wouldn't stumble across them.

I hurried downstairs to the kitchen. Esther had been busy. The fridge was stuffed, probably for Zac's arrival. I finally settled on a turkey sandwich and a brownie. After packing my lunch in a brown paper bag and grabbing a bottle of pop, I checked the living room. Esther and Zac weren't there. I heard voices coming from the second floor. They must be in his room. I suddenly realized Zac and I would be together upstairs. Wonderful. All I could do was hope he'd leave me alone. I didn't want to be scrutinized by a reporter.

I scooted out of the house, got into my car, and drove back to the church. When I got there, I noticed Pastor Troyer's buggy was gone. Maybe he'd gone to lunch in town. Had he locked the church? I got out of my car and checked the front door, breathing a sigh of relief when I discovered it was open. I stopped by Pastor Troyer's office anyway, thinking maybe his wife had taken the buggy, but no one was there.

Although it felt strange to be in the building alone, I headed downstairs. I'd been hoping I could get done today, but it looked as if I'd need at least one more day to make it through all the books. I felt an urge to hurry in case Chase really was in Sanctuary and was suspicious about me. What if he suddenly took off? I needed to work faster.

"Once again into the breach," I whispered as I entered the door to the basement. Great, now I was talking to myself. "Stop it, Sophie," I said without thinking. For some reason, saying my name felt good. I was tired of being Emily. I just wanted to get finished here and go back to my life. Since coming to Sanctuary, my world had been turned upside down. Even my affirmations weren't working anymore. I hadn't even listened to them today—and I didn't want to. "I need to get out of this place," I said to no one.

Shaking my head and questioning the wisdom of having a conversation with myself, I sat down at the desk and opened my paper bag. I'd eaten half my sandwich before my stomach stopped growling. Ever since coming to Sanctuary, I'd been eating more than I ever did at home. Thankfully, my jeans still fit, but I'd have to leave Sanctuary before I turned back into that unhappy, overweight girl from Kingdom. I could feel her watching me. Waiting for the chance to take her life back. But that wasn't going to happen. I knew I'd blamed a lot of my insecurity on my weight. Over time, I'd learned that the real reason for my pain had been my shattered self-image. I'd met several very successful women at work who were overweight, yet they were happy and self-confident. They didn't define themselves by the way they looked. They were self-assured in who they were as people. I wanted to be like them, but I wasn't there yet.

As I ate, I looked around the room. I'd been concentrating on the files, but there were a lot of other things stored down here. Although it was difficult to see clearly into the corners of the dark room, I spotted stacks of hymnals and other books on metal shelves that began in the middle of the room and stretched almost the entire length of the basement. Against the wall, there were folding chairs and tables and a couple of old wooden pews. The room reminded me of a library. Files and a desk on one side of the room, shelves with books and supplies on the other side. I thought about looking around some, but it was just too dark. The basement of a church shouldn't be intimidating, but for some reason, this one was.

I finished my sandwich, wolfed down my brownie, and drank about half of my pop before going back to work. I finished 2013 and started to work on the last book. Frankly, I had very little confidence that Chase would have come here after 2012, but I felt I should go through everything. I didn't want to leave any stone unturned. Besides, I still needed to know who had left Sanctuary in the last few years. That could be very important if I had to look for Chase somewhere else.

I worked as quickly as I could. I only had one more year to go, but my eyes were shot. I put all the books back in the filing cabinet, making sure they were in order, then I cleaned up the desk and took a moment to glance around the room once again. Even though it was a little spooky, it had been a welcome place to hide from the people in Sanctuary. Especially

Jonathon. I took a deep breath and stared at the door. One more day here, and I'd be done. After that, Esther's house would be the only place I could hide. But now Zac was there. Couldn't he have waited another week to visit?

With a sigh, I picked up my purse, turned off the desk lamp, and had started for the door when the dim light overhead turned off. I jumped, almost dropping my purse. The room was plunged into total darkness. Although I wanted to believe it was a power failure, I'd heard the distinct *click* of the light switch before everything went black. Someone was in the room with me.

"Who's there?" I called out. My voice was thin and high, powered by fear. I could feel my heart pounding in my chest, and I had to take a deep breath because I suddenly felt lightheaded.

There was no answer.

I put my hand out in an attempt to hold on to something, but I felt only air. Trying to see the room again in my mind, I moved slowly to my left until my fingers touched one of the metal shelves. I couldn't see anything, but maybe whoever was in here couldn't find their way around any better than I could. I gently set my purse on the nearby shelf so my hands would be free.

"This isn't funny. Please, who's in here with me?"

Although I knew it was probably a waste of time to call out again, a part of me wanted to believe Pastor Troyer had a weird sense of humor and thought scaring people in the basement might make them more amenable to church. Of course, I knew that was a long shot. The note I'd received yesterday suddenly seemed much more ominous.

I felt my way to the end of the shelving and moved as quietly as I could around the unit. Then I crouched down, trying to hide, although the person in the room with me would have to be wearing night-vision goggles if he had any chance of seeing me. After what seemed like hours but was probably only a few minutes, I heard a noise. It was close. Not knowing what else to do, I felt my way to the next aisle. I suddenly remembered a small flashlight I kept for emergencies in my purse. As much as I wanted it, trying to go back seemed like a really dumb thing to do. Panic had seized my body, and I couldn't stop shaking. Although I was trying to be quiet, it was difficult to keep my breathing slow and silent. I wanted to take big gulps of air, but I couldn't risk letting anyone hear me.

Another noise. It seemed to be coming from behind me somewhere. I stood up and began to feel my way along the shelves again, trying to get closer to the door. My fingers touched something on the shelf. I couldn't tell what it was, but it felt like a candlestick. Metal, heavy, and probably the best thing I could find down here to use as a weapon. I picked it up slowly, trying to be as quiet as possible. I made an effort to calm myself and figure out just where I was. If my calculations were correct, I was between the first and second rows of shelving—and about halfway down the row. That meant the door should only be about twenty feet away. Not knowing what else to do, I decided to make a run for it. I wanted my car keys so I could get to my car and drive away, but the keys were in my purse. Pastor Troyer should be in his office now, but that wasn't very comforting. Since I had no idea who was after me, I probably shouldn't count on the slight, skinny Mennonite pastor being able to subdue him.

I waited several seconds but didn't hear anything more. Then, after taking another deep breath, I moved as quickly as I could, still holding on to the shelf so I wouldn't get lost in the dark. At the end of the shelf, I let go and headed toward what I hoped was the door. I held the candlestick in one hand and kept my other hand in front of me. I felt something hard, but it wasn't the door. It was the concrete wall. Surely the door was just a few feet to my right. I began to fumble my way along the wall, but before I could find the door, I stumbled over something on the floor and fell to my knees. Then a burst of pain exploded in my head, and I felt myself drift away.

CHAPTER TWELVE

"Emily? Emily, can you hear me?"

I tried to force my eyes open, but I had the worst headache of my life, and my eyes felt like they were glued shut.

I jumped when someone stroked my face.

"Can you open your eyes?"

"Y-yeah," I mumbled. "I'm okay." I forced my eyelids apart, even though it hurt. Although at first everything was blurry, I realized I was looking straight into Jonathon's eyes. "What . . . what are you doing here?" I tried to move my head to see around me. "Where am I?"

"Hush. Don't move. You're in Pastor Troyer's office. We found you in the basement and brought you here. You fell and hit your head."

"No . . . no, someone hit me. There was someone in the basement."

Even peering through eyes only halfway open, I could see the look of skepticism on his face.

"Really. Someone was in there. I tried to get away, but . . ." A wave of pain hit me, and I cried out.

"Let me look at her," another voice said.

Jonathon turned his face away for a moment and then squeezed my hand. "We sent for the doctor. He needs to check you over."

I grabbed his hand as he started to pull it away. "Please. Please don't leave me."

"I'll be right here, Emily. It's okay." He stared at me strangely for a moment then got up and stepped back a few feet.

An elderly man sat down in the spot Jonathon had just occupied. I realized I was on the couch in Pastor Troyer's office. The lights were off in the room, but the door was open a little so we could see. I was thankful because the light hurt my eyes.

"I'm Dr. Watson," the man said. "I need you to look at me. I'm going to shine a small light in your eyes. I know it will be uncomfortable, but I need to find out if you have a concussion."

I nodded slowly, every move of my head causing pain.

"Try to focus on me," he said calmly.

I did my best, but when he shone the light in my right eye, it closed immediately. I forced it back open even though the pinpoint of light was excruciating. Then the doctor swung the light to my other eye.

"Any nausea? Confusion?"

"N-no, I don't think so," I said.

"Can you tell me your name?"

I opened my mouth, ready to tell him my name was Sophie Bauer, when I suddenly remembered. "Em . . . Emily McClure."

"Where are you from, Emily?"

"St. Louis. I'm in Sanctuary to find some information about my family."

He smiled at me, and his gray mustache seemed to curl upward with his lips. "Good. Now, any numbness? Can you move your arms and legs for me?"

I did as he'd asked. "Everything seems to be fine, Doctor, but I have an awful headache."

"I'm not surprised. Let's see if you can sit up."

He stood up and took my hand, pulling me to an upright position. The pain seemed to be less than it had been while I was lying down.

"So does she have a concussion?" Jonathon asked.

The doctor shook his head. "I don't see any sign of it." He leveled a serious look at me. "If you have any trouble with your vision, or if you start feeling sick, I want you to call me. When do you plan to leave town?"

"I don't know," I said slowly. "Could be a few days. A week at the most."

"Make sure you see your regular doctor when you go home. You can't be too careful with a head injury." He turned toward Jonathon and Pastor Troyer, who stood a few steps away, concern evident in their expressions. "Is there someone who can keep an eye on this young lady for the next couple of days?"

Jonathon nodded. "She's staying with Esther Lapp."

Dr. Watson nodded and turned back to me. "Good. She'll take great care of you. Now remember, any unusual symptoms, you call me right away. Okay?"

"Yes, I will. Thank you so much."

"You're very welcome." He shook hands first with Jonathon and then with Pastor Troyer. "Can one of you also check up on her once in a while? Just to be safe?"

"I will," Jonathon said quickly. "No problem."

Dr. Watson said good-bye and left.

Great. One more reason for me to see Jonathon. I suddenly thought of something. "My purse. Did anyone see my purse?"

Pastor Troyer shook his head. "I did not see your purse when we found you. Did you have it with you?"

"Yes, I . . ." Then I remembered. "Actually, when the lights went off, I put it on a shelf. The one closest to the desk."

"The lights went off?" he repeated, looking confused. He glanced over at Jonathon, and I saw him shake his head slightly.

"Yes," I insisted. "Someone turned off the lights. I tried to hide, but when they got too close to me, I made an attempt to get to the door. I tripped and fell, and then whoever it was hit me on the head."

"I will go downstairs and look for your purse," the pastor said. "Will you stay here with her, Jonathon?"

"Of course," he said, "and when she's ready to go, I'll drive her home."

The pastor left the room, and Jonathon sat down next to me again. "Emily, you tripped over a mop bucket and hit your head on a metal chest near the door. That's where we found you."

I grabbed his arm. "Jonathon, someone was in that room. I'm not delusional. He turned off the light, and when I tried to get away, he hit me with something."

"Why would anyone want to hurt you?"

"I—I don't know. But it's what happened."

Back in Kingdom, Jonathon had watched over me. He'd been the one person I could count on. I needed that now, but it was out of my grasp. I was no longer that shy, awkward, unloved teenager he took pity on. For just a moment, I almost wanted to be her again so I could rely on his help and protection for a little while. But that wasn't going to happen.

He leaned over and checked my head. "You've got a nice bump. I'm sure it hurts."

"I don't suppose the doctor gave you a prescription for a pain reliever."

"Sorry. You'll have to do with over-the-counter medicine."

"Great." Actually, I had some leftover pain pills from having two wisdom teeth pulled. The bottle was in my purse. Correction. *Hopefully,* the bottle was still in my purse. I reached up and touched my head. Sure enough, there was a good-sized lump. "Did it occur to you that if I tripped on something and fell, I should have hit my forehead? Not the back of my head?"

He frowned. "I hadn't thought about it, but . . ."

Whatever he planned to say next was interrupted by Pastor Troyer, who came into the room, carrying my purse. "It was on the floor, not far from where you fell," he said, holding the purse out to me. "You must have dropped it when you tripped."

Shaking my head, I took the purse from his hand. I quickly looked through it. My notes were gone. All my work. The person who'd attacked me was after the information I'd found. That meant he was probably worried I might find Terrance Chase. Or he might *be* Terrance Chase. Chase must be in Sanctuary, and somehow, he knew why I was here. That knowledge frightened me and thrilled me all at the same time. But how could he know? Suddenly, Donnie's words came back to me. Someone had beaten Tom, and there was no way to know what he'd told them. So either Chase was behind this or someone else who wanted Chase's money had taken my notes, hoping he could find the robber first.

Something else occurred to me, and I quickly checked my wallet. The picture of Chase was gone, as well.

"Is everything there?" Pastor Troyer asked.

I nodded. "Nothing seems to be missing," I lied. I couldn't tell him about the notes and the picture. It might reveal what I'd really been doing in the church basement. No one would knock me out and steal notes about the Byler family. The idea was ridiculous. I pushed a few things aside, and my fingers closed over the bottle of pain pills. "Could I have a glass of water?" I asked.

"Of course. I will be right back." He hurried out of the room.

"As soon as you're ready, I'll take you home," Jonathon said. "You need to lie down and take it easy for a while."

"I will. With this headache, I don't think I'm up to doing much else today."

"You told the doctor you were going to stick around for a while?"

"Yeah. I would like to meet some of the people in Sanctuary. People who actually knew my great-aunt—and my grandmother. Before I leave, I'd love to have a better idea about what kind of women the Byler sisters were."

He nodded. "I understand. You know, the church supper would be a great place to talk to people about Miriam and Clara. But that's a pretty big knot you've got going there. If you're still hurting, please stay home. Don't push yourself, okay? You can always meet people at church on Sunday."

I didn't say anything, just smiled and nodded my head. With the help of my pain pills, I'd be at that church supper tomorrow. A large collection of Sanctuary residents all in one place. I couldn't miss it.

Pastor Troyer came back with a glass of water. I thanked him and quickly took two pain pills, knowing they'd probably knock me out. But by the time they hit, I'd be tucked into bed at Esther's. I was suddenly grateful for impacted wisdom teeth.

"Are you ready?" Jonathon asked.

"Yes. Thank you for taking me to Esther's. I hate to leave my car here, but I really don't feel like driving right now."

"I understand. I'll walk back and get your car after we get you home."

"Okay."

He stood up. "If you get dizzy, let me know, okay?"

"Sure." I took the arm he extended to me and slowly stood to my feet. I didn't feel dizzy. My only problem was the pounding pain that made my head feel as if it were trapped in an ever-tightening vise.

Pastor Troyer rushed over and took my other arm. We began a slow processional to the front door of the church. When we stepped outside, I was thrilled to find that it had turned cloudy. The last thing I needed now was the bright sun shining in my eyes. Rain sprinkled lightly on us as we made our way to Jonathon's truck. The two men helped me into the passenger's seat.

"I will be praying for you," Pastor Troyer said. "God will watch over you, Emily. I am certain you will recover completely."

"Thank you," I said.

Jonathon walked around the truck and climbed into the driver's seat. After saying good-bye to the kind pastor, we began the short drive to Esther's.

I turned toward Jonathon, trying not to move my head too much. "I really appreciate your help."

He shrugged. "That's the way we are in Sanctuary. People helping people."

His tone had a slight edge to it. Was he angry at me for some reason? Had my story about the attack in the basement made him suspicious? I wanted to tell him everything. Ask for his help. But how could I? Jonathon was a pastor. A man dedicated to the truth and to taking the moral high ground. I couldn't expect him to lie to people for me. Or to sanction my reason for being in his beloved town. There was no way he could do anything except expose me and ruin my chances of ever finding Chase. I was certain he would not only reject my reason for being here, he would turn his back on me, as well. And I couldn't blame him.

We didn't talk the rest of the way. When we got to Esther's, he came around to help me out of the truck. We were walking up the steps to the front door when Esther came out, her face creased with worry.

"Oh my. Is something wrong? Are you sick, child?"

"She fell in the church basement and hit her head," Jonathon said before I could respond.

"Oh dear. Can you get her upstairs? She needs to be in bed, and I am not strong enough to support her."

"Sure," he said. "Doc Watson says you need to keep an eye on her. She doesn't seem to have a concussion, but he wants to make certain. If she seems confused or nauseated, or if she can't seem to remember things, we've got to let him know."

Esther nodded. "I understand."

As we entered the living room, we found Zac coming in from the kitchen. "Are you okay?" He hurried toward me. "You look awful."

"Gee, thanks. Just what every girl likes to hear."

"Can you help me get her upstairs?" Jonathon asked Zac.

"You bet." He put down the glass he had in his hand and moved over to my other side. Slipping his arm around me, he let me put my hand on his shoulder so I could support myself. The three of us slowly climbed the stairs.

"Can I get you something?" Esther called from behind us.

"Maybe a glass of hot chocolate?" I replied. "For some reason, I'm so cold. Hot chocolate sounds wonderful."

"You get in bed," she answered. "I will be up in a few minutes with your cocoa."

Although I didn't enjoy being in pain, the pills started to kick in, and with them, a slight feeling of euphoria. Snuggled in bed on a rainy evening, sipping hot chocolate, sounded just perfect. I usually worked so hard I didn't get much time to simply rest.

When we got to the top of the stairs, Jonathon and Zac helped me to my room. Once inside, Jonathon asked if I wanted to change out of my clothes.

"Yes. I have some sweats in the drawer." I looked at the men. "You can go now. I don't need help changing clothes."

"I'm going to stick with you for a while," Jonathon said. "I'll wait out in the hall."

I sighed. "Okay." I turned my attention to Zac. "Could you go downstairs and wait for my hot chocolate? I don't trust Esther on those stairs."

"Sure. I'll be back in a minute." He left the room. Jonathon was quiet as I gathered my clothes.

"I need to make a trip to the bathroom," I told him. "I'll just change in there."

"Do you need help getting down the hall?"

"It's just a few steps away. I'll be fine."

"Okay. I'll wait for you here."

"Thanks, Jonathon. This certainly hasn't been one of my better days."

He smiled. "I think that's an understatement."

The pain pills were making me groggy, but I walked slowly to the bathroom on my own. I changed my clothes and then went back to my room. Jonathon was standing next to the bed, my purse lying open on top of the quilt. He held my wallet in his hands. It was flipped open.

"What are you doing?" I said sharply. "Put that down."

When he finally looked at me, I recognized the expression on his face. I'd seen it before.

"I told you I'd only met one other person with amber eyes," he said in a tight, controlled voice. "In Pastor Troyer's office, when you were lying on his couch, I began to notice other similarities to the girl I used to know, and I decided I had to know the truth. You may have changed on the outside, but you're still a liar and a manipulator, aren't you, Sophie?"

CHAPTER THIRTEEN

"Here's your hot chocolate."

I jumped involuntarily at the sound of Zac's voice. He'd been so quiet I hadn't heard him enter the room. I walked over to the small stool Jonathon had put next to the bed so I could climb in.

"I'll take that," Jonathon said, sounding tense. "We need a few minutes, Zac. Do you mind?"

Zac looked back and forth between us. "I—I guess not," he said, handing the cup to Jonathon. He nervously cleared his throat and looked at me, confusion on his face. "I'll be downstairs if you need me."

"Thank you. I'll be fine."

Jonathon didn't say anything as Zac left the room. We could hear his steps going down the stairs. I climbed up on the bed, put the pillows behind my back, and pulled the covers over myself. Try as I might, I couldn't think of anything to say. My trip to Sanctuary had come to an end. There was no way I would be able to stay here now. I'd have to go home a failure. Something I was used to.

Jonathon threw my wallet on the bed next to me. "I need you to explain what you're doing here. Did you come to Sanctuary to find me?"

My mouth dropped open. "Of course not. I had no idea you were here."

"Then what's going on?"

"I'll tell you everything, but not right now. I took some pain pills, and I'm so sleepy . . ."

"Give me the short version. Then when you're feeling better we'll talk more."

I quickly ran through my reason for being in Sanctuary. My meeting with Tom and my need to find Terrance Chase for a story. "And that's it. I'm not here to hurt anyone, or to cause trouble. I'm trying to track down a murderer. Someone you shouldn't want hiding out in this town. After I find him, I'll be gone."

"You just want the story. You don't care about this town any more than you cared about Kingdom."

Maybe it was the pills, but tears filled my eyes and spilled down my cheeks. "That's not fair. I cared enough to leave. I know what I did was wrong . . ."

"You burned down our church," Jonathon stated emphatically. "You could have killed someone. I had to run inside to save Pastor Mendenhall. That's not some kind of youthful stunt, Sophie. It could have been a terrible tragedy."

"I know that," I said, the words slurring. "Tom told me to do it . . ."

"You can't blame Tom for everything you did."

"I'm not. It was my fault. I wrote a letter to Pastor Mendenhall and told him what I'd done. I asked for forgiveness, and I left town so I wouldn't hurt anyone else." I wiped tears from my face with the back of my hand. "I've changed, Jonathon. I'm in college, working toward a degree. I'm educating myself, and I've been trying to make something out of my life. I'm not the same person."

He shook his head. "How can you say that? You're here under false pretenses. You're lying to everyone, including Esther."

"Esther knows the truth."

His eyebrows shot up. "You told her?"

"No. Turns out Clara Byler couldn't have children. My story fell apart."

He stared at me through narrowed eyes. "Why didn't Esther throw you out?"

I couldn't hold back a sob. "Because she thinks God sent me here for a reason. She wants to give me a chance."

"And do you think God sent you here, Sophie?"

"No. I told you, I don't believe in God. I've rejected the idea of a God who allows children to be abused and abandoned. God never showed me any love. I prayed and prayed for help. None came. Now I trust myself. No one else."

Although I understood my last words, I knew they were garbled. I was barely conscious. "I—I have to sleep. I'm sorry. I know you hate me, but I can't help it. If it makes you feel any better, I hate myself, too."

I pulled my pillows down and collapsed into them. As I drifted off, I thought I felt someone stroke my hair.

When I woke up, the room was dark except for a night-light plugged into the wall by the bed. Although it was hard to see, I leaned over to check the clock on the nightstand. It was only nine o'clock at night. Even so, Esther would be in bed by now. I needed to go to the bathroom, and I was hungry, but there wasn't anyone here to help me. I'd have to take care of myself—as usual. I sat up in bed and swung my legs over the side.

"You're awake."

The voice from the darkness made me cry out. I looked over toward the fainting couch and saw Jonathon sitting there.

"You scared me to death." I gasped for breath.

"Sorry." He stood up and walked toward me. "I felt someone should be with you. Make sure you're okay."

"I'm fine. Except for the mild heart attack you just gave me. I thought someone was after me again." Although I tried to calm myself down, my voice trembled.

"We need to talk," he said.

"What I *need* to do is go to the bathroom and get something to eat."

"How does your head feel?"

I hadn't even thought about it. "It's better," I said with relief. I reached up and touched the spot where I'd been hit. It was still tender, but the swelling had gone down quite a bit. "Seems the patient will live. Sorry to disappoint you."

"Don't be stupid," Jonathon said sharply. "Go to the bathroom. I'll wait here."

He came over and pushed the stool next to the bed. I put my feet on it and started to step down, but I suddenly lost my balance. Before I fell, Jonathon reached out and caught me, wrapping his arms around me. Surprised, I looked up into his face. I saw something in his eyes that made my breath quicken, but as quickly as it came, it was gone. Chalk it up to my imagination. I planted my feet firmly on the floor, and he let me go.

"Sorry . . . I . . ." My mind was blank, and I fled the room. When I reached the bathroom, I closed the door and leaned against it. I could still feel his arms around me. It was something I'd dreamed of for so long. An old, familiar ache sprang to life inside, but I pushed it away.

"Stop it, you idiot," I scolded myself softly. "You're not going to make a fool of yourself again. Not ever again."

Before I went back to the bedroom, I checked my image in the mirror. There were dark circles under my eyes, and my hair looked awful. Thankfully, I'd left my makeup bag in the bathroom, so I took a few minutes to brush my hair and fix my face. When I was done, I looked more like myself, not the scared and confused kid Jonathon had known in Kingdom.

I tried to focus on my investigation. Would I have to leave town? My only chance was to convince Jonathon to let me finish my business in Sanctuary. Although I'd lost my notes, I had the names of most of the men who were most likely to be Chase on my laptop and stashed under my mattress. I wanted to make one more trip to the church to go through the last book. I needed to see if there were any more single men who'd left town. Then my list would be complete. It was clear someone didn't want me here. First the note and now the attack in the basement. But did it have anything to do with Terrance Chase? I still wasn't sure.

I took several deep breaths, trying to control my shattered nerves. I attempted to whisper my affirmations, but once again, they seemed powerless. In fact, I felt as if they mocked me. "It's in your head, dummy," I said to myself. "You're intimidated by this town, and it's going to stop. Right now."

I gathered my determination and willpower and headed back to my room. I had to keep reminding myself that I was no longer Sophie Wittenbauer, pathetic and uneducated. I was Sophie Bauer, a writer for the *St. Louis Times*. I was here on a story, and that story came first. Any other feelings or concerns needed to be imprisoned in the dark place where I kept the rest of my emotions. I had a job to do, and I intended to do it.

When I reached my room, Jonathon was sitting in an overstuffed chair near the bed. "Do you want to go downstairs to eat, or would you like me to bring you something up here?"

"I can make myself something," I said hurriedly. "I'm fine."

"Okay, but I'm still going to hang around until I'm certain you're really okay."

I shrugged. "Help yourself. Does Esther know you're here?"

"I told her you needed someone to watch you. Someone who could stay awake. She wanted to do it but was afraid she'd fall asleep."

"Well, Zac is next door, you know. He could have checked on me."

"I convinced her you'd be more comfortable with someone you knew."

"You—you didn't tell her . . ."

"No. I didn't tell her about Kingdom. Just that I knew you and that I was at the church when you were . . . injured."

"Okay. Good." I was relieved. Sharing what had happened in Kingdom wasn't something I planned to do. Ever. Of course, now that Jonathon knew who I was, every time I looked at him, I was faced with the shame of my past.

I wanted to change my clothes, but I'd just be going back to bed, so I left my sweatpants and sweatshirt on. I pulled off my socks, found my flip-flops, and slid those on.

Jonathon was silent as he followed me downstairs to the kitchen. As I fumbled around in the refrigerator, he sat down at the kitchen table and watched me. His presence made me nervous, but I tried to ignore him. I found some chicken salad, so I made a sandwich. Then I sliced some strawberries and poured a glass of tea.

"Can I get you anything?" I asked.

He shook his head. "Esther made me dinner while you were sleeping."

"Then you talked? About me?"

"Yes."

I put my food and tea on the table and sat down next to him. "May I ask what you said about me?"

"Just that I knew you a long time ago. That you and I are from the same town. And that I never thought I'd see you again."

I took a bite of chicken salad, chewed, and swallowed it. "You mean you *hoped* you'd never see me again."

"No. To be honest, I've thought about you a lot since you left Kingdom. Prayed for you many times. A lot of people in Kingdom prayed for you, Sophie."

"I find that hard to believe. I'm sure they were thrilled to see me go."

"You need to give them more credit than that. People cared about you."

I drank some tea. For some reason, my mouth was horribly dry and the tea was incredibly soothing. Probably the pills. "And what did you pray?"

Jonathon sighed. "I prayed that you would find your way. And that you would discover the path God has for you."

I couldn't help but laugh. "I found my path, but God had nothing to do with it."

To my surprise, he smiled. "So you think coming to Sanctuary and finding me was just . . . dumb luck?"

"I'm not feeling very lucky right now."

"What do you mean?"

I took another bite of my sandwich and stared at him while I chewed. "Let's see," I said after I swallowed. "I came here on a pretext to find an infamous thief and murderer. My cover story has been blown, I've been threatened, hit on the head, and I ran into you. I don't think you can call any of that *lucky*, do you?"

"Maybe not. It's almost like it was . . . planned."

I grunted. "Please don't tell me you've bought into Esther's belief that I'm here for a reason, and before I leave, I'll understand it all."

"Maybe."

"Then you're as delusional as she is."

"Sophie, your parents were . . . well, awful. Selfish, cruel, terrible people. As examples of God, they failed miserably. But you shouldn't judge God by them. It's something a lot of people do, but people aren't perfect. Even when they call themselves Christians. They still have free will and can choose wrong things."

His words made my blood boil. "I'm not judging God by them. I'm judging God by God. I prayed and prayed for help. All I got back was silence. Explain that to me."

He hesitated a moment before responding. "That's not an easy question to answer. I've been asked it before. All I can tell you is that parents have authority over their children. Because of that, they have the ability to mistreat them. But that certainly isn't God's will. You keep saying God didn't help you, but you were never alone. A lot of people watched over you. I was one of them. And when you were ready to leave town, Lizzie Housler gave you money so you could get away."

"Yes, she did."

"Why don't you judge God by those people?" he asked gently. "Instead of by the parents who failed you?"

"God says He's our father," I spat out, unable to control my anger. "The only father I've ever known abused me." I pointed my finger at him. "In ways you don't know anything about. No one does."

His eyes widened, and I was shocked to see them turn shiny with tears. "Sophie, you don't mean . . ."

"Yes, I do mean. So parents have authority over their children, huh? Do they have the authority to do . . . that?"

Jonathon got up from his chair and walked to the window. He didn't say anything for a while. I assumed he was so disgusted with me now, he'd just leave. It was the reaction I expected—and the reason I'd never told anyone what my father was doing.

Finally, he turned around, and his eyes met mine. The expression on his face made my heart beat faster. "If I'd known, I would have been tempted to kill him."

My mouth dropped open. "I—I don't understand."

He came back over and sat down, a terrible look on his face. "I may be a pastor, Sophie, but I'm still a man. I would have done something. I would have stopped him somehow." He shook his head. "Did your mother know?"

I wiped away a tear that dripped down one of my cheeks. "I honestly don't know. She didn't act like she did, but sometimes I felt she suspected something wasn't right."

Without thinking, I reached out and touched his hand. "You wouldn't have killed him, Jonathon. You're a good man."

He sighed. "I probably wouldn't have killed him, but it would have crossed my mind. I'm human, Sophie. That means I'm not perfect." He cocked his head to the side. "Is that what you think? That Christians have to be perfect?"

I withdrew my hand and picked up my sandwich. "Isn't that what the church teaches? That you're supposed to be like Christ? I could never do that. Never come close to that."

"No church should make you feel you have the ability to be righteous by yourself. Our righteousness comes from Jesus. He gives it to us when we become His. You don't have to *try* to be perfect. When God sees you, He sees Jesus. You're already perfect in His eyes."

His words were like arrows piercing my heart. "That's ridiculous. So I can act any way I want to, and God will accept me? No matter what awful things I do?"

"No. You're putting the cart before the horse, Sophie. Allowing God in your life means He comes in and changes you—if you let Him. Too many people are trying to be *good.* But we can't do that without Him." Jonathon crossed his arms and leaned back in his chair. "The Bible tells us that it's the goodness of God that leads to repentance. If you'd had a good father—a loving father—you'd want to please him. Be like him because he loves you and you love him. That's what love is. But your father didn't love you. He hurt you, so you rebelled. Unfortunately, now you're angry at the Father who wants to give you the love you've missed. That's a terrible mistake."

I sighed. "Look, I know you're trying to help, but I'm just not interested. I like the life I have now. I've worked hard, and I know what I want. This church and God thing? It's just not for me. Being around judgmental people who always know what I should and shouldn't be doing? Never again. I'll figure things out on my own. I'm the only one who truly has my best interests at heart."

I knew Jonathon believed what he said, but I didn't. And I never would. I'd spent my life being judged by *church people,* and I'd come up wanting. I was done with that. I expected him to get angry about what I'd said, but he just smiled.

"Let's get back to the reason you're here," he said. "You explained some of it earlier, but I have a few questions."

I picked up my plate and carried it to the sink, where I rinsed it off and set it on the counter. "I'm still tired, Jonathon. Can we talk about it tomorrow?"

"Sure. It's just . . . I'll need more information . . . if I'm going to help you."

I turned around to gape at him, but I moved too quickly. A wave of dizziness hit me, and I grasped the countertop, trying to steady myself.

Jonathon jumped to his feet and took my arm, helping me back to my chair. "Are you all right?"

"I'm . . . fine. Those pills. Maybe I shouldn't have taken two." I waited until he sat down. "I don't understand. Did you say you're going to . . . help me?"

"I'm as surprised as you are. But yes, I'm going to help you. Finding an evil man and bringing him to justice is . . . praiseworthy." He pointed at me. "But no more lies, Sophie. I mean it. Not one. If you lie to me, I'm done." He glanced at his watch. "Let's get you to bed. I'm going to ask Zac to keep an eye on you the rest of the night. When you get up, if you feel the least bit dizzy, you call him for help getting downstairs." He picked up a slip of paper. "Here's his cell phone number. I'll stop by his room on the way out and let him know. In the morning, I've got to help prepare for the church supper. But let's talk after that. Say around two? I'll have some time before I have to get back to the church. You bring me up to date on everything you've found. And tell me what you need to know. I'm not a longtime Sanctuary resident, but I'm acquainted with people who are. Together, we might be able to figure out if this Chase guy is really here. Why don't you meet me at The Oil Lamp? If you feel up to it."

"I don't know what to say. Th-thank you."

"You get some rest." He stood up and offered me his arm. I took it, and together we made our way up the stairs. After he deposited me in my room, I heard him walk down the hall and knock on Zac's door. Although I couldn't make out the words, I could hear them talking.

I climbed back into bed and lay there for a long while, trying to make sense out of the strange turn my life had taken. But try as I might, I couldn't figure it out.

CHAPTER FOURTEEN

I woke up the next morning feeling pretty good, but I'd been plagued all night by strange dreams. I was lost inside a big house. Every time I thought I'd found a way out, the doors disappeared. Sometimes the house changed, as well. No matter what I tried, I couldn't find a way of escape. When I opened my eyes, my first impulse was to seek safety. But then I remembered where I was—and what had happened the night before. Jonathon knew who I really was, and instead of telling me to leave town, he'd decided to help me look for Terrance Chase. It was still almost impossible for me to believe.

After lying in bed for a few minutes, I decided to get up and take a shower. I gathered my clothes together and headed to the bathroom. After my shower, I felt much more human. The pain pills had really knocked me for a loop. They were probably the source of my weird dreams.

After brushing my teeth, putting on makeup, and fixing my hair, I went back to my room. In the hallway, I heard voices coming from downstairs. Zac and Esther. I wondered if she'd told Zac why I was really here. I hoped not. I'd wanted to keep my reasons for being in Sanctuary to myself, but now two people knew my secret. That was two too many. Besides, Zac worked for a television station. I couldn't allow him to scoop me.

I was getting ready to go downstairs when my phone rang. Donnie's number. Make that three people who knew the truth. Before long, I might as well take out an ad in the local newspaper and make sure everyone was up to date on my reason for being in Sanctuary.

Ignoring the call for the time being, I quickly straightened my room then went downstairs. I found Zac and Esther in the kitchen, sitting at the table.

"There you are," Esther said when I came into the room. "Zac was getting ready to check on you."

I smiled at her. "I'm feeling much better."

"Good," she said, returning my smile. "You sit down. I'll get you some coffee and something to eat."

"Thanks, Esther, but I'm not hungry. I came down here last night and made a sandwich. Just some coffee, please. That's all I really need." I craved a kick of caffeine to push away the final cobwebs from the day before.

"Of course," she said. "Have a seat, and I will pour you a cup."

Zac pulled out a chair for me. "Glad you're feeling better."

"Thank you." I sat down and waited while Esther got a jadeite mug from the cupboard and filled it with her delicious coffee. When she put it in front of me, I picked it up and took a sip. A sigh of satisfaction slipped out.

Zac laughed. "Esther's coffee will cure anything. I thought

the only coffee in the world was from Starbucks. Until I tasted this."

I grinned. "I know exactly what you mean."

"I buy coffee almost every morning when I'm working," he said. "It gets my day going in the right direction. Don't know how I'd get by without it."

Seemed we had something in common. "So do you enjoy working at a television station?"

"I love it. Every day is different. They're letting me work with the reporters now. Besides taking pictures and video, I get to do some research."

"Sounds great."

"Esther tells me you're an accountant?"

Obviously, Esther had kept my secret. I breathed an inward sigh of relief. "Yes. I'm afraid it's not as exciting as your job. But I enjoy dealing with numbers, and I like the people I work with."

Zac took a sip of his coffee as he looked me over. "You don't seem like someone who would be an accountant."

What in the world did people see that I couldn't? "You're not the first person to say that. I'm not sure what an accountant looks like."

He grinned. "A little man with glasses and a bow tie. His best friend is his calculator."

I laughed. "Sounds like an old movie."

"You're probably right. I love old movies."

"I do, too." After I left Kingdom, I discovered television for the first time. I couldn't believe some of the things I saw on TV. Although it helped teach me about modern hairstyles, fashion, and makeup, the regular shows were too graphic for me. So I'd found channels with old movies that kept me entertained and intrigued. I'd cried over Cathy's death in *Wuthering Heights* and laughed at Jimmy Stewart in *Harvey* and Cary Grant in *Arsenic and Old Lace*. Of course, I didn't admit to watching those movies with the people at work. I just smiled and nodded during conversations about their favorite shows.

Esther put a plate with pancakes and bacon in front of Zac. He added butter and syrup then began to eat. Although it looked delicious, it reminded me of my mother. She'd loved anything sweet. Especially fattening cupcakes and desserts. Sometimes I snuck some of her food since she was selfish with it. In a weird way, I guess I'd been trying to find some kind of control by taking the things she loved. My mother's food gave me a rush. Made me feel better. It wasn't until I left Kingdom that I realized food had become a drug. Something to dull the pain—and it had taken over my life. Rather than giving me control, it controlled me. It took a lot of work to change my habits. I had no plan to ever again use food as a panacea for the hurt in my soul.

"What are your plans for the day?" Esther's question brought me back to the present.

"I have some work to do on my laptop. And then I'm meeting Pastor Wiese later today."

"You have accounting work to do on vacation?" Zac asked, looking confused.

I thought quickly. "It's March," I said. "April is right around the corner."

"Oh. That makes sense."

I nodded as if it actually did.

He got up and poured himself another cup of coffee. Then he held out the coffeepot. I stuck out my cup, and he filled it.

"More coffee, Esther?" he asked.

She shook her head. "I have a lot of baking to do. I need to get at it."

Zac put the pot back on the stove and sat back down in his chair. "Jonathon's a great guy, isn't he?"

I nodded, not knowing what to say. Zac must have heard our angry confrontation last night. Surely he was curious about it.

"He needs to find a wife, though," he continued. "There are a lot of women interested, but he doesn't really date. Seems to be waiting for the right person."

I frowned at him. "He knew my grandmother. We're just planning to talk about her."

"Oh." He turned his attention to Esther. "Do you mind if I hang around and help you get ready for the church supper? I don't have anything else to do."

She reached out and patted his hand. "I think you could find something if you wanted to. It is more likely you are concerned I will work too hard, and you plan to keep an eye on me."

Zac's eyebrows shot up. "I'm wounded to the quick. How can you be so suspicious?"

He winked at me, and Esther saw him. We both laughed.

"You are welcome to stay and keep me company," she said. "As long as you know that you have not fooled me."

"I'm sure I have no idea what you're talking about," he said innocently.

How wonderful it would be to have such an easy friendship

with someone. Although I had acquaintances at college and at the newspaper, I didn't really have any friends. I told myself I didn't need them, yet I couldn't help but envy Esther and Zac. Despite their age difference, they got along famously.

"I need to get to work." I got up and went over to the coffeepot. "Can I help with the dishes, Esther?"

"No, honey. Zac loves to do dishes. You go on and get your work done. We'll be leaving for the supper around five o'clock. If there's not enough room in Janet's car, Zac will drive you over."

"Yeah, I'd be happy to."

"Thanks, but I'll probably walk to the church after my meeting with Jonathon. If I'm not here at five, just go without me."

After filling my cup one more time, I went upstairs to my room. I couldn't help feeling unsettled. I needed to be careful from now on. Make sure I stayed around other people and didn't get into vulnerable situations. The only comfort I had was that whoever hit me had only been interested in my list and my picture of Chase. If they'd wanted to permanently put me out of commission, they could have—yet they didn't. After thinking about it, I decided it was best to let everyone think I'd tripped. That I'd just imagined someone hitting me. Except for Jonathon. If he brought it up again, I'd stick to the truth. If I changed my story now, he might think I was being deceitful and decide not to help me.

I really wished I had something more to go on than old church records and staring at men in town, trying to figure out if they looked anything like Terrance Chase. I should have worked out a better plan. I'd been so excited about coming here, maybe I hadn't done enough research. Would an experienced investigative reporter have come up with something better? It was possible, but the trail was so cold I was pretty certain anyone would have had trouble figuring out how to track down Chase.

I grabbed my laptop and plopped down on the fainting couch. Then I scooted around and got comfortable. There were twelve names on my list. Three of the men had left town. Three had died. That left six men who still lived in Sanctuary. Of course, Chase could have been one of the men who'd moved away. Or maybe he'd died, although that was less likely. He wasn't an old man, and if he'd passed away, it was possible his true identity would have been discovered. I really needed to go back to the church and look through the final book. It was possible Jonathon or Esther might be able to fill in the blanks, but I couldn't take the chance that someone might slip through the cracks. I'd come too far and worked too hard to leave any loopholes. I had to make sure my list was accurate.

I stared at the list, and my mind drifted to the incident yesterday. Whoever took my notebook had these names—and a few others, the names I'd written down yesterday. If it was someone looking for Chase, would my attacker find him before I could?

I studied the names and recognized one of them. Reuben King. Esther had told me he was the man the other Emily had married. I started to mark his name off but decided to wait until I saw him, although he was probably too young to be Terrance Chase. Chase was forty-two when he robbed the armored car company. That meant he was now around fifty. Esther had mentioned that Emily, or Wynter, was near my age. I doubted she would marry someone so much older than she was, but I couldn't be sure.

Jonathon's name was on my list, so I crossed him off. For a second, I wondered if he might be in danger from whoever had stolen my notes, but he was way too young to be Chase. Anyone looking for the elusive criminal would know that.

One of the names, Peter Bakker, sparked something. Where had I heard that name? Suddenly, I remembered. The post office. The clerk's last name was Bakker. Sarah Miller had mentioned an Evan Bakker who was smoking a turkey for the church supper. The postal clerk couldn't look less like Chase if he tried. Besides, Chase had no relatives, and Evan Bakker had a brother. In researching Chase, I'd found that his parents had died when he was young. He'd lived with his grandmother until he was eighteen. Not long after he left home, she'd passed away. There was no one else. I didn't feel sorry for him. Being alone doesn't give you the right to take the lives of innocent people.

I quickly wrote the remaining names down in another notebook I'd brought with me. I needed to talk to someone about each of these men. Esther was out because she was spending the afternoon with Zac. I had a meeting with Jonathon at two. He'd be able to help me some, but he hadn't been here that long. I'd just have to do the best I could with his help until I could get some time alone with Esther.

I put the notebook in my purse and then spent some time figuring out what I was going to wear to meet Jonathon. The last thing I wanted to worry about was what he thought about me, but I couldn't help it. I would probably never stop loving him. My love for him was like a fire burning somewhere deep inside—in a place I couldn't find and couldn't control. It was something I'd have to learn to live with, along with the pain that fueled the flames. I finally settled on a black leather jacket to wear over a dark green sweater and jeans. It was simple, but the black emphasized my blond hair, and the sweater highlighted my eyes.

By the time I got ready to leave, I knew I looked good, but no matter what I wore or how I fixed up my outside, I was certain Jonathon would always see me as the person I'd spent the last few years trying to destroy.

CHAPTER FIFTEEN

A few minutes before two o'clock, I told Zac and Esther I was leaving and would probably meet them at the church.

It was two on the button when I pulled up in front of The Oil Lamp. Jonathon's truck was already there. I went inside and found him sitting at a table in the back corner of the restaurant. I'd just sat down when Randi came up and asked me what I wanted.

"Just iced tea," I answered.

"Bring us both a piece of your great coconut cream pie," Jonathon said.

I started to protest, but he held up one hand.

"Trust me. You've never had coconut cream pie like this. If you can't finish it, I'll eat it for you."

Randi laughed. "He means it, honey. That's how he gets extra pie without looking like a pig." She shook her head. "I thought gluttony was a sin, pastor man."

Jonathon grinned. "Just fetch the pie, woman."

Randi chuckled, patted Jonathon on the shoulder, and walked away.

"I take it she doesn't go to your church?" I asked when she was out of hearing range.

"Yes, as a matter of fact, she does. Why do you ask?" His confused expression cleared. "Oh, I take it you're still bugged by the lack of formality I have with my parishioners?"

I shrugged. "It's not my business."

Jonathon took a sip of his coffee. "What do you care, Sophie? You don't believe in God anyway, right?"

"Like I said, it's none of my business what you do."

"According to you, pastors teach others to believe in someone who doesn't exist. Doesn't that make us . . . phonies? Liars? Why should we get any respect?"

I scowled at him. "I never said that. You're putting words in my mouth."

"No, I'm not. If there's no God, then I'm lying to the people who attend my church."

I sighed. "Obviously, you're trying to make a point. Why don't you just say it? Get it over with?"

"I'm not trying to make any point except this—I think you do believe in God. If you didn't, you wouldn't be so angry. Why be upset with someone who isn't real? It doesn't make sense."

I felt my face flush with anger. "Then you explain to me where He's been all my life, Jonathon."

He reached out and grabbed my hand. "Right there with you. He never left."

I pulled my hand away. "Then He stood by and did nothing."

Jonathon started to say something else, but I waved his

comment away. "You asked me to meet you because you said you'd help me go through these names. Was that true or not?"

He frowned. "Yes, it's true. But one thing before we start. I need to apologize to you. If I'd been the right kind of friend, you could have told me what was happening at home. What your father was doing to you. I let you down, and I blame myself. You should have been able to come to me for help."

I blinked back the tears that sprang to my eyes. "I wouldn't have told you, no matter what you did. I was ashamed. Afraid people would blame me. Hate me."

"How could you think that? What happened wasn't your fault."

"That isn't what my father said. He counted on my shame to keep me quiet." I wiped my eyes. "Look, I've worked through a lot of stuff over the last several years. I appreciate what you just said, but it truly had nothing to do with you. You were my savior. The one person who didn't seem to mind having me around. Until I ruined everything." I took a deep breath and let it out slowly. "I didn't come here to talk about my father. You said you'd help me with my story. If you don't mind, I'd feel more comfortable if we could drop this subject. It's personal. I shouldn't have said anything about it in the first place."

"I disagree," Jonathon said softly. "I think you need to talk about it. Dismissing it isn't the way to heal, Sophie. You've got to face your feelings. Your anger. Maybe I wasn't there for you when it happened, but I'd like to be here for you now."

Before I could respond, Maxie came up to the table with my tea and our pie. Toasted coconut covered the rich, thick meringue, and the filling spilled out onto the plate.

I thanked her and waited until she walked away before framing a response to Jonathon's comment. "I—I really appreciate your offer. But to be honest, I just don't think I could talk to you about this."

His eyebrows drew together. "Why not? Because you know me? Wouldn't that actually make you more comfortable?"

I couldn't tell him it was because I still cared for him. He might feel some compassion, but he'd never have romantic feelings for me. "No, I don't think so." I sighed. "Look, let's get to the list. Maybe we can talk about other things . . . later."

He studied me for a few seconds. "All right. If that's what you want. But please remember what I said. I'm completely serious."

"I will. Thanks." I took a bite of my pie and washed it down with a sip of tea. The pie was incredible.

Jonathon grinned when he saw my expression. "I take it I don't need to finish that for you, after all?"

"Not unless you want a fork in your hand."

"I'll pass, thanks." He took a bite of his own pie and then put his fork down. He stared at me with a weird expression on his face. "I know you're Sophie Wittenbauer, but it's so strange. Sometimes I see you, some fragment of the girl I knew. And other times . . . you're not her. You're someone else. Someone I don't know. It's unsettling."

"I don't want to be that girl anymore. I've done everything I can to get rid of her."

He stared down at his plate for a moment, not saying anything. When he looked up, there was something in his eyes that made me catch my breath.

"I cared about that girl. I'm afraid I can't just dismiss her like you have. She may have been confused, but there was something special about her. A fire. A determination. I felt drawn to that . . . and to her." He looked down for another long moment before lifting his eyes and meeting mine. "You've always been beautiful, Sophie. You were a beautiful child, and now you're a beautiful woman. Beauty isn't something you wear on the outside. It shines from the inside. I see that in you now—and I saw it in you back then."

I couldn't tear my eyes away from his, and I couldn't think of anything to say. It was as if the right words didn't exist. We kept staring at each other until someone at the table next to us dropped a utensil on the floor. The clanging made us both jump. I picked up my glass and forced myself to take a drink, trying to concentrate on the cold liquid coursing down my dry throat instead of the searing heat that seemed to flow through my body.

As I put my glass down, I tried to calm my trembling body. "Let's talk about Terrance Chase, okay?"

"Okay," he said in a low, husky voice. "Tell me the names you have. Let's see if we can narrow them down."

I picked up my purse and pulled out my notebook. Then I searched for a pen. My hands shook so badly, it was difficult to grasp. "Whoever knocked me out took my other notebook so some of the names were lost. Also, I still have one record book at the church I need to go through. The sooner, the better."

"You never mentioned that someone took your notebook," Jonathon said after swallowing another bite of pie.

"I didn't want Pastor Troyer to know what I was really doing in his basement. If I'd told him about the notebook—

the one he thought I was using to do research on my supposed family—he would have become suspicious."

"At first, I didn't believe you. I thought you'd simply tripped and hit your head. If someone really was in that basement, it means you might be in danger, Sophie. Someone is trying to stop you from finding the truth."

"I realize that, but if they'd really wanted to hurt me, they could have finished me off. They didn't. All they took was my notebook and a picture I had of Terrance Chase. Thankfully, I'd removed my notes from yesterday morning and left them in my room. The only thing I don't have is yesterday afternoon's names. All my other previous work is on my laptop."

"So now that they know you're going through the records, probably looking for Chase, what do you think they want? I mean, I assume they realize you could have saved the information somewhere else. Stealing those notes won't stop you from continuing your search."

"I don't know what they want. Maybe it's someone just trying to figure out what I'm up to. Maybe it has nothing to do with Chase."

"Maybe." His forehead wrinkled in thought. "I have a tough time believing Chase is in Sanctuary. It might sound ridiculous, but I like to think I'd know if someone that evil was living in my town." He leaned toward me. "You shouldn't take this attack so lightly, Sophie. Whoever it was hit you pretty hard. Maybe they meant to do more than just knock you out."

"I didn't get that impression, Jonathon, and I'm fine." To be honest, I *was* a little worried. I knew I was taking risks, but I really wanted this story. I had to keep Jonathon from contacting the police before I was able to find Chase. Trying to change the subject, I reached down, picked up my purse, and took out my phone. After bringing up my pictures, I found Chase's mug shot and handed Jonathon the phone.

He stared at it. "I don't know," he said finally. "I mean, I know some men with his coloring. It's just too hard to tell from this picture. It's too fuzzy."

I put my phone back in my purse. "That's why these names are so important. It's been a long time, and he probably changed his appearance. When I first came here, I really thought I could recognize him. But I was being naïve. That's why narrowing it down through these lists is so important. If I can find someone on the list who might be Chase, then I can probably use the mug shot to confirm my suspicions." I sighed. "I was really relying on that picture. It was a copy of the last known picture of Chase. I've stared at it long enough to memorize it, so I'm not sure why I'm so upset. I guess it was kind of my security blanket."

"What happens if you decide Chase was here and is already gone?"

"I try to track him down."

Jonathon was silent for a moment. "Sophie, I think it might be time to contact the authorities. I don't want you to put yourself in any more danger. I know this story is important to you, but it isn't worth your life."

There it was. The reaction I'd been dreading. "Look, at least I need a name. A possible suspect. I'm so close. If I can't figure out who Chase is for certain—or if it gets too dangerous—I'll call the police."

Jonathon sighed and shook his head. "I'm not convinced,

but we'll talk about it later." He pushed away his pie plate and leaned toward me again. "Are you checking men who have died?"

I nodded and read him the list.

"I either know those men or know of them. None of them would fit your scenario. One of them, August Metzger, was here a couple of years ago. His background was checked during the murder investigation. He's not Chase."

"Someone was murdered in Sanctuary?"

"Same thing happened in Kingdom. No place is immune from evil."

"I guess not." It seemed there should be a place on earth where people could live in peace and safety.

"Why would Terrance Chase stay in Sanctuary?" Jonathon asked. "When he felt he was safe, wouldn't he leave town and go somewhere else? Someplace where he could spend the money?"

"Yes, that's certainly possible. That's why the names of the men who left are so important. I'm even looking for men who came here single and left married. I agree it would be odd for him to stay—unless he likes it here. Of course, I think people would notice if someone tried spending millions of dollars in Sanctuary."

"I agree. So you want to recopy the names you lost and bring your list up to date so you can see who left town?"

"Exactly. Maybe after the supper I'll see if Pastor Troyer will let me go back to the church and finish up."

"You're not going alone," Jonathon said emphatically. "I'm going with you."

"Thank you. I really would feel better if you did. I don't want to be there by myself."

"I intend to keep a close eye on you from now on."

I studied him for a moment. "You know, I'm still having a hard time seeing you as a pastor. It's quite a change from the Mennonite rebel you used to be."

"I rebelled against some of the self-imposed rules from our church because I love the truth, and I wanted to serve God honestly." His eyebrows met as he looked at me. "Look, Sophie, I'm not knocking the good people in Kingdom. Some of them were the best Christians I've ever known. I . . . just wanted more freedom. I think the grace of God justifies that."

"All those rules didn't make my father a good man." I picked up my iced-tea cup and stared into it. "Yet people like Lizzie, Hope, Ebbie . . . and you . . . were wonderful people who truly cared about others."

"But the rules didn't cause that. We just loved God and wanted to be like Him. And He isn't a God of rules."

I grunted. "The Old Testament is full of rules."

"As a way to show us we couldn't be righteous by keeping them. Jesus fulfilled the law, bringing us into grace. The law isn't needed anymore because the law of love has been written on our hearts."

"Not on my father's."

"I know," Jonathon said. "Your father used religion to satisfy his desire for control. You think he got away with it, but he didn't, Sophie."

"Whatever." The direction of our conversation was making me uncomfortable again. "Why don't you save your sermons for church?" My comment sounded harsher than I meant it, but I really wasn't interested in being preached to.

"Okay," he said affably. "Read me the rest of the list."

I picked up my notes. I hadn't meant to snap at him and was relieved he didn't seem offended. "Well, I think we can automatically rule out one of the names. Jonathon Wiese."

He gave me a lopsided smile. "Gee, thanks."

"What about Reuben King?"

"Too young. Besides, he's a longtime resident. He moved away for a while. College and a job, but he came back several years ago. He's married now. That might not be in the records because it happened recently."

"I guess I also missed the entry about his living in Sanctuary before."

Jonathon shrugged. "Well, the family owns a farm outside of town. That might explain it. Maybe whoever kept the records didn't consider him an actual resident."

That information concerned me. Maybe the church records weren't as accurate as I'd hoped. I crossed Reuben off. "That leaves these names." I read the remaining names out loud.

"Well, let's see. Why don't you repeat them one by one?"

"Okay. Let's start with Norman Yoder."

Jonathon laughed. "Norman is eighty-three and came here about five years ago to live with his niece who was born in Sanctuary. Again, not really the criminal type."

I crossed his name off. "What about Joshua Franklin?"

Jonathon shook his head. "He moved away to live with his uncle in Cape Girardeau. Besides, he's only in his late twenties. He would have been too young in 2008."

I sighed and crossed off another name. "You know, there really aren't that many single men who've moved here and stayed."

"Is that a surprise? Most single men aren't looking for small-town life."

"Well, you're here."

"True. But I was raised in a small town. I didn't want something different. I just wanted a place that was . . ."

"Different?" I said with a smile.

He chuckled. "Okay. Point taken. What about single men who came here and got married?"

"I have a small list with those names, alongside the men who came here, got married, and left. To be honest, I just don't think Chase would risk marriage. Too legal. Too easy to be found out. But just in case, I wrote them down. There are only four on that list."

"You might as well read them."

I rattled off each one.

"No, forget them. I know two of them, and I know the families of the other two. All of them are young."

"All right, let's go back to the list of single men still here. The next name is Ben Johnson."

"Well, Ben is about the right age. In his fifties." Jonathon was silent for a moment. "When did he come here?"

"According to the records in the church, he moved to town in 2010. About a year and a half after the robbery."

"He works with Abner Ingalls in the hardware store. Sleeps in a back room Abner set up for him. Keeps to himself. I get the feeling he has something in his past he's trying to deal with."

"Like murder?"

Jonathon stared at his coffee cup for a few seconds before picking it up. "I hope not. I like the guy."

"Okay. There are three men who have died. Jacob Vogel, Arthur Deering, and Leo Moreland."

"Jacob and Arthur were very old. They actually came here to stay with family so they would have someone to take care of them. I didn't know Leo, but I know his sister. He couldn't be Chase."

I marked off those names, feeling a sense of relief. My story wouldn't be as dramatic if Chase had died. "Martin Hatcher?"

Jonathon considered this. "Keep him on your list. Martin owns a saddle and tack store at the end of Main Street." He pointed to my list. "When did he come here?"

"2009."

He nodded. "I always thought he was a little odd. I've stopped by to talk to him several times. Nice enough, but when I invite him to church, he shuts down on me. I asked him once if he had any family. He acted like I'd asked him if he was an ax murderer."

I put a star next to Martin Hatcher's name. "What about Steven Reinhardt?"

"No." Jonathon answered so quickly it startled me.

"Wait a minute," I said. "Tell me more about him."

"Trust me. He isn't Terrance Chase. First of all, he's too young. Only in his twenties. Steven's had a tough life. He came to Sanctuary to get a fresh start."

"Okay. No problem." I scratched the name off my list. "The next name is Peter Bakker."

Jonathon thought for a moment. "I never met him, but he's about the right age. He moved away not long after his brother came here. According to Evan, their mother was ill and Peter went home to Ohio to care for her. Evan had been her caretaker for many years. Once Peter took over, Evan decided to stay in Sanctuary. Nice man who has had a very lonely life. He seems happy here, though. Not really the bank robber type." He grinned. "If he has millions of dollars, I'll eat one of the bowties he wears every day."

I crossed his name off my list. "Terrance Chase doesn't have a brother." I looked over what was left of my list. "So I only have two names as possible candidates for Terrance Chase. Ben Johnson and Martin Hatcher. That narrows it down quite a bit. And they're both still here. That's good. I don't suppose either one of these guys has a cleft chin?"

"I have no idea. They both have beards."

"Oh, great. I don't suppose you can ask them to shave?"

Jonathon grunted. "Oh, sure. That wouldn't look suspicious." He frowned. "Can someone have a cleft chin fixed?"

"Yes. I did some research about that on the Internet. It's possible Chase had it altered. I mean, it would be a lot harder to identify him if he has a normal chin."

"So what do we do? With their beards, we can't get a good look at their chins."

I shrugged. "I'll have to study their faces. You can't change bone structure."

"Will you let me see that picture again?"

I got out my phone and brought up the mug shot again.

"Not what you'd call a good-looking man."

"No. Frankly, there's nothing that stands out about him—except for his red hair. I bet he's colored it. Or shaved it off."

"That's why I wanted to see this again. I hadn't really noticed the first time. Martin has red hair."

"Really?"

"Does that move him to the front of your list?" Jonathon asked.

"Maybe. Sanctuary isn't St. Louis. I'd be surprised if anyone here knows who Terrance Chase is. He might be more inclined to relax and keep his normal hair color."

"By the way, I should mention that there are a couple of other single men who've come to town recently. They're not likely candidates, but I didn't see them on your lists."

I frowned at him. "I thought all the names of new residents were added to the population records."

"Most of them, but for example, there's a young man living at the church right now. His car broke down out on the main road a couple of days ago, and he couldn't afford to get it fixed. He had nowhere else to go, so I offered him some work at the church—along with a place to sleep. He wouldn't be in the records. Not only because he just got here, but also because he's not officially a resident. Then there's another guy who came to town last year to visit his sister. He's still here, but he's not a resident. Even though it's been a while, he's not planning to stay."

I nodded. "Okay, I get it. Neither one of them could be Chase."

"I agree. Just wanted to make sure you knew about them." He paused for a moment before saying, "Has it occurred to you that if Chase does know that you're looking for him, he may have taken off already?"

"Yes. But that would actually point us right to him, wouldn't it? So if one of our possible suspects suddenly disappears, there's a pretty good chance he's our man."

"You're right." Jonathon took his keys from his pocket. "Now, I've got to get to the church and help set things up. You're coming, aren't you?"

I nodded. "Tonight I'd like you to point out the two men on our list if they show up at the supper. Even if he's using a disguise, I'm still hoping I'll recognize him."

"Okay, but we'll have to be careful. I don't want these guys to think we're talking about them."

"But we will be."

"I realize that. You know what I mean."

I nodded. "I'll use caution."

"You realize that whoever attacked you might be at the supper."

That idea made my stomach clench, but I kept my face expressionless so Jonathon couldn't see how much it worried me. "I doubt they'll bother me with so many people around. But we should probably keep our eyes peeled. Watch for someone acting suspicious. Especially if we notice strange behavior by Ben Johnson or Martin Hatcher."

Jonathon fiddled with his keys "Look, whoever confronted you in the basement had to have been watching you. They knew where you'd be and when. If it's Chase, he'll want to protect himself. If it's someone looking for Chase, or for the money, they'll want to find him or it before you do." He stared into my eyes. "I know you don't want to contact the authorities yet, but I have a friend, Paul Gleason. He's a deputy sheriff here in Madison County. He'll be at the supper. I'd like you to talk to him. At least let him know what's going on."

"No." The word came out loud enough that a couple at

the table near us turned to look at me. "No," I said again, more quietly. "Like I said, I want to at least have a name to give him. Right now I have nothing. Talking to him at this point would be a waste of his time."

"Are you saying that because you really don't think you have enough information to make it worth his while or because you're protecting your story?"

"Both." I reached over and grabbed his hand. "Please, Jonathon. This is important. It—it's everything to me. This will pull me out of the muck my life has been and into something new. Something better. I want to be able to hold my head up and be someone. Someone worthwhile." I also wanted to find Chase so I could help Tom, but I decided not to tell Jonathon about Tom being attacked in prison. After what had happened in the basement, I was afraid he'd contact his deputy sheriff friend without my permission, and I couldn't risk that.

Jonathon sighed deeply. "Oh, Sophie. I'm afraid you're confusing *what* you do with *who* you are, but I don't have time to tackle that topic right now." He gently pulled his hand from mine and grabbed his keys again. "Okay. For now I won't tell anyone. But if one more thing happens. One more threat. One more dangerous situation, I'm talking to Paul myself. Do you understand?"

"Yes, I get it."

He glanced at his watch a second time. "I've got to go. I'm running late. If you want to come with me, you could help set up for the supper."

"I'd like that, but let me finish my pie first. I'll walk to the church when I'm finished."

"Okay." He stood up, took out his wallet, and tossed some money on the table. "I'll see you there. And Sophie, tonight you are to stay within my sight at all times, do you understand me? I mean it."

"I will. And Jonathon," I said softly, "you've started calling me Sophie. Please don't make that mistake at the church, okay?"

"I'll try my best. If I mess up, you have my permission to kick me."

I smiled. "That will be my pleasure."

He didn't laugh, just shot me one more concerned look and walked out of the restaurant. I was more determined than ever to find Terrance Chase. No matter who threatened me. I'd made a promise to Jonathon that I had no intention of keeping. I would do everything possible to keep Paul Gleason from interfering in my investigation. I couldn't allow anyone to stop me from achieving my goal.

Not even the man who held my heart in his hands.

CHAPTER SIXTEEN

After finishing my pie, I left the restaurant. The sidewalks were full of people walking toward the church, some of them carrying food. I walked the two blocks to the large building on the edge of town and saw cars and buggies parked next to one another. I was still rather impressed that the two churches did things together. It was a testimony to the kind of spirit I always thought churches should have.

I was grateful Jonathon was trying to help me. I didn't feel so alone, but I regretted telling him about my father. It was the elephant in the room. A wall that I'd erected because I'd accidentally shared something I had no intention of ever telling anyone. And of all the people to reveal my shame to, it had to be the one man I really cared about. Jonathon would never see me the way a man should see a woman he could love. Jonathon was a man of God, and I was a woman of . . . nothing.

Tears pricked my eyelids, and I blinked them away. I had to concentrate on my goal. The possibility that Terrance Chase could be in the crowd tonight had me feeling exhilarated. This dinner might finally bring me everything I'd wanted for years. My father's face flashed in front of me. *"You ain't nothin' but trash, girl. And you ain't never goin' to be nobody."* But I *would* be somebody. I would be the reporter who found Terrance Chase. Something even the FBI couldn't do. Something no other reporter in the world had been able to accomplish.

I followed the people going through the front door of Agape Fellowship. The interior was extremely attractive. Walls painted light beige with dusky blue carpet on the floors. Pictures used to decorate the foyer showed Jesus, but they were like nothing I'd seen before. In one painting, a small child sat on Jesus' knee. In another, Jesus was laughing. Conservative Mennonites didn't have pictures of Jesus, but if they had, I was pretty sure Jesus wouldn't be laughing. It wasn't until I'd left Kingdom that I began to see images of Christ. They all seemed pretty much the same. The Last Supper, a side view of Jesus looking up, paintings of the crucifixion by some of the great masters. For some reason, I found them all flat and uninspiring. But these more contemporary paintings were different. There was something almost alive in them. I was just turning away to follow the crowd heading through a door I assumed led to the room where the supper was being held, when I noticed one other painting. A young girl looked up to Jesus, a tear running down the side of her face. He cradled her face in His hands and stared into her eyes, as if trying to comfort her. I was shocked by the image. The little girl was the spitting image of me as a child. I couldn't tear myself away, and I stood there, unable to move, until I realized someone was touching my elbow.

"Emily? Are you okay?"

I turned to see Jonathon gazing at me with concern. "Uh, yeah. Sorry." I took a quick breath and tried to regain my composure. "I—I was trying to figure out where to go."

He pointed to the large open door I'd seen people entering. "It's here. Are you sure you want to help set up?"

I nodded, not trusting myself to speak.

Jonathon kept his hand on my arm and accompanied me through the door and into the community room. Long tables that were obviously set up for food were lined up in the middle of the room. The rest of the large area was full of round tables with chairs. There wasn't much space between the tables; it was clear they were expecting a large crowd. Even though it was at least two hours before the supper began, there were quite a few people already seated.

"What do you want me to do?" I asked.

Jonathon pointed toward a man walking out of the kitchen at the back of the room and waved him over. The man put down a stack of paper plates and quickly made his way over to us.

"Emily McClure, this is Nate Reynolds. If you want to help, Nate's your man. He's overseeing the food tables and supplies."

Nate was a handsome man with sun-bleached blond hair and green eyes. His easy smile spread from his mouth to his emerald eyes. "Happy to have the help, Emily. I promise not to work you too hard."

I smiled back at him. "I'll try to keep up."

"I'll leave you in Nate's capable hands." Jonathon turned when someone called his name and started to leave, but I grabbed his arm.

"Where do I sit?" I asked. "I—I mean, I don't really know anyone except you and Esther."

"But now you know me," Nate said. "You can sit with me, okay?"

Jonathon nodded. "Just follow Nate, Emily. He'll keep you company." He gazed into my eyes for a moment. "I won't be far away. If you need me, come and find me, okay?" When he walked away, there was a part of me that felt a little hurt and abandoned. After all, he'd promised to keep an eye on me during the dinner. But I was being silly. Jonathon was a busy pastor, and he had to visit with other people, too.

I swung my attention back to Nate. "Okay, so what do I do?"

"All I can do is share what Randi told me." He took a deep breath and pointed at the long tables in the middle of the room. "People are going to be bringing food. According to Randi, we need to make sure it's in the proper place. You know, main dishes in one area, side dishes in another, bread and desserts somewhere else."

"Okay, I get it. Now, tell me how you got stuck with this job."

Nate rolled his eyes. "Randi's busy cooking. I was lucky enough to be standing nearby when she was talking to Jonathon. Big mistake. My close proximity earned me this incredible honor."

I smiled at him. "We'll get through it. I've been around a few church suppers. Together we can carry this off."

"Good. Why don't you start working on arranging food

in the right places while I get the rest of the paper products ready? They'll be at the front of the two tables." He hesitated a moment before saying, "And why don't we put all the drinks on that other table against the wall? That way we won't have people spilling their drinks around the food, and it won't hold up the food lines."

"You sound like a pro."

"I must be a really good actor, then. Either that or I'm afraid of Randi. She really does scare me a little."

I chuckled and followed him as he started walking toward the food tables. "You can see we're trying to divide the different kinds of food, but as people come in, they set their dishes down anywhere. If you could redirect them a little, that would be helpful."

"As long as you don't ask me to strong arm any little old Mennonite ladies."

He laughed. "I think it's safe to say your pastor wouldn't look on that favorably."

"Jonathon's not my pastor." I said the words without thinking.

Nate looked at me curiously. "Are you new in town? I mean, you said you didn't know many people."

"I'm not a resident. I just came here to do some research on family members who used to live here."

"Well, we definitely need to stick together, then. I'm new, too. I've only been here a couple of days. Ended up in town after my car broke down. Jonathon offered me a job and a place to stay until I decide what to do next."

"Oh." I suddenly remembered Jonathon telling me about a man he was helping at the church.

Nate looked around and noticed more people heading toward the tables. "I'd be happy to tell you about it sometime, but I think we're about to be inundated with tuna casseroles and several different varieties of chicken."

I glanced at my watch. "Isn't it a little early for some of this food? I mean, shouldn't meat dishes be kept warm?"

Nate snapped his fingers. "Oh, man. I forgot about the hotplates. Please don't tell Randi. She'd have my head. Follow me."

I trailed behind him as he hurried into the kitchen, where several women bustled around. I could tell some of the food was being kept hot inside the two ovens. Nate grabbed some large metal heating trays and pointed toward a couple smaller ones.

"Can you carry those into the other room?"

"Sure. Is there somewhere I can put my purse?"

A woman standing close to us opened a door under a counter. "You can put your purse here, dear." Several other purses were already stored there. I thanked her and slid mine in with the rest. Then I grabbed the hotplates.

"Randi told me to put these out first," Nate said, "but I spaced it. Thank goodness you thought of them. This could have been a huge disaster. Food poisoning is never pretty. Even with a prayer covering on top of it."

I laughed as we hurried out to the tables. Working together, within a few minutes we'd hooked up the hotplates and transferred the main dishes that should be kept warm.

"I wouldn't worry about anything else coming in," he said when we finished. "People will start eating early, so any food that comes after this should be fine." He winked at me.

"Besides, a little poisoning is usually expected at a church dinner, right?"

I laughed again as he left to get more paper plates and plastic utensils. For the most part, all I did over the next hour was tell people where to put their food. I relocated a few dishes dropped off when I wasn't looking, but it was far from a labor-intensive job, and I was happy with the way things were working out.

Although I watched the crowd, most of the people who came early and brought food were women. As the men began to arrive, I scrutinized them the best I could without making anyone suspicious. I quickly found out that watching for men with beards was a huge waste of time. Most of the men sported facial hair, and I began to wonder if it was a prerequisite for males living in Sanctuary.

I spotted Jonathon talking to an elderly couple on the other side of the room, but even though he gave them his attention, every once in a while, his eyes wandered over to me. As he'd promised, he was watching me, making certain I was safe.

I was putting a tray of deviled eggs on the table when I heard someone say hello. I looked up and saw Evan Bakker from the post office. I smiled and returned his greeting.

"So nice of you to help out," he told me. "I hope you're enjoying your visit to Sanctuary."

"Thank you. I certainly am."

He held a large metal pan in his hands. "I'm sorry to run late, but this turkey took longer than I thought it would."

"Let's take that to the table with the main dishes." He followed me to the front of the two tables. I moved a few things over. "How about here?"

"That's fine."

He put down the pan and peeled back the tinfoil that covered it. The turkey looked awesome and smelled out of this world.

"Wow. This will certainly be popular."

His blue eyes twinkled behind his glasses. "I'm not a cook, but I can smoke a turkey. Hopefully, no one ever gets tired of me bringing the same thing to these church suppers."

"I doubt that's possible."

"Well, nice to see you again. Guess I'd better find a place to sit."

"Nice to see you, too."

I spotted Pastor Troyer and Dorcas talking to Jonathon. Dorcas saw me and waved. I smiled and waved back. The mixing of people in regular clothes with those who were obviously Conservative Mennonites touched me for some reason. Everyone seemed relaxed and friendly.

"Emily?"

I jumped when Nate said my name. I'd been so focused on the crowd I hadn't noticed him come up next to me.

"Sorry," he said quickly. "I didn't mean to frighten you."

I waved my hand at him. "Not your fault. I wasn't paying attention."

"Everything's ready. I thought I'd show you to my table."

"Okay." Since almost every table looked full, I'd hoped he'd saved something. Sure enough, his table had a *Reserved* sign on it.

"This table is near the food so volunteers can help serve if necessary. Some of the residents are elderly or disabled. Jonathon said we should make them a plate and take it to them."

"I can do that." In the back of my mind, I was thinking this would provide me a great way to get a closer look at those attending the supper.

"Why don't you sit until we're ready to serve? How about a cup of coffee or some tea?"

"I can get it myself," I replied.

"You'd better take me up on the offer now. You'll need your energy."

I pulled out a chair. "Okay. I'm sitting. And coffee would be great. Black, please."

I watched as he walked over to the area where the drinks had been set up. Tall, good-looking, with an easy gait and manner—if I'd met him in St. Louis, he would have been someone I'd want to get to know. But realizing I wouldn't be in Sanctuary much longer, I pushed that thought out of my mind. I wasn't looking for a boyfriend. In fact, I wasn't sure I would ever allow myself to get romantically involved. All I really cared about was my career. And Jonathon. A man I could never have.

I turned my attention back to the crowd. Not one man looked like Terrance Chase. At that moment, it occurred to me that I really didn't have a backup plan if I didn't find him. I'd left St. Louis hoping he was here and planning to track him if he wasn't. Going back to the paper without my big story hadn't crossed my mind.

I noticed a man walk into the room wearing a sheriff's department uniform, Sarah Miller's arm linked through his. This had to be Paul Gleason. They walked over to the table behind mine. I realized Esther and Janet were at the same table. Although I wanted to say hello to Esther, I wasn't thrilled about meeting Paul. I could only hope Esther or Jonathon wouldn't decide to tell him why I was in Sanctuary.

At six o'clock, Jonathon walked to the middle of the room and asked for everyone's attention. After welcoming those attending, especially members of Sanctuary Mennonite Church, he led a brief prayer and then pointed at each table around the room, giving them numbers and asking people to get their food one table at a time to avoid congestion.

"And if you need help, please raise your hand. We have volunteers who will find out what you want and fill a plate for you." His gaze swept the crowd. "Table number one, you can get started."

I watched for hands going up and helped Nate and a few other volunteers fetch plates for those guests. I saw Esther raise her hand, but I turned the other way and assisted an elderly Mennonite man instead.

Once it seemed everyone had been served, I went through the food line myself. There was so much food, it was ridiculous. I finally picked some smoked turkey, a couple spoonfuls of corn relish, and some marinated cucumbers, red onions, and tomatoes. When I got back to my table, I found it occupied with other volunteers. I was happy to see Mary and Rosey, so I sat next to Mary. We talked a bit, and then Nate joined us.

"Wow, I'm beat," he said, plopping down into the chair on the other side of me. "I may be too tired to even open my mouth."

Mary laughed. "You filled your plate pretty full for someone who can't eat."

Nate picked up his fork. "I'm just trying to keep up my strength."

"Well, that should do it," Rosey said, grinning.

"I take it you've all met?" I asked.

Mary nodded. "Pastor Jonathon brought Nate to the restaurant yesterday. That's the fastest way to get to know new people in Sanctuary. Since we don't get that many newcomers, they kind of stick out like sore thumbs."

Nate leaned over toward me. "She's calling me a sore thumb. Not the way a newcomer wants to be described."

Mary chuckled. "I could have described the pain you cause in another part of the body, but I believe I exhibited great restraint."

Everyone laughed, and for the first time since coming into the church, I started to relax. Although I hadn't spotted anyone who looked like Chase, I continued to scan the crowd. When Nate and Rosey stood to get seconds, I leaned close to Mary.

"Mary, do you see Ben Johnson or Martin Hatcher? Jonathon mentioned them, and I wanted to put faces with the names."

She began to look around at the crowd. "There's Ben, sitting with Abner Ingalls." She indicated a table on the other side of the room. "Ben's bald and has a beard."

I spotted the man she pointed out, but he was too far away for me to see him clearly.

"Martin won't be here. He never comes to social functions. Since he's single, he eats at the restaurant quite a bit, but he's not big on church gatherings."

I remembered Jonathon telling me that Martin had red

hair. He seemed to be the person most likely to be Terrance Chase.

A few minutes later, Nate and Rosey returned.

"Mom, you've got to try Ethel Brucker's chocolate bread pudding." Rosey held a plate near her mother's face. "We need to get this in the restaurant. It's awesome."

Mary smiled. "I've asked Ethel for her recipe many times. All she says is, '*Ach,* Mary. Family recipes must stay in the family, *ja?*'"

Mary's impression of Ethel must have been right on the mark because Rosey laughed so hard she almost choked on her food. Mary slapped her on the back and handed her a glass of water. "Sorry, honey."

Rosey croaked out, "Don't you ever let Ethel hear you do that. She would be . . . mortified."

"I won't. I wouldn't do anything to hurt her feelings."

Rosey reached over and patted her mother's arm. "I know that, Mom."

"Hello, everyone."

I turned in my chair to see a young man and woman standing behind me. He was very good-looking, with sandy hair and a friendly face. The woman was striking, too. Blond hair and deep green eyes.

Mary smiled. "Hi, Wynter. Haven't seen you much lately."

"Sorry," the woman said. "I've been holed up trying to write the next great American novel." She sighed. "It's a lot harder than I thought it would be."

"I'll bet it's wonderful," Rosey said.

Wynter laughed. "I'm not sure about that."

"But I am," the man said, wrapping his arm around Wynter. "She's allowed me to read some of it, and I think it's great."

"But what does he know?" Wynter quipped. "He writes how-to manuals about tractors."

Everyone laughed.

Mary introduced me. "Wynter, this is Emily McClure. She's staying with Esther."

Wynter turned her incredible eyes on me. "So you're the other Emily."

I smiled at her. "I guess I am. But everyone calls you Wynter?"

She nodded. "It's confusing, I know. My real name is Emily. I used to work for a TV station in St. Louis, and my professional name was Wynter. I've used it so long, it seems to have stuck."

"Well, I like it. It's nice to meet you."

"Thank you. And this is my husband, Reuben."

So this was Reuben King. I shook the hand he extended.

"Happy to meet you, Emily. Esther has wonderful things to say about you."

I was surprised and touched. "She's very kind."

Wynter smiled. "Yes, she is. And she's a very good judge of character."

Although I appreciated her comment, I certainly didn't feel I deserved Esther's positive opinion.

"Any news about the reclamation?" Mary asked

"We have an abandoned mine outside of town that's caused some trouble," Rosey explained to me. "Reuben is working with the Missouri Department of Natural Resources to get the mine filled and reclaim the land."

"Really?" I knew something about the program from stories at the paper. Missouri was rife with abandoned mines. A lot of them had been coal mines, but there were also quite a few lead mines. Although some were still in operation, most of them had been forsaken when their resources played out.

"It's a rather long process," Reuben said. "The government is very careful to keep anything toxic or dangerous from affecting the surrounding land. The goal is to fill the mine and then treat the land. Bring back the grass and trees."

"Sounds like a great program," I said.

"It is," Reuben agreed.

"So now what?" Rosey asked.

"They intend to fill the space and seal the entrance Monday morning. After that, they'll begin to restore the land."

"I'll be so glad when it's completed," Mary said.

Wynter nodded. "All of us will breathe a sigh of relief. That mine has been nothing but trouble. Especially for Sarah and Cicely."

Reuben looked at his wife. "Well, we'd better get back to Esther. Nice to see you all. And very nice to meet you, Emily."

"Thank you."

I envied Wynter. She seemed so close to the elderly Mennonite woman. Once I had my story, I'd leave this place behind. I had no plans to come back, but I had to admit I'd miss Esther.

"Oh, Emily. I almost forgot." They started to walk away, but then Reuben stopped and came back to our table. He dug in his jeans pocket and pulled out a folded envelope. "One of the women in the kitchen found this on the counter. You're the only Emily volunteering."

He handed me an envelope with *Emily* written on the outside. I stared at it for a few seconds, before excusing myself from the table. There was a side exit not far from where we sat, so I opened the door and stepped into the dusk. The sun was almost down, but there was a light over the exit. I opened the envelope and pulled out a piece of paper. With trembling fingers, I opened it.

Go home, Sophie. Before it's too late.

I dropped the note as if it were on fire.

CHAPTER SEVENTEEN

"Is everything all right?"

A small scream escaped my lips. I hadn't heard Nate follow me out the door. Before I could move, he bent down and picked up the piece of paper. He frowned after he read it. "What does this mean?" he asked. "And who is Sophie?"

Unable to come up with an explanation, I grabbed the note from his hand and shoved it back into the envelope. "I—I don't want to talk about this, Nate."

I turned toward the door, wanting nothing more than to escape back into the crowded room where I felt safe. Nate stepped in front of me, blocking my way.

"Emily, it sounds like a warning. A serious warning. You need to explain what's going on."

"I can't. I appreciate your concern, but you've got to trust me. This is something I can't talk about."

Instead of moving, he stayed right where he was. "If you're in trouble, Jonathon's friend Paul is right inside. You can talk to him."

"No." I stared up into Nate's green eyes, full of concern for me. "I can't do that. Please, just let this go."

"I'm sorry, but I can't." He took a deep breath. "Look, Emily, not long ago I lost someone. He got himself into a bad situation. I should have done something. Should have stepped in. But I didn't. I decided it was his business, and I was wrong."

"I—I'm sorry. But this isn't the same thing. Honestly."

"Then you're going to have to explain it to me. The truth. When you're finished, I'll decide whether or not I think we need to talk to Paul."

I could tell by the look on his face that he was serious. That he had no intention of changing his mind. "All right. But not here. It's cold and dark. I'm . . . afraid."

At first, he looked confused. "Of me? Do you think I wrote this?"

"I don't know you, and I have no reason to trust you."

He was quiet for a moment. "Fair enough. Let's go to one of the classrooms. One close to the main hall, if that makes you feel better."

I nodded. "It does."

He stepped away from the door and opened it. I went back inside, glad to be around people again. Although I was confident Nate hadn't written the note since he couldn't possibly be Chase, standing outside had made me feel . . . vulnerable. And that was something I hated more than anything else. Feeling as if I was at someone's mercy.

"Follow me," Nate said once the door closed behind us.

He headed toward the foyer where I'd first come in. I noticed Jonathon talking to a group of kids. He was concentrating on them and didn't see us walk by him. Once we were outside the community room, Nate pointed to a door on the other side of the stairs.

"Let's go in here. Most of the other classrooms are upstairs, but I think you'd feel better if we stayed down here."

I didn't confirm his suspicions, but he was right. I wasn't really afraid of Nate, but the note made me nervous. Who was writing these things? And why?

We went into the empty classroom, and Nate closed the door. Chairs were arranged in a circle in the middle of the room. I slumped down into one of them, and Nate sat down on the other side of the circle, facing me.

"Okay, now tell me what's going on. Why would someone care if you're trying to uncover your family history? Was your family involved in something . . . dangerous?"

"No, it has nothing to do with my family." I stared at him, trying to figure out what to say and what to keep to myself.

"Tell me the truth, Emily. If you don't . . ."

"I know, I know. You'll pull Paul Gleason into this, and I'm just not ready for that." I took a deep breath and let it out slowly while I considered my options. In the end, I decided on partial truth. "Here's the deal. I'm actually a reporter trying to find a criminal I think might be hiding out in Sanctuary. I'm not sure he's here, but if he is, it would be one of the biggest stories of the year. It would make my career. I have no idea who sent this note, but they're not going to hurt me. They just want to . . . derail my story." I crossed my arms. "And that's all there is to it."

He frowned. "So your name really is . . . Sophie?"

"Yeah. Sophie Bauer. I'm with the *St. Louis Times*."

He shook his head. "Just when I think I understand this place, something weird happens. Who else knows who you are?"

"Jonathon and Esther Lapp. They both know the truth, and neither one of them plans to tell Paul Gleason anything . . . yet. I need you to do the same. If Paul found out Terrance Chase might be hiding out in Sanctuary, he'd go after him, and my story would be ruined. I need to have some solid evidence before I contact him, and I don't yet. In fact, Chase might not be here at all." Although I said it, I didn't believe it. I hoped Nate would.

Nate's eyebrows shot up. "Terrance Chase? The guy who robbed the armored car company?"

"Yes. How do you know about him?"

"I'm from Missouri. It was a big story when it happened, but I also saw a special on TV a while back. The police looked everywhere for him and . . . some other guy. I can't remember his name. But aren't both of the robbers dead?"

"Well, almost everyone thinks so."

"But you think he's here? In Sanctuary?"

I shrugged. "I'm not sure, but I have to find out. I know he was headed here at one time. It's possible he never made it, but I'm trying to uncover the truth." I tried to sound nonchalant, but the note had frightened me. Someone knew who I was. This time they'd used my real name. I knew it wasn't written by Esther or Jonathon. The printing matched the first note—block letters with nothing unusual that could point to the writer. Plain white paper without any kind of watermark or design. Whoever penned these warnings was making sure there wasn't anything about them I could use to track their origin.

"That doesn't make sense," he said. "Why would someone who took that much money hang out in Sanctuary? I'd be long gone. Might even go to another country."

"It might be a little hard to get out of the country with so many people looking for you. Look, I'm not sure if he's here or not, but I have to find out. If you bring Paul into this, he'll handle it like any official investigation. If Chase *is* in Sanctuary, it will scare him off, and we may lose him forever. And if Chase doesn't get away, and is arrested, the story isn't mine anymore. Trust me, if I find him, the first thing I'll do is call Paul. Then, before anyone else gets it, I'll write my story and turn it in."

"But how do you intend to find him? Do you know what he looks like?"

I rattled off a quick description of Chase. Coloring, height, even the cleft in his chin. "I've seen photos. If I can get close enough to look at the men who *might* be Chase, it's possible I'll be able to end the mystery of what happened to him after the robbery."

"Okay, I understand what you're saying." He pointed to the envelope in my hand. "But what about this? Who do you think wrote it?"

"I don't know. Look, whatever it means, I'll be fine. Jonathon is keeping a close watch on me. I'm not in any danger."

Nate studied me a moment. "Is this the only warning you've gotten?"

"Yes," I lied. "Please, you've got to keep this to yourself, Nate. I'm serious. The only way for me to figure out who sent it is to keep the upper hand. Keep the lid on my investigation. If the truth gets out, things will spiral out of control fast."

He was quiet for a moment, but finally he nodded. "Okay, I'll keep your secret. For now. But on one condition."

I raised my eyebrows and stared at him. "And what's that?"

"You keep me updated on . . . everything. I want to know where you're going, what you've found out . . . and if you're threatened again." He raised his hand toward me when I started to protest. "No. That's it, Emily . . . I mean, Sophie. That's my arrangement. If you don't agree, I go straight to Paul. Immediately. I'm not going to stand by and see you get yourself hurt. The only reason I'm not doing that now is because Jonathon knows what's going on. He doesn't seem like the kind of person who would allow you to get yourself into a dangerous situation."

There was nothing I could do but nod. One more person who knew the truth. Things were unraveling fast. I needed to find Chase before it became impossible, before my cover was completely blown. I wondered if other investigative reporters went through situations like this. If so, I had even more respect for them.

"What are your plans after the dinner?" Nate asked.

"Jonathon and I are going to the church. I need to get some names from the church records they keep in the basement. I—I'm trying to complete my list of possible suspects."

"So Jonathon will be with you the entire time?"

"Yes, the entire time."

"I'm going to keep my eye on you," he said in a serious tone. "I don't want you to venture out alone, okay?"

Two people in one day who'd promised to watch over me.

Great. "Really, Nate. I don't even know you, and you've appointed yourself my personal bodyguard. Don't you think that's a little weird?"

He looked down at the floor. "Maybe," he said finally, "but if I'd been more watchful over my . . . friend, he would still be alive."

I leaned back in my chair. "You forced me to tell you my secret. Now you're going to have to tell me yours. Who was this guy?"

He crossed his arms over his chest. "Just someone I knew. Someone I cared about." His gaze strayed to the ceiling. "Sorry, but I can't talk about it."

His voice cracked, and I realized he was still traumatized by whatever had happened. "I'm sorry," I replied quickly. "You don't have to tell me. But if you want to talk, I'm here. You'd be surprised how much I understand about loss."

"All right. Thanks." Nate stood up. "Let's get you back to the community room before someone thinks I kidnapped you."

I stood up and started for the door, but before I opened it, I turned back to look at him. "Thank you for keeping my secret. Finding this man is more important than I can say. And not just because it will make me famous. He's a very bad man."

Nate looked at me strangely. "I was beginning to wonder if that meant anything to you. If the guards who died were important . . ."

I nodded. "They are. I know sometimes I get focused on what catching this guy will do for my career, but I realize finding him is even more important to the families of the guards."

"I'm glad to hear you say that. You're obviously a good person, Sophie."

"Not many people would agree with you about that. And please don't call me Sophie in public, okay?"

"Okay."

I walked out of the room with Nate following behind me. As we made our way toward the community room, someone called my name. We stopped and turned around. Jonathon was walking toward us, and he didn't look happy.

"I've been looking for you two everywhere," he said. "Where did you go?"

"We . . . we needed to get away from the noise," I said quickly. "Just taking a break."

Jonathon came up to us and looked back and forth between Nate and me. He seemed upset, and I assumed it was because he hadn't known where I was.

"Did something happen?" I asked. "I thought everyone had been helped."

"No, everything's fine." Without saying another word, he walked away.

"That was odd," I said softly.

Nate laughed. "It's not that odd. He obviously likes you."

I didn't respond to his comment. "Let's get back. Maybe we can help serve dessert."

"My feet are starting to hurt," Nate grumbled. "I don't think I'll ever be a waiter."

"Believe it or not, I used to work as a waitress. Obviously, I've gotten out of shape."

We went back to the community room and spent the next two hours fetching drinks, desserts, and picking up dishes.

By the time everyone left, my legs were stiff and sore. I sat down in one chair and put my feet up on another. Nate came over and slumped down next to me.

"I think I know how I'm going to feel when I'm eighty," he said. "And it isn't good."

I shook my head. "Not good at all."

Jonathon walked up to us. "You two look beat. Can't keep up?" His good mood seemed restored, and I was relieved. I hadn't meant to upset him.

"Hey, don't hassle the help," Nate said. "We almost ran our feet off."

Jonathon smiled. "You'd better start heading home," he said to Nate. "You've got a long way to go."

Nate turned to me. "He thinks he's funny. I'm staying in a room downstairs."

"To be honest, even that sounds too far away right now."

Nate stood up slowly. "You're right about that. Might as well get it over with. If I don't show up in the morning, you might send someone to see if I'm still alive."

Jonathon chuckled. "We will definitely check on you if you don't come upstairs for breakfast. If you turn down breakfast at The Whistle Stop, I'll know you're dead."

"For sure." He waved at me. "See you tomorrow, Emily."

"See you tomorrow."

Jonathon watched as Nate left the room. When the door closed behind him, he sat down in the chair Nate had just vacated. "I talked to Jacob. He gave me the keys to the church's back door. After I check things here, I'll come and get you. Then we'll head over to the church."

Every part of my body wanted to tell him I wasn't up for

it, but I knew I had to go. "Okay. But until then I'm just going to sit here and suffer."

"Would a cup of coffee ease your suffering?"

"Somewhat. But if it were accompanied by a serving of chocolate bread pudding it would go a long way toward my complete recovery."

He glanced around the empty room. "I'm sorry, Sophie, but all the food is gone. I'm afraid you missed out."

I grinned at him. "Check the refrigerator. There's a foam box inside with *Leftover grease* written on the top."

"You hid a piece of bread pudding in the fridge?"

"As you know, I can be very devious."

"In this case, I'd say you were brilliant."

I laughed and watched him walk away. This had been a strange night. It was even more important now that I find Terrance Chase and get out of this place. I didn't like having to trust so many people. Esther, Jonathon, and Nate knew the truth now. Well, at least the truth I was willing to give them.

As I waited, I remembered my purse. I called out Jonathon's name, and he poked his head through the door.

"Could you also grab my purse? It's under the counter next to the sink."

He nodded and disappeared for a few minutes. When he came out, he was carrying the box of bread pudding, a cup of coffee, and my purse. The strap was slung over his shoulder.

"Don't tell anyone you saw me with a purse," he said when he got to my table. "It will ruin my manly reputation."

"You have my word. My lips are sealed."

"Thank you." He handed me the box. Inside were the bread

pudding and a plastic fork. He set the coffee cup in front of me and put my purse on the table.

"I'd offer you some, but . . . I'm not going to." I smirked at him.

"Gee, thanks." He patted his stomach. "I guess the two helpings I had earlier will have to suffice."

"No wonder it went so fast." I took a bite, and just as Rosey had said, it was incredible. I closed my eyes and chewed slowly, savoring the taste. "I think I could live on this."

"So did you learn anything new tonight?" Jonathon asked.

"Not much, unfortunately. I saw Ben Johnson. He's bald and has a beard. Might be a good disguise. Didn't get close enough to see his eyes."

"Martin Hatcher wasn't here, was he?"

I shook my head. "I hear he eats at The Whistle Stop a lot, though. All in all, tonight was a major disappointment. I'm realizing more and more how clueless I've been. Just coming here and hoping to run into Terrance Chase was . . . dumb."

"I'm not sure what else you could have done," Jonathon replied. "If you thought he was here, it was worth checking out. You just have to go with what you've got."

"But I need something solid," I shot back. "I can't throw away my career on a *maybe*."

"So what do you intend to do?"

"First of all, I need a close look at both of these men. Chase can change some things, but he can't change everything. Eye color, the shape of his face, his hairline. If only I could see his upper arm. There should be a scar. Chase got a bullet in the arm during the robbery."

"He could be wearing contacts."

"After all these years? I doubt it."

"Okay, if one of them looks like Chase to you, will that really be enough?" Jonathon asked.

"Not really," I admitted. "I need DNA. Fingerprints. Some kind of forensic evidence."

Jonathon sat down in a chair next to me. "Listen, Sophie. You may not be able to gather that kind of evidence yourself. You told me if you narrowed it down to a strong possibility, you'd be willing to talk to Paul. He could provide the final proof you need. It might be the only way to catch Chase and write your story."

I couldn't argue with him. For the first time, I started to see the wisdom in bringing Paul in on my quest. As long as he promised to let me break the story. And I might have a decent chance of getting his agreement because of his relationship with Jonathon.

"You may be right, but I can get fingerprints without Paul's help. I've been thinking about it, and I believe I've got it figured out."

"And how are you going to do that? Just walk up to him and say, 'Excuse me, but I think you're wanted for murder, and I'd like to have your fingerprints so I can prove it?'"

I rolled my eyes. "Of course not. I'll get his fingerprints and send them to a guy I know at the paper. He works with the police and FBI. He can have them checked. You have my word. If Chase is here, I'll figure out how to catch him."

Jonathon was silent for a moment. "Finish that. I'm tired. If we're going to the church, we need to hurry up."

I wolfed down the rest of the bread pudding and chased it with coffee. After cleaning up my mess, Jonathon turned off the lights, and we left the community room. While he checked all the doors, I stared once again at the painting in the lobby. Something about it made me hurt inside. Why wasn't Jesus there for me when I was a child? For a few short moments, that question was more important than anything else. Even finding Terrance Chase.

CHAPTER EIGHTEEN

I retrieved my car from The Oil Lamp and followed Jonathon to the Mennonite church. The night had turned bitterly cold. Thankfully, I'd tossed my coat in the back seat, so I was as warm as I could be in the frigid night air. The drive to the church was so short there wasn't time for my car heater to warm up.

As we approached the building, I noticed a glow on one side of the building. Pastor Troyer must have left the lights on. Strange, since Jonathon had only asked him tonight if we could get in. The closer we got, the more my heart began to race. The light was flickering and moving. This illumination wasn't from lights. The church was on fire!

I pulled up behind Jonathon, who jumped out of his truck and raced toward the back of the building. I opened my door and willed my legs to move, but I felt paralyzed. Flashbacks of the fire at the church in Kingdom overwhelmed me. People screaming, running, Jonathon rushing into the building, trying to save the pastor. I held onto the car door, unable to believe what I was seeing.

Jonathon came running around the side of the building. "Sophie! Help me!"

It took every ounce of strength I could muster to finally move my legs and start to run toward him. When I reached him, he grabbed me by the shoulders. He had a water hose draped over his arm.

"Help me get this hose untangled!"

I grabbed it and began to unravel the rolled-up hose while Jonathon pulled on it until it reached a water spigot on the side of the church. Once he hooked up one end of the hose, he helped me finish untangling the rest of it.

"When I yell, turn on the water," he said. Then he took off for the back of the church. A few seconds later, I heard him call my name, and I attempted to turn the handle. I strained, trying to get it to move. It seemed to be frozen. I gave it everything I had, but it wouldn't budge. I could hear Jonathon still shouting in the distance, but I couldn't respond. All of my strength and attention was concentrated on that stubborn faucet. The fire in Kingdom raged in my head. It was as if I could make the destruction I caused go away if I could save this church. Finally, I felt some movement. I got on the other side of the faucet and pulled with every ounce of energy I could muster. The knob kept turning. When it was open all the way, I collapsed on the cold ground, crying. I felt completely drained. Eventually, I forced myself up and hurried to the back of the building. The back door was open, so I followed the hose down the stairs to the basement. I found Jonathon spraying water on smoldering embers. I ran over and switched on the light that sat on the desk. Then I jogged over to the other door and flipped on the light switch. By the time I got back to where Jonathon stood with the hose in his hands, the fire was almost completely out.

"I don't understand," I said. "How could we see the fire from outside? The windows are painted over."

Jonathon crooked his head toward the side of the room. "That glass was broken out."

I went over to the area Jonathon had indicated. Sure enough, there was glass on the floor and an opening near the top of the basement wall. Apparently someone had broken the window, dropped down onto an old church pew directly underneath, and started the fire. I went back to Jonathon, who was making sure the flames were out.

"Those are the records I've been working with," I told him. "Someone took them out of the cabinets, threw them on the floor, and set them on fire."

"I think that's obvious, don't you, Sophie?"

Although I could barely see him in the dim light, he looked angry. "I—I didn't do this, Jonathon." My voice trembled, and my knees felt weak. "I really didn't do this. I—I wouldn't set this church on fire. You've got to believe me." I could feel tears running down my cheeks. Memories of Kingdom and that terrible night were flashing through me as if I had been transported back to that moment in time. The worst moment of my life. I reached out and grabbed his arm. "You've got to believe me. This wasn't me." The last words came out in a raspy whisper.

Jonathon dropped the hose and grabbed my shoulders. "Oh, Sophie. I didn't mean . . . I wasn't saying you set this fire. I know you didn't. That wasn't what I meant . . ." He looked down at my hands. "What have you done? Your hands are bleeding."

Before I knew what was happening, Jonathon pulled me close to him and kissed me with a passion I'd never experienced before. Desire for him exploded inside me, igniting the love I'd carried for so many years. But suddenly, fear overpowered everything else. Fear of losing him. Of being hurt again. Of not being good enough. The barrier of protection I'd built for myself closed around me like a prison door. I pushed him away, tears running down my face. Although I wanted nothing more than to return his kiss, I couldn't.

Not knowing what else to do, I turned and ran for the basement door. I flung it open and hurried up the stairs. At the top, I ran right into Jacob Troyer.

"Emily? Is that you? Are you all right?"

I nodded, but I couldn't stop sobbing. I pushed past him and ran out the front door and got in my car. I fumbled around in my purse and found my keys. The cuts on my hands were getting blood on everything I touched, but I didn't care. Before I could put the key in the ignition, Jonathon came running out of the church. He sprinted to my car and opened my door.

"Sophie, wait. Please don't go. I'm so sorry. I shouldn't have done that. Please, please forgive me."

The interior light in my car highlighted the distress on his face. Instead of making me feel better, it hurt to see him like that. I wanted to be in his arms, and I wanted him to kiss me. But I knew it was wrong. Jonathon was a man of God, and I wasn't good enough for him. Never would be. My love for him was so strong I couldn't allow him to throw his life away with someone like me. He needed a woman who could live up to his standards. Someone he could be proud of. I wasn't that woman. "It's not your fault," I said between sobs. "I just can't. . . . I can't . . ."

Jonathon gently pulled me from the car and helped me to my feet. Then he wrapped his arms around me. "I understand, Sophie. I really do. I'm here for you. No matter what." He let me go and held my face in his hands. "You have my word that I will never kiss you again—unless you ask me to. I promise. You have nothing to fear from me." He took one hand off the side of my face and wiped my cheeks with his fingers. "I don't believe you started that fire, and nothing could convince me otherwise." He put his hand back on my cheek. "I want to be your friend . . . if you'll let me. I'm not going to lie to you. I'm falling in love with you, Sophie. But I know you've got to heal from all the damage your father caused. I shouldn't have pushed you before you were ready. It won't happen again."

Jonathon thought my reaction was caused by my father's abuse. I decided it was better to let him believe that. If I told him the truth, I was afraid he'd argue with me. Try to tell me I could be the kind of woman he needed. And I just couldn't accept that.

"Tonight when I saw you with Nate, I realized how much you mean to me." He took a deep breath. "I know God has to be the center of any relationship I have. And it should be the same for you. So until that happens, just let me be a part of your life. A friend you can always count on. Someone who will be there whenever you need them, okay?"

As I nodded slowly, the painting at the church popped into

my mind. Jesus holding the little girl's face as if He wanted her to know how much He loved her. I realized that Jonathon was holding me the same way. My tears began again, but this time it was for a completely different reason. Suddenly, I could feel God's presence, wrapping me in love and telling me that He'd never left me. That He'd always loved me. I pulled Jonathon's hands down and wrapped my arms around him again. He held me for quite some time. Finally, I pulled back, wiped my face on my coat sleeve, and offered him a shaky smile. "I love you, Jonathon. It feels like I've loved you forever. But I'm realizing there are some dark places inside me that have to heal. And not just from my father." I lightly touched his face, something I'd wanted to do ever since I'd seen him again. I removed my fingers quickly, not wanting to get blood on his cheek. "God and I have some work to do. Right now, I'm not good for you. Or for anyone. Even myself. I would love your friendship—and your prayers. Maybe someday I can be the kind of woman you deserve. Right now, I'm not even close."

He started to say something, but I shook my head. "If you really do care for me, please don't argue. If I've ever been sure about anything in my life, I'm sure about this."

"I wasn't going to argue with you, Sophie. I just wondered why you mentioned God. I thought you didn't believe in Him."

I sighed into the darkness. "I'd convinced myself I didn't, but it seems He didn't go away just because I turned my back on Him. I still can't explain some of the things I had to endure, but ever since I set foot in Sanctuary, I've seen Him. In this town, in these people. But most of all, I see Him in you."

A tear snaked down the side of Jonathon's face, and he nodded. "I understand." He took my hands and stared down at them, highlighted by the light from my car. "You've got to wash your hands and put some disinfectant on them, okay?"

"I will. As soon as I get back to Esther's."

He hugged me one more time and then helped me back into my car. "Go home and get some sleep. I'm going to help Jacob clean up. I'll talk to you tomorrow."

As he walked away, I wanted to call him back. Tell him the whole truth. About Tom being attacked, the notes, everything. But fear held me captive. "If you want me to tell Jonathon everything, God," I whispered, "You'll have to give me the strength to do it. I'm just not there yet."

As I drove to Esther's, two emotions battled for my heart. Love and fear. Each so strong I couldn't control them. I really had no idea which one would win.

CHAPTER NINETEEN

I didn't sleep well Saturday night. I finally nodded off around three in the morning, but I was awake again a little after six. I tried to go back to sleep, but I couldn't, finally crawling out of bed around six-thirty. Being as quiet as I could, I went down the hall, took a shower, and got dressed for church. I'd treated my hands the night before and was glad to see the cuts weren't as deep as I'd first thought. Although the scratches were still visible, I didn't think they'd cause me too many problems.

I'd brought only one nice outfit with me, since I hadn't planned to go anyplace where I'd have to dress up. It was a simple black dress with long sleeves and a sweetheart neckline. Even though the neckline wasn't really low, I felt uncomfortable wearing it to church, so I draped a black and silver pashmina over the front. I added silver earrings and a silver bracelet. When I looked in the mirror, I felt overdressed. In the end, I took the dress off, pulled on a white, lacy camisole, and put the dress back on over it. With a little adjusting, it looked perfect. I took off the dangly silver earrings and put on small pearls. With plain black pumps, I felt I looked church-worthy.

Today would be the first time I'd taken part in an actual church service since I'd left Kingdom. Not only was I nervous about the experience, I was anxious about seeing Jonathon again. Last night had shaken me. Had he really told me he loved me, or had I dreamt that? To be honest, I wasn't completely sure when I first woke up. I was afraid to believe it was true. And I was even more afraid to believe it wasn't.

When I went downstairs, I headed to the kitchen. Esther was standing at the stove, and Zac was sitting at the kitchen table. His eyes widened when he saw me.

"Wow. You look great. Are you going to church?"

I nodded. "Jonathon invited me."

"Why don't we go together?"

"That would be nice." I was relieved I wouldn't have to walk into the service alone, but on the other hand, getting too close to Zac still made me a little nervous. What if I said or did something that made him suspicious?

Esther allowed me to get away with just a roll and coffee. Of course, she talked me into smearing the roll with her homemade strawberry jam. It was so good I almost wished I hadn't insisted on just one. I drank another cup of coffee while I waited for Zac to get ready. Esther left before we did, picked up by someone in a buggy. We'd all decided to meet at The Oil Lamp after church, and Esther had told us that Wynter and Reuben would be joining us. About ten minutes before the service at Jonathon's church was set to start, Zac came bounding down the stairs. I was surprised to see him wearing jeans. He noticed my surprised look.

"A lot of people wear jeans to Agape," he said.

I glanced down at my dress. "Is this . . . too much?"

"No, some people dress up. Some don't. You'll love it. It's an awesome church, and Jonathon is a terrific pastor."

"We'd better get going. I don't want to be late."

"It only takes about three minutes to get to Agape. One of the great things about small towns."

"I'll drive," I said. My car was a midsized sedan and had more room than his Mini Cooper. I didn't feel like being squeezed into a tiny space with him.

"Sure." He swung open the front door and bowed. "After you, m'lady."

I smiled, although I was a little irritated with his casual attitude. I didn't like to be late to anything. Especially church. The last thing I wanted was for people to stare at me when I walked in after everyone else was already seated. My parents had been late to church almost every Sunday. I could still hear the whispers and see people shaking their heads when the Wittenbauers strolled in after the service had already started.

As Zac had said, it only took a few minutes to drive to Agape. The parking lot was packed with cars. Zac asked if I would like him to drop me off near the front door so I could go inside while he looked for a parking space. I was grateful and took him up on his offer. Maybe I'd be on time, after all. But much to my surprise, the lobby was crowded with people talking and laughing. No one seemed in a rush or appeared worried that they might have trouble finding a place to sit.

Near the entrance to the community room, I glanced up

at the painting of Jesus with the little girl. Just the sight of it made me emotional again. I could almost feel Jonathon's hands on my face. My cheeks felt warm, as if he were still touching me.

I turned left and entered the sanctuary. It was the first time I'd seen it, since the doors had been closed the night before. Although it was large, it was casual and comfortable. Nothing ostentatious or formal. Maybe not as simple as the Kingdom church, but I didn't feel out of place. There were other obvious differences. In Kingdom, men sat on one side of the sanctuary and women on the other. Here, families stayed together. Men and women sat next to each other. People seemed happy to be in church. They were talking and laughing as they greeted one another. Our services in Kingdom had been very subdued. Members came in, sat down, and waited quietly for the pastor or elder to come to the front.

I made my way to a row about halfway up the aisle and sat down. Feeling that I should save a place for Zac, I put my purse on the pew next to me. There were musical instruments on the stage, and the musicians had just begun to take their places when Zac walked up. I moved my purse and put it down on the floor so he could sit down. He'd just taken his seat when a young woman walked up to the podium and asked us all to stand. Although I liked music, it wasn't allowed in our services back home. I'd heard some contemporary Christian music since I'd left Kingdom, but I couldn't say I'd paid much attention. I assumed that's what I'd hear this morning.

After the woman asked us to stand, the crowd became quiet, respectful. Although I'd told myself I probably wouldn't like the music much, as the first strains began, I felt overwhelmed by something powerful stirring within my heart. A feeling of love filled the room. As people began to sing the words that were projected on two big screens mounted on the walls, I could hear the adoration and passion for God in their songs. As the music swelled and the voices blended together, worshipers began to lift their hands. I'd never seen this before, but it seemed so natural. So right. I remembered a passage in the Bible about people lifting holy hands to God, and I found my hand slipping upward. It was as if I were directing this wave of praise to Him. I tried to sing along, but I was too overcome by emotion. I couldn't get the words out, so I just read them as the congregation poured out their praise to God. After a couple of songs with a faster beat, the music slowed down. I was touched by words that declared God was the very breath we breathe.

I was surprised when the strains of a song I'd heard back in Kingdom drifted gently from the stage—"'Tis So Sweet to Trust in Jesus." At first I was afraid it would take me out of the glorious atmosphere and bring back dark memories from the past, but instead, the words ministered to me. I felt God's arms around me the same way I had last night. There was something about praising Him with all these people that seemed to make His presence so strong and personal. I snuck a look at Zac. His eyes were closed, and I could tell that he wasn't just mouthing the words. He was in communion with God. I glanced around me and saw the beatific faces of the people near me. God was here. Their praise wasn't coming forth because it was expected or because it was time to sing. It came from hearts full of worship for a Father who adored His children.

When the swell finally slowed, the woman leading the service left the podium. Even this was something I'd never seen in our church. Women didn't talk during the service. And they certainly weren't leaders. I couldn't help but wonder if this was wrong, but how could it be? How could anything so beautiful, so full of God, not be His will?

Then a man went up to the podium and led a prayer. Afterward, he told us we could sit down. When we were seated, he mentioned several things going on in the church. I was surprised by all the small groups offered to the members and was impressed when he talked about their large youth group and an upcoming missions trip that summer to Uganda. This congregation was certainly active.

Then Jonathon came up on the stage. He was wearing black slacks, a blue shirt, and a dark-blue tie. He looked so handsome I couldn't take my eyes off of him. Memories of his kiss distracted me from what he was saying, and I fought to focus on his words, trying to forget the feeling of his lips on mine.

He began to talk about how God has a plan for everyone's life, and that we can slow down His plan by living in the past. "Whether our pain is caused by something we did, or something that was done to us, looking backward can keep us from moving forward. The apostle Paul spent many years aiding in the persecution of Christians. He stood by while Stephen was stoned to death. But on the road to Damascus, he discovered God's plan. God called him to spread the truth of Christ to the Gentiles. I'm sure Paul felt great conviction about his past and regretted his actions. But he had a choice. Either he could turn his eyes on Jesus and away from the things he'd done before he met Christ, or he could spend his life suffering for those mistakes. When faced with that choice, he said this: 'One thing I do: Forgetting what is behind and straining toward what is ahead, I press on toward the goal to win the prize for which God has called me heavenward in Christ Jesus.' Paul's decision was vital to his calling. If he'd allowed his painful past to overshadow his faith in God's love and forgiveness, he never would have stepped into a ministry that changed the world."

Although I wasn't near the front of the church, I was almost certain Jonathon was looking at me as he said, "God has something wonderful for you. Turn from the past and step into the freedom and power found in Him. People need the gifts that have been hidden inside you. You're important to the church. To the world. And to the people who love you. God has called you to touch lives. And you can't fulfill that calling if you're imprisoned in the past."

I only half listened to the rest of his sermon. Was Jonathon really talking to me? There was nothing I wanted more than to leave my past behind. It was the reason I'd left Kingdom. But had I just dragged it with me? I was still the injured child. Angry, hurt, defensive. That wasn't who I wanted to be. But how could I simply turn off the past and be free from what my father had done? The negative image I had of myself? Would God just zap the past away? Was I supposed to pretend it hadn't happened? Jonathon's words rang true, yet I had no idea how to get from where I was to where I needed to be.

Before I knew it, the service was over and people were beginning to walk out. I stood up, picked up my purse, and began to follow Zac out of the sanctuary. I was almost to the door when I heard someone call my name. I turned around and found Nate standing behind me. He looked great in jeans, a chambray shirt, and a black leather jacket.

"Wow, you clean up great," he said with a smile. "Do you have plans?"

"I guess we're all going to The Oil Lamp for lunch," I told him. "You're welcome to join us."

He frowned. "Are you sure? I don't want to intrude."

"It's nothing formal," Zac interjected. "Everyone's welcome. You can ride over with us if you want."

Nate zipped up his jacket. "Okay, sounds great. I'd love to. Thanks."

"Have you two met?" I asked.

"Yeah, last night," Zac said. "Nate saved me a piece of pecan pie, so I guess we're best friends now. Nice to see you again."

Nate laughed. "You too. Thanks for letting me tag along."

Zac grinned. "The more the merrier. As long as Randi doesn't run out of food, we're good to go."

As we walked out the sanctuary doors, I glanced back and saw Jonathon standing at the front of the sanctuary, a small crowd of people around him. It was clear he was very popular with his congregation. Although I wasn't certain, I thought I caught him looking my way. The flow of people pushed me toward the lobby, so I couldn't be sure.

Zac, Nate, and I got into my car and made the short drive to The Oil Lamp. We weren't the first car to pull in, and more cars were coming behind us.

"I'm going to run in and get us a table." Zac had his door open before I'd come to a full stop in the parking spot. He jumped out of the car and sprinted toward the front door.

"He seems worried about not getting a table." I looked at Nate in my rearview mirror. "We could go to Mary's place if The Oil Lamp gets too full."

Nate looked across the street. "I think Mary closes on Sundays."

Sure enough, there was no one there.

"Then I'm glad Zac's willing to fight the crowd for us."

"Me too."

I put my hand on the door handle, but Nate stopped me. "Jonathon mentioned the fire last night. Did it have anything to do with what you're doing?"

"I—I don't know." I stared into his green eyes in the mirror, and I saw concern etched on his face. "We need to get inside. Can we have this discussion later?"

He paused and looked out the window for a moment. "You need to know that Jonathon and I talked before the service. He asked me what you'd shared with me, and I told him. I hope you're not angry, but I couldn't lie about it."

"I'm not mad. I was going to tell him anyway."

"He's very concerned about you, and so am I."

"I know," I said. "Hopefully this will be over soon."

"What makes you say that?"

"Well, I'm hoping Martin Hatcher and Ben Johnson will be at the restaurant today. For now, they're my prime suspects. I'd like to get a closer look at them."

"And then what?"

"I'm not sure. No matter how Chase has changed the way he looks, I think I can still recognize him. I have to try. It's all I've got."

I'd told myself—and Jonathon—this same thing more than

once, but I suddenly realized that Jonathon hadn't recognized me when he'd seen me again. Had I put too much stock in being able to identify Chase by sight?

"You don't sound very confident," Nate said.

"I know. Look, let's get inside. If I don't get a good look at Hatcher and Johnson inside the restaurant, I'm going to track them down this afternoon. If it's not too late." I didn't say it, but the notes, the fire . . . all these things pointed to someone who knew exactly what I was up to. Add that to all the people who knew what I was really doing in Sanctuary, and it made getting my story before everything blew up in my face almost impossible.

We got out of the car and went into the restaurant. I gazed around the packed room and saw Zac sitting at a large table, waving us over.

"Man, what took you guys so long?" he asked as we sat down. "I thought I was going to have to fight several little old ladies for this spot."

As I slid into my chair, I noticed some people standing at the front of the restaurant, shooting us looks that weren't appropriate for a Sunday.

"Who are the other chairs for?" I asked.

"Esther, Wynter, Reuben, and Jonathon."

"Jonathon?" I gulped. "Did he say he was coming?"

Zac looked at me like I was crazy. "No. It's my psychic ability kicking in." He laughed. "Yes, he grabbed me when I was coming in today and asked where we were going after church. I told him we were having lunch here, and he asked me to save him a seat."

I just nodded and turned my attention to the menu sitting

in front of me. I wanted to see Jonathon, but a part of me was afraid. Afraid he was sorry about last night.

I was trying to decide between chicken and dumplings and fried catfish when someone sat down in the chair next to me. I looked up from my menu and found Jonathon gazing at me. I could swear my heart stopped beating for a moment, although I was fairly certain that wasn't really physically possible. After giving him a quick smile, I turned my attention back to the menu. Unfortunately, I couldn't make sense of the words any longer. The only thing I could think about was how near he was to me.

"Great sermon today, Jonathon," Zac said from across the table. "It really spoke to me."

"I'm glad," Jonathon said. "We all have things from the past we have to deal with. It's a pretty universal struggle."

"I agree," Nate said softly.

I glanced over at Nate and could tell by the expression on his face that something in Jonathon's sermon had hit home. Seemed Jonathon was right. Very few people had perfect lives.

Jonathon touched me lightly on the arm, and I jumped. I turned to look at him and found him looking past me.

He leaned in close and whispered, "That man over there. The one sitting alone—that's Martin Hatcher."

I went back to staring at my menu for a few seconds so it wouldn't look suspicious if he was looking our way. When I finally lifted my head and turned toward the spot Jonathon had indicated, I found myself staring into the face of a man who could easily be Terrance Chase.

He was the customer in the post office who'd seen my picture of the missing criminal.

CHAPTER TWENTY

I turned back quickly to Jonathon. "I saw him in the post office," I whispered. "I accidentally mixed up my picture of Terrance Chase with my mail. I think he saw it. He could have figured out what I was up to the day I arrived here. I think he's behind everything that's happened."

Jonathon put his hand on my arm. "Don't overreact. He's looking over here."

"What's going on?" Nate asked.

I turned away from Jonathon. "See the guy sitting by himself? Against the far wall? That's Martin Hatcher."

"Does he look like Chase?"

I nodded. "Red hair. Square-shaped face. I can't see if he has hazel eyes or a cleft in his chin from here. Especially since he's wearing glasses."

"You people are starting to make me feel insecure." Zac frowned. "Are you talking about me? Do I look funny or something?"

"I'm sorry," Jonathon said. "No, we're not talking about you. And you don't look any funnier than normal."

Zac rolled his eyes. "Gee, thanks. I feel so much better now."

"We'll talk about this later, okay?" Jonathon said to Nate and me.

"Sure. Sorry, Zac," I said.

Zac picked up his menu but kept his eyes on us. "Is anyone going to tell me what's going on?"

"That man over there looks like someone I might know," I said, "but I'm not sure. I didn't want to say anything to him in case I'm wrong."

To my horror, Nate got out of his seat and walked over to Hatcher's table. He leaned over and said something. Hatcher looked up at him and nodded. Nate picked up the bottle of ketchup on the table and brought it back toward us. It was then that I noticed Nate had removed the ketchup from our table and put it on the floor near his chair.

"What is wrong with you?" I hissed when he sat back down next to me.

He put the bottle on the table and smiled. "You wanted to know his eye color and if he has a cleft chin, right?"

At that moment, the front door swung open and Esther came in, accompanied by Wynter and Reuben. As they made their way toward our table, I glared at Nate.

"You should have asked me first."

"Do you want to know the answer?"

I glanced over at Esther. They were almost halfway across the room.

"Yes. Tell me. Quickly."

"Hazel eyes. Cleft chin. I could tell since his beard is trimmed short. I believe you've found him."

"Found who?" Zac said, frustration in his voice.

"Later, okay?" Jonathon said under his breath.

Zac nodded, just as Esther got to the table. She sat down next to him. Wynter and Reuben took the last empty seats.

"I am sorry we are late," Esther said. "Surely you all did not wait for me."

"No one's taken our order yet," Jonathon told her. "It's pretty busy."

At that moment, Maxie stepped up to the table. "So glad to see you, Esther." She smiled at the old woman. "What can I get you to drink?"

Zac grinned. "Now I know how to get great service. Just eat with Esther."

Maxie reached over and slapped him lightly on the arm. "I was on my way over before Esther got here. But I do have to admit that she's better lookin' than you."

The rest of us laughed while Zac struck a comical pose, his bottom lip sticking out. "And I thought you loved me, Maxie."

I tried to take part in the friendly banter, but I couldn't look away from Martin Hatcher. Was I staring at Terrance Chase? Had my search finally come to an end?

Hatcher seemed to be concentrating on his meal, so I prayed Nate's ploy hadn't tipped him off. Although he'd appeared to be looking at me earlier, now he seemed oblivious to the people around him. With everything that had happened—the attack in the basement, the threatening notes, and the fire—his nonchalant attitude seemed odd. Shouldn't he be worried I was closing in on him?

Jonathon was talking to Wynter and Reuben about the mine reclamation and Nate had gotten up to go to the bathroom when Zac leaned toward me and whispered, "When he leaves, get his glass. I'll take it back to St. Louis tomorrow. The police can get fingerprints."

I stared at him in confusion. "What are you talking about?"

He grunted. "I work for a television station, and I help with investigations. It's obvious you're interested in this guy. Nate was trying to get a close look at him. I assume you're trying to figure out who he is?" He raised his eyebrows. "I'm right, aren't I?"

I could only open my mouth in surprise. I didn't know what to say.

"Look, you don't have to tell me who you think he is, but if you really want answers, this is the way to get them. I'll try to keep the results quiet. Unless he's a famous fugitive. Or Jimmy Hoffa. Then the police will be all over him. But I'll give you a heads-up before that happens. Will that work for you?"

I nodded, unable to find the words to thank him. This was the answer to my dilemma. As long as Zac was telling the truth, I'd finally be able to prove whether or not this man was Terrance Chase. And if the results turned out the way I suspected they would, my days of writing obituaries would be over.

Zac jabbed his index finger at me. "Just promise me you're not a hit man tracking down your next victim."

I snorted. "You have my word. I'm not a hit man."

"That's all I need to know. You can keep your secret. I'm not interested in exposing it—or you."

With that, he turned his attention to Wynter. She looked at us strangely for a moment but then appeared to dismiss our brief exchange and joined back into the conversation about the mine outside of town.

"I did some research about it," she said. "It was originally dug in the 1850s. It produced a decent amount of coal, but it was abandoned in the 1970s."

"I remember that," Esther said. "It was called the Gabriel Mine. When it closed, many people moved out of Sanctuary. We worried the town would die, but eventually we grew again. Not as large as we used to be but enough to support those who want to live here."

"I can't believe that mine's been sitting there all these years," Reuben said. "It's unsafe. Dangerous. We've had several close calls. Many of the tunnels have already collapsed. Thankfully, it will be filled this week. I'm told we won't even be able to tell a mine used to be there."

Esther nodded. "I know Sarah and Cicely will be happy when the mine no longer exists."

This was the second time I'd heard someone make that comment. I wanted to know what Esther meant but decided to wait until later to ask her about it.

Maxie brought our drinks and took our orders. I kept my eye on Martin. When he got up to leave, I excused myself. As he made his way to the front register, I went to his table, quickly dumped the remaining water in his glass into a bowl, touching only the bottom of the glass, and then put the glass in my purse. When I reached the bathroom, I looked back to see if anyone had noticed me, but no one appeared to be interested in my actions. After I closed the door, I removed the glass from my purse with a paper towel, careful not to smear the fingerprints, then I slid it into one of the plastic bags I kept in my purse for leftovers. Since I'd started writing restaurant reviews for the paper, I'd begun carrying the bags since I didn't usually eat a complete dinner. Although I could ask for a carryout box from most restaurants, some of the so-called gourmet places frowned on it. On my salary, I couldn't afford to leave food behind, so the bags came in handy. I could slip leftovers into my purse without being obvious. Right now, I was really grateful for that part of my job. The bag was the perfect way to protect the prints that could confirm Martin Hatcher was actually Terrance Chase.

I left the restroom and went back to the table. On the way, I passed Sarah, Janet, and Cicely. After stopping briefly to say hello, I scooted back into my chair. Zac winked at me, acknowledging that he'd seen me collect the glass. As I sat down, Maxie came to the table with part of our food. After another trip to the kitchen, everyone had been served.

"Does anyone mind if I pray?" Jonathon asked.

"It would be appreciated," Esther said.

We bowed our heads, and Jonathon prayed over our food, thanking God for good friends. We all said, "Amen," and started to eat. I'd just taken a bite when Jonathon nudged me. He nodded toward a man walking past our table. This was the man we'd seen at the supper last night. Ben Johnson. He had brownish hair, mixed with gray. Although I couldn't see his eyes, I could tell by the shape of his face that he couldn't possibly be Chase. I looked at Jonathon and shook my head. He nodded his agreement. Frankly, I was pretty confident I had Chase anyway. When I got back to Esther's, I was going to work on the story I'd give to the newspaper. As soon as Zac's police friends confirmed my suspicions, I'd hit *Send* and email my story to the editor of the *Times*. Besides scooping everyone else, I would be the reporter who helped to bring Chase to justice. I'd finally have everything I'd always wanted.

So why did I still feel so empty?

CHAPTER TWENTY-ONE

When Zac and I pulled up in front of Esther's house after lunch, I took the glass out of my purse and gave it to him. "You've got to promise me you'll tell me the results as soon as they're in and before you tell anyone else," I said. "It's really important. After that, I don't care what you do."

"I already told you I would. This isn't some kind of personal vendetta, is it? I mean, this guy didn't date your mother and dump her or anything, right?"

I laughed at the image of anyone dating my mom. "Not even close."

"Odd actions for an accountant." He held up the bag and stared at the glass. "You're not from the IRS, are you?"

"No," I said emphatically. "Look, I'm not a hit man, I'm not from the IRS, and this man didn't date my mom. The truth is, he might be a really bad man. A criminal. You're doing a public service by getting that glass checked out."

"Okay, I'm leaving this afternoon so I can be at work in

the morning. Give me your cell phone number, and I'll call you as soon as I get the results."

I rattled off my number while he wrote it down on a small notepad he carried in the pocket of his jeans. "One of these days you've got to take me out for dinner when you're back in town and tell me . . . everything."

"You've got a deal," I agreed. "And thanks for understanding, Zac."

He shrugged. "This is my life. Sneaking around, trying to figure out what people are up to. It's what people in the news business do."

I wanted so badly to tell him who I really was and what I actually did, but I didn't dare. If he found out I worked for the paper, he might be tempted to scoop me. I liked him, but that didn't mean I could completely trust him.

We got out of the car, and Zac hurried upstairs to pack while I went to my room to start writing. I'd wanted to talk to Jonathon after lunch, but he was still talking to Reuben when I left.

I changed my clothes, grabbed my laptop, and plopped down on the fainting couch to write. I'd barely started when someone knocked on my door. Figuring it was Zac, I called out, "Come in!"

The door swung open, and Jonathon came in. Surprised, I swung my legs over the side of the couch and sat up, putting my laptop on the couch next to me.

He walked toward me but left the door open. "I'm sorry we didn't get to talk more. Are you busy now?"

Even though I wanted to get going on my article, I still had the rest of the day. "No, I'm fine."

He glanced around the room, looking uncomfortable. "Could we go somewhere else? I don't think we should be in your . . . I mean . . ."

"It's a bedroom, Jonathon. Yes, we can go somewhere else. Esther said she was going over to Reuben and Wynter's house for the rest of the afternoon, and Zac is getting ready to head home. Why don't we just go downstairs to the living room?"

"That sounds good."

He went out through the door before I could say anything else. I was touched by his desire to keep everything above board. I put on my shoes and followed him downstairs. When I reached the living room, he was sitting on the couch, still looking decidedly uncomfortable.

"Can I get you something to drink?" I asked. "Esther's got some apple cider in the refrigerator. How about a glass?"

"Sure, thanks. Can I help?"

"No, I think I can handle it. Be right back."

As I walked toward the kitchen, I wondered why he seemed so nervous. I took a pitcher out of the fridge, filled two glasses with ice, and poured in some cider. By the time I finished putting the pitcher back, I was convinced he'd come over to tell me last night was a mistake. That he didn't really have feelings for me. I had the urge to run out the back door of Esther's house and keep going. But that was childish. I'd already told myself that a relationship between us wouldn't work. I was going back to St. Louis after I'd finished what I needed to do here. What did it matter?

I took a deep breath and carried the glasses to the living room. Jonathon was standing up now, gazing out the front window. He turned when I cleared my throat.

"Oh. Thank you."

When he reached for his glass, our fingers touched. My eyes met his. "Is something wrong? You seem . . . upset."

He took his drink over to the couch and sat down again. "So you think Martin Hatcher might be Terrance Chase?"

I sat down in the chair near him, holding on to my glass like it was a life preserver. "I—I don't know. I think it's very possible. He saw my picture of Chase right after I got to town, Jonathon. It would explain all the weird things that have been happening, wouldn't it? He's trying to stop me."

"All the 'weird things' . . . does that include the note from last night?"

Obviously, Nate had told him about the note. "I was going to tell you . . ."

"I hope you're being honest with me, Sophie."

I wanted to tell him that was my intention, but it would have been another lie. I decided to change the subject. "I picked up Hatcher's glass from the restaurant. Zac is going to have it checked for prints. I don't want to accuse Hatcher for no reason, but he really looks like Chase. Nate got close to him. He has hazel eyes and a cleft chin. I really think it's him, Jonathon."

Jonathon stared at the glass in his hands. Finally, he looked up. "I'm proud of you, Sophie. I really am. You might just bring a murderer to justice. There are families out there that will finally have closure. That's awesome."

"That's a nice thing to say, but I don't deserve your respect. The families haven't been the most important part of this for me. And they should have been."

"Why are you always so hard on yourself? If you didn't

care about the families, you wouldn't feel badly now. I've never met anyone who judged themselves as harshly as you do. Didn't you listen to my sermon today?"

I reached over and put my glass on the table next to my chair. "Yes, I did, and I'm trying. But you know what I've done and why it's hard to forgive myself."

"Do you know what I've done? The things I'm ashamed of?"

"You're a good man, Jonathon. You can't put yourself in a class with me. You've never burned down a church, have you?"

"No, you're right." He peered at me through narrowed eyes. "I only tried to kill a man."

"I—I don't understand."

"When you saw me here, did you expect to see Hope, too?"

"Yes. I thought you two were getting married."

"So did I. You know why Tom went to prison, right?"

"I know he attacked Hope. Lizzie told me about it when I was getting ready to leave."

"And that's it?"

"She said his father shot him. That's all I know about it." I frowned at Jonathon. "How does this involve you?"

He leaned back against the couch. "The only reason I didn't kill Tom is because Sheriff Ford took the shot first. Tom was threatening to kill Hope, and I wanted him to die. I had my gun pointed at him, and I planned to pull the trigger."

"There's nothing wrong with that. You were trying to save the woman you loved."

"I was Mennonite. You know what we're taught."

"Non-resistance," I answered. "But how could you stand by and watch her die?"

"Ebbie Miller had the same choice to make. Instead of

choosing violence, he tried to goad Tom into shooting him. He figured the noise of the shot would bring help."

"I—I don't understand. What are you saying?"

He sighed and looked down at the floor. "Ebbie was willing to put his life on the line for his beliefs. In the end, Hope chose him because of his integrity."

"Oh, Jonathon."

"What I'm trying to tell you is that everyone has had . . . moments. Made choices we're not proud of."

"So what are you saying? If you'd been a better man, you'd have let Tom kill you?"

"No," he said sharply, raising his head and staring at me. "I'm not saying that. But I am telling you that I went against everything I believed—at that time—because I was under stress. What you did was the same thing, Sophie. Your life was falling apart. What your father did to you . . . you never had a chance to react normally to the rest of the world. Getting involved with Tom and his buddies happened because you were hurting. In pain. I can understand that."

I felt tears fill my eyes. "I knew it was wrong to set the church on fire. I did it anyway."

"Will you come over here?" He motioned toward the seat beside him.

Trembling, I stood up and walked over to the couch.

"Sit down, please."

When I sat down next to him, he took my hands in his. "When God looks at you, all He sees is Jesus. Whatever you did, whatever you're ashamed of, Jesus paid the price."

"But . . . I should be punished."

"No, you shouldn't. That's what I'm trying to tell you.

Jesus was already punished. There's no penalty left to pay. And if you won't forgive yourself, aren't you saying that what Jesus did wasn't enough?"

"But our pastor could have died, Jonathon. You said that yourself."

"I know, and I'm sorry. I was angry." He squeezed my hands. "Sophie, when I left Kingdom, I thought my heart was broken. All I could think about was Hope. But after I'd been in Sanctuary for a while . . ." He looked away for a moment then faced me again. "You may not believe this, but after a while, my feelings for Hope dwindled. I kept thinking about . . . you. I know that doesn't make sense, but I felt such a burden to pray for you. And I did. Day after day, I lifted you up in prayer. You know that picture at the church? The one you were staring at?"

"Yes." My voice came out in a whisper.

"I bought that with my own money. The church board was supposed to pick out paintings for the lobby, but I had to have that one. I couldn't quite figure out why it spoke to me the way it did. Until I saw you standing next to it."

"It looks like me when I was a girl," I said softly. "I noticed that right away."

He nodded, and then he let go of one of my hands and rested his hand against my face. "I realize now that's why it called to me. Because I saw you in it. The girl with amber eyes." He took a deep breath. "When you left Kingdom, I felt a real loss. Since then, you've never really left my thoughts. Now that I'm with you again, I have feelings I can't explain. But I'd like to find out why. Maybe God brought us together again for a reason."

"I can't believe God would want you involved with someone like me, Jonathon. You should have someone strong. Someone godly who can help you be everything you're called to be."

"If God has a plan for us, you'll be that, Sophie. And more. Look. I realize you're not ready for any kind of a romantic relationship. You have a lot of healing to do. No pressure, okay? I just felt I had to be honest with you."

Relieved, I nodded. "Can I ask you one thing?"

He took his hand off my face and smiled. "You can even ask me two things."

"Why did you kiss me last night?"

He let go of my other hand. "Do you mean, was I caught up in the moment? Am I sorry I kissed you?"

I nodded again, too unsure of myself to say anything.

Jonathon put his hands on my shoulders. "I meant it, Sophie. I love you. And if the time should ever come when you're ready to accept that love, I'll be waiting." He lowered his head to look deeply into my eyes. "Does that answer your question?"

"Yes." A sensation ran through me. Something I'd never felt before. It was joy. Pure happiness.

We were staring at each other when we heard someone clear his throat. Jonathon let go of me and turned to look at Zac, who stood in the living room, holding a suitcase.

"Uh, sorry to interrupt," he said. "But I'm leaving. Not that you two would notice or anything."

"S-sorry." Feeling flustered, I shakily stood up. "I'm glad I got to meet you, Zac. And thanks again for helping me out. How long do you think it will take to get results back on the glass?"

He placed his suitcase by his feet. "I'm not sure. Could take a week or two. Or they might be able to get to it right away."

"If you can encourage them to hurry it up . . ."

"If this guy is someone who might be important to the police, they could get to it right away. Otherwise we just have to take our chances."

I nodded. "It's possible he would be important to the police, but I'm not completely sure."

He studied me for a moment before saying, "Look, Emily, someone at the police department owes me a favor. Let me see if I can get this rushed through."

"That would be great. Call me with the results as soon as you can. Please."

He frowned at me. "Okay, but if there's a story here, I'd appreciate you returning the favor. Give me a shot at it after you do whatever you need to do."

Relieved, I smiled. "You've got a deal."

"And don't forget our lunch when you get back."

"I won't. I promise."

"Hey, I'll walk you to your car, Zac," Jonathon said.

Zac grabbed his suitcase and followed Jonathon out to the Mini Cooper. As I watched, Jonathon said something to Zac, but I couldn't hear it. Whatever it was, Zac seemed to take it seriously. Then he tossed his suitcase into his trunk, shook Jonathon's hand, and took off.

I stepped out onto the front porch and waited for Jonathon.

"It's nice out," he remarked as he came up the steps. "Why don't we sit on the porch for a while?"

"Sounds good." I sat down in one of the rocking chairs and Jonathon sat in the other. "What were you saying to Zac?"

"I just asked him to do everything he could to get the information to you as quickly as possible."

"I'm a little afraid he'll go after the story himself if the prints belong to Terrance Chase."

Jonathon leaned his head back on the rocking chair. "Don't worry about that. He promised he'd contact you first. He'll keep his word. Zac's a good guy." He turned his head and looked over at me. "Is there anyone you trust, Sophie?"

"I—I'm trying to trust God again."

"The best place to start."

"I'm sorry, Jonathon. I wish I wasn't so mistrustful. I'm sure I'm hard to deal with sometimes. It's got to be frustrating for someone like you."

He smiled. "Every human being on the face of the planet makes a daily choice to trust. Life doesn't really encourage it, you know."

"You think it's a choice?"

"Sure. Trust doesn't just jump up and overtake you. You have to choose it. When you're whole again, you'll find the ability to trust people."

"I've never thought about it that way before."

"Well, if you go outside in the summer and get a sunburn, what are you going to do? Never go outside again?"

"No, I'd stay inside until I recovered. Then I'd go outside again. But I'd probably wear sunscreen this time."

"Look at God as your sunscreen. When you're healthy, you'll go outside again. But this time, you'll have a covering. The grace, love, and protection of God."

"I like that. It makes me feel hopeful that someday . . ."

I stopped talking when an odd expression crossed Jonathon's

face. I turned to look at the road. Zac was driving back toward the house. Had he forgotten something?

He pulled up in front of Esther's house and got out of the car, his expression tense.

Jonathon stood up and began to walk toward him. "Is everything all right?"

Zac shook his head. "Uh, no. There's a crowd gathered at the church. That guy? Nate? He's holding some guy hostage inside the building."

CHAPTER TWENTY-TWO

We all squeezed into Zac's car and raced to the church. Jonathon seemed dazed. When we pulled into the parking lot, a car from the sheriff's department was there, its lights flashing.

Jonathon leapt from the car and ran over to a crowd gathered outside the building. I sprinted after him but had a tough time keeping up. Spotting Reuben, Jonathon grabbed his arm. "What's going on?"

"I'm not actually sure." Reuben glanced at Zac and me as we jogged up to join them. "Paul got a call that there was a man with a gun inside the church. When he got here, he found that guy you've been helping—Nate? He's holding a gun on Martin Hatcher. Since I know Martin as well as anyone does, Paul called me."

"Did you say Martin Hatcher?" I couldn't keep the shock out of my voice. "I—I don't understand."

Jonathon pulled Reuben aside, away from the crowd. Zac and I followed him. "I have no idea why Nate would do something like this, but we think Martin Hatcher might be wanted by the police." He jerked his head my way. "Sophie . . . I mean, Emily has reason to believe he's Terrance Chase. The guy who robbed that armored car company back in 2008."

Reuben looked at us like we were crazy. "Terrance Chase? You think he's Terrance Chase?"

"Yes," I assured him. "I discovered Chase planned to hide out here after the robbery. Hatcher came here not long after that. He looks like Chase. Same coloring. Same features."

Reuben shook his head. "Look, I don't know how this relates to this situation, but I can assure you that Martin Hatcher isn't Terrance Chase." He leaned in as if he was going to tell us a secret. "You know there are people in Sanctuary that have . . . pasts, right? Well, Martin is one of those people." He looked down at the ground for a moment, as if contemplating something. "I know this because . . . because I helped to relocate him here." He met Jonathon's eyes. "Martin Hatcher was a witness against a gang member who killed a cop. His testimony helped to put the guy away. He came here for his own protection. I shouldn't even tell you this much, but it looks like I have no choice. You can't repeat this to anyone, and that means you, too." He directed his last comment toward Zac and me.

"I won't," Zac said. "You have my word."

"Are you sure?" I asked. "I mean, absolutely sure?"

"Beyond a shadow of a doubt. He was placed here by the U.S. Marshals. Paul and I are . . . *were* the only people who knew the truth."

"Okay," I said slowly. "So why is Nate in there with a gun? I don't get it."

"Could he think Martin is this . . . Chase guy?" Reuben asked.

"Yeah," I said. "But why would he care? He doesn't know Chase, and he has no connection to the case."

Reuben studied me for a moment. "You've struck up a friendship with Nate. You need to tell him Martin isn't who he thinks he is."

"I can do that," Jonathon said. "I don't want her anywhere near a gun."

"No," I said, determination filling my voice. "It has to be me. I mean, he likes you, Jonathon, but he'll trust me."

Jonathon took my arm. "I don't like this."

"We'll be careful, Jonathon," Reuben said. "I won't let anything happen to her. I promise."

Jonathon wrapped his arm around my shoulders. "I'm going with her. No argument. I gave Nate a place to live, and I think he trusts me, too."

"All right." Reuben pointed to Zac. "You stay here."

"Is there anything I can do?" he asked.

Reuben nodded. "Keep this crowd back. And call Wynter. She's at our house with Esther. She wanted to come when Paul called me, and I don't want her to worry. Let her know I'm okay and that everything's going to be fine."

"All right," Zac said in a low voice. "You just make sure I'm telling her the truth."

Reuben clapped Zac on the shoulder. "I will. You have my word." He looked at me. "Come on. We need to get in there before something happens we can't fix."

Jonathon and I followed him into the church and toward the sanctuary. I could hear voices coming from inside.

When we got to the sanctuary doors, Reuben slowly opened one of them. "Paul, it's me, Reuben," he called out. "I've brought Emily and Jonathon. They'd like to talk to Nate, if it's okay."

As the door opened all the way, I saw Nate at the front of the sanctuary, near the stage, with a gun in his hand. Martin Hatcher was on the floor with his hands up. Paul was about halfway down the center aisle, his gun drawn. As we stepped into the room, Nate looked directly at me. The twisted expression on his face frightened me, and I wondered if he was mentally unbalanced. Why would he go after a man he didn't even know? It didn't make sense.

"Nate," I called tentatively. "What's going on? What are you doing?"

He said something, but I couldn't hear him very well.

"I can't hear you," I told him. "Is it okay if I come closer?"

He nodded, and I started down the aisle. I turned and found Jonathon right behind me. I put a hand on his chest. "Stay back. I don't want to spook him. Please." I could see the concern on his face, and it meant a great deal to me, but Nate seemed to be standing on the edge of a precipice, and I didn't want him to step over it.

"Sophie . . ."

I shook my head and didn't look back at Jonathon, just kept walking slowly up the aisle. When I reached Paul, he stepped in front of me.

"I don't think you should go any closer," he said softly.

"I'm going all the way. I know I can talk to him. You've got to let me try."

"All right. But whatever you do, don't get in my way." From the expression on his face, I knew he would shoot Nate if things got out of hand.

"Okay. But please don't overreact. Give me a chance."

"Backup is on the way. If you don't get him to put the gun down, I can't guarantee a good outcome. Do you understand me?"

I nodded. His message was clear—and frightening. I couldn't believe I was in this situation. Why in the world would Nate do this? Because I told him I thought Martin Hatcher was Terrance Chase? It didn't make any sense, yet I knew somehow I was partially responsible for what was happening. I had to try to talk to Nate.

I continued walking toward the front of the church. Martin was clearly terrified, afraid Nate was going to kill him. When I finally reached the men, my entire body felt numb from fear and stress. I sat down on the pew in the front, mere feet away from Nate.

"I'm sorry about this, Sophie." His eyes were wide with emotion. "I know your story is important, but I have to kill him. I can't take the chance he'll get away."

"Nate, I don't understand." I made my voice as gentle as I could. "Why in the world would you take this so personally? You don't know this man."

Tears made his eyes shine. "Yes, I do. I've known him for a long time. He killed my brother."

For the first time, Martin spoke. "I told him I don't know his brother. I've never killed anyone in my life."

"Liar!" Nate screamed the word so loudly, it made me jump.

Martin cringed and shielded his head with his hands.

"Nate, what are you talking about?"

"My real name is Donald Abbott. Charles Abbott was my brother."

My mind raced, trying to figure out what he was telling me. Who was Charles Abbott? Suddenly, I understood. "Charles Abbott? One of the guards killed in the armored car robbery?"

"Yes." He glared at Martin. "This man talked my brother into letting them into the building that morning. Charlie was supposed to get a cut of what they took. He—he was getting ready to lose his house to the bank. He thought this was his only way out. When he admitted to me what he'd planned, I told him it was wrong. That no amount of money was worth his integrity. I begged him to contact the police, but he wouldn't do it. I should have called them. I could have stopped it. If I had, Charlie would still be alive."

I realized he'd been talking about his brother at the church supper. He felt guilty for not stepping in and contacting the authorities.

Nate—now Donald—looked at me, grief etched in his features. "He changed his mind. Told this slimeball he wouldn't help him. But they came anyway. And they shot him."

"I—I'm sorry. But I still don't understand. How did you end up here?" All of a sudden, everything became clear. It was just like in a cartoon. I could swear a light bulb switched on over my head. "You're Donnie."

He nodded. "I decided to follow Charlie's lead and become a guard. But I applied to work at a prison. In Kansas. What were the chances I'd meet someone who had an idea where to find the man that killed Charlie? It was like . . . it was meant to be. When I found out Tom knew where Chase was, I told him I'd make sure all his mail got out without being intercepted by the office. I planned to get him to tell me what he knew. I even sent him a threatening note so he wouldn't talk about Chase to anyone else. But I had no idea he'd mailed one letter on his own. To your paper. So I decided to wait until after he talked to you. I couldn't take the chance he'd figure out who I was and refuse to tell me what I wanted to know."

I glanced at Martin. He was staring at me, panic on his face. I knew he wanted my help, and I was going to do everything I could to save him. Donnie thought he was avenging his brother. If this situation didn't resolve itself, he would become another of Chase's victims. And I didn't want that.

"Donnie, is Tom all right?"

"Yes. I paid a couple of guys to start a fight and get him thrown into solitary. But he's fine. I needed to keep you and him apart so I could find this . . . this animal. I tried to get Tom to tell me where you were, but he got suspicious. He began to suspect me."

That must have been what Tom was trying to tell me on the phone. Not to talk to Donnie. "But when I called, you got me to tell you where I was."

"Yeah. Then I tried to talk you into letting me come here and help you. But you wouldn't budge. So I came here anyway and made up a story about my car breaking down and needing help. The pastor let me stay. Where I could wait until you found the answers I'd been searching for." He lowered the gun for just a moment. "I sent the notes to you, Sophie. The first one was to make you think you were close so you wouldn't give up."

"And the second?"

"So you'd tell me the truth. Let me in. It was the only thing I could think of."

"I understand, Donnie. I do. But this man isn't Chase. I was wrong about him."

"You're lying." His body suddenly shook with rage, and I was afraid the gun might go off accidentally.

"Look at me, Donnie."

He turned his face my way.

"I'm not lying. I swear to you. Reuben and Paul know this man. They helped bring him here. You've got to listen to me. I jumped to conclusions because he moved here after the robbery, and he has the same coloring as Chase. Just like a lot of people do. This is my fault. I was so obsessed with finding Chase, I turned Martin into him. Without any evidence. Without proof." I leaned toward him. "If you hurt an innocent man, Donnie, you'll be dishonoring your brother. You don't want to do that."

"How can I know you're telling me the truth?"

I tried to find an answer to his question, but in the end, I couldn't. "I don't know," I said finally. "You'll just have to trust me. You'll have to decide if your hate for Terrance Chase is stronger than making a huge mistake and taking this innocent man's life. If you shoot him, and then find out you were wrong, how will you deal with that? You will have done to him what Chase did to your brother. Is that what you want?"

He lowered the gun a few inches. "No." His eyes locked on mine. I stood up slowly and took a few steps toward him. "This has gone too far, and I'm sorry. It's all my fault. I see that now. I wanted a story. Something to help my career. And all I've done is cause confusion and pain. Please, Donnie. For me. Please give me the gun. If you hurt Martin, I won't be able to live with it."

The battle raging inside was evident on Donnie's face. Finally, he lowered the gun a little more. "Okay. But will you promise me something?"

"Sure. As long as it's something I can do."

"Will you keep looking? Find Chase? I want him to pay. I want my mother to have closure."

How could I promise that? All I wanted right now was to get out of this town and forget all about Terrance Chase. But I had no choice. I had to tell him what he wanted to hear. "I promise, Donnie. We'll find him."

He hesitated, and for just a moment, I was afraid he might turn the gun on himself. But finally he held it out toward me. I came up next to him and took it from his hand. Martin Hatcher broke out in sobs and scrambled away, running over to Jonathon while Paul ran up to us and put Donnie in handcuffs.

As I tried to reassure Donnie that everything was going to be all right, I handed Paul the gun. I promised Donnie I'd visit him as soon as I could and then watched as Paul escorted him out of the building. Feeling completely drained of energy, I collapsed onto the pew next to me.

Jonathon talked to Martin for a bit. When Martin left, Jonathon came over and sat down beside me.

"That was really brave," he said. "I'm so proud of you."

"There's nothing to be proud of," I countered. "I almost cost Martin Hatcher his life. I'm done. I know what I told Donnie, but I can see now that my secrecy and selfishness has caused nothing but trouble. If Donnie had shot him . . ."

"Then it would have been Donnie's fault, not yours."

I turned to him. "Will you stop being so nice to me? Why don't you tell me off? Be honest? I jumped to conclusions, and I was wrong."

"I guess it's because I see something in you that you don't. You're used to envisioning yourself through the eyes of your parents, Sophie. But God's eyes are different. You'll never be whole until you can picture yourself through the eyes of your heavenly Father instead of through the eyes of imperfect people."

"I want to do that, Jonathon, I really do. But it's hard."

"I know. But I'll help you if you'll let me."

I shook my head, not knowing what to say.

Jonathon looked at something behind me, and I turned my head to see Paul coming up the aisle.

"You two okay?" he asked.

"She's a little shaken," Jonathon answered, "but she'll be fine." Paul walked around and stood in front of me.

"Thank you for what you did. I want you to know that if I'd felt at any time you were in danger, I would have taken that shot."

"I know," I said. "But I'm certainly glad you didn't have to."

He sat down on the other side of me. "Donald Abbott is being transported to our office. He'll be charged with threatening Mr. Hatcher's life. We'll also check to see if he has a permit for that gun. He'll be spending some time in jail until we get this all sorted out."

"I understand," I said, "but I really feel sorry for him. He thought he was getting justice for his brother."

Paul grunted. "Justice comes from finding Terrance Chase

and putting him through the court system. It doesn't come from threatening innocent people. If he doesn't learn this lesson now, he may ruin his life. His mother doesn't need that."

What Paul said made sense, but I still felt badly for the man who was grieving for his brother. Because of this, he would probably lose his job at the prison. And it was all my fault.

"Now, I have some questions," Paul said.

I nodded.

"Who are you, Sophie? And why are you really in Sanctuary?"

CHAPTER TWENTY-THREE

I poured out the entire story. Why I was here. What I'd been looking for. I even told Paul that Jonathon and I knew each other from the past, although I didn't go into details. When I finished, he sat there looking stunned.

"Why didn't you just come to me at the beginning? You're not trained to look for criminals on the run. You almost got an innocent man shot." He glared at Jonathon. "You should have known better, Pastor. When you found out what she was up to, you should have contacted me right away."

"He wanted to." I scooted closer to Jonathon. "But I talked him out of it. I wanted to locate Chase first—or at least narrow it down to a good suspect. I was afraid I'd lose the story if I brought you in too soon." I shook my head. "It was selfish and stupid. It's been kind of a theme ever since I came to town. But I'm done. I don't think Chase is here. Martin was the only person who seemed to fit the profile. The time he came to town, the way he looks, even the way he acted.

Seems he was hiding out, all right, but not because he was Terrance Chase."

"Have we ruined things for him?" Jonathon asked Paul.

Paul glanced toward the back of the sanctuary. "No, I don't think so. To be honest, I think any real threat to Martin ended several years ago. He's still here because he wants to be." He turned back to me. "I talked to Donnie for a few minutes before they drove him away. He asked me to give you his apologies. He mentioned he felt bad about sending you those threatening notes."

"Notes?" Now Jonathon was staring at me, too. "How many were there?"

I looked away, afraid to answer.

"Why didn't you tell me?" Frustration laced his words.

"I was afraid you'd force me to call Paul."

He didn't say anything, but I could tell he was upset I hadn't told him. Add it to the list of my many mistakes.

"Look, it's over now," I vowed. "No more investigating. I'll give you everything I have, Paul. If Chase was ever here, you can track him down. Frankly, I'm beginning to believe this was a complete waste of time. I came here because of a story someone told me. No one at my paper followed the lead. They must have known how flimsy it was." I sighed and looked at Jonathon. "I still think Tom believed what he told me. Even if he was wrong. I promised him I'd try to get his sentence reduced. Telling him I lied about that will be hard. He'll be hurt and disappointed."

"Do I have your word that this is over, Sophie?" Paul said.

Turning back to Paul, I held up one hand, palm out. "Absolutely. I'm heading back to my job at the paper, and I'm going to gladly accept the assignment of reviewing restaurants. I still want to be an investigative reporter, but I'll just do my time and wait for a promotion like everyone else. Obviously, I still have a lot to learn." I looked from Paul to Jonathon. "I really wish I could do something to help Tom, though. Maybe one of these days you could visit him?"

Paul stood up. "I'll let you two sort all that out. I'm going back to the station. I'll keep you updated on what happens to Donnie." He stabbed his index finger toward Jonathon and me. "You both stay out of trouble, okay?"

"Sounds good," I said, giving him a sheepish smile. "Frankly, I need a good long nap."

Paul tried to hide a grin. "I'm sure you do."

He said good-bye and left.

"Well, you've certainly had a busy, busy day. Are you done?"

I snorted. "I certainly hope so."

Jonathon stood, reached for my hand, and pulled me to my feet. "I have a suggestion. Why don't you go home and get some rest? Then tonight, let me take you to dinner. *Not* in Sanctuary. Let's drive to Fredericktown. They have a great little Mexican restaurant. It might do you good to get out of town."

"You don't have a church service tonight?"

"Nope. We like to give members a chance to spend the rest of Sunday with their families."

"I like that idea."

He smiled. "So do I. Especially right now."

I followed Jonathon down the main aisle. "I love Mexican food, and getting out of Sanctuary for a bit sounds wonderful. I mean, I like it here, but . . ."

"You need a break?"

I laughed. "I definitely need a break."

"Good. I'll pick you up around six." He glanced down at his watch. "That will give you a little over three hours to rest."

"Maybe I'll take a catnap. Which at Esther's is easy because there are always cats around."

Jonathon gave an easy laugh at my lame joke. "Do you need me to drive you back to Esther's?"

"I'll check to see if Zac is still waiting outside. If not, I'd rather walk. A little fresh air sounds heavenly."

"Okay. I'm headed home, too."

I glanced out one of the church windows. Looked liked most of the crowd had dispersed. "You know, Jonathon, I've never asked where you live."

"The parsonage is next door."

"You mean that cute bungalow? The one with the red door?"

"Yeah, that's me. The red door wasn't my idea. Since the church owns the house, they maintain it. The last time they painted the house, I came home and discovered my door was red. I was told that red 'made it pop.' What could I say?"

I laughed. "Well, I like it. I'd love to see the inside sometime."

"Sure. But remember, I'm a man. I'll need to clean up first."

"Deal." I hesitated a moment. "Thanks, Jonathon. I mean, for walking me through this. For trying to help me. For . . . everything."

"Of course." He took my hands. "We have a lot to talk about, Sophie. I don't want to lose you . . . as a friend. And maybe as someone who might be more someday. Again, no pressure. But I'd like you to think about what you want out of life. If it's going back to St. Louis and pursuing your career, that's fine. You could still come to visit, and I can drive up to see you sometimes. I just want you to consider what happens next."

"I know. And I am. We'll talk about it more tonight, okay?"

"Okay."

I slowly pulled my hands from his and walked toward the door of the church. I was almost ready to push it open when I stopped, turned, and then ran back to Jonathon. When he saw me coming, he held out his arms, and I fell into them. He held me for quite a while. I felt warm, safe, and happy there. When I stepped back, he released me. I looked up and saw tears in his eyes. I wanted to tell him how much I loved him, but I couldn't right then. I wasn't the woman he needed in his life. But with God's help, maybe someday I would be. For now, I hoped the hug said everything I wanted to.

This time I didn't look back as I walked out of the church and onto the sidewalk. Paul was still there, and I spotted Zac, leaning against his car, obviously waiting for me. As I started toward him, a small group of people stopped me. A couple of them were strangers, but I recognized Mary and Rosey, as well as Evan Bakker.

"Is everything okay?" Mary's forehead wrinkled. "Someone told me you were inside, and I was so worried."

I held my arms away from my body to show I was unharmed. "I'm fine. Thanks, Mary."

"Martin said you thought he was some kind of famous criminal?" Rosey told me. "Terrance Chase?"

So Martin was spreading the story around town already. Great. Now everyone in Sanctuary would know the truth. Who I was and what I'd been up to.

I blushed. "Yes. But I was wrong. I feel stupid. I'm sure everyone thinks I'm an idiot—and a troublemaker."

Evan cocked his head to the side and peered at me though his thick glasses. "I don't believe anyone thinks that. For my part, I'm grateful you cared enough about justice to try to catch that man." He scratched his head. "I remember the story. He robbed something . . . was it a bank or . . . no, it was an armored car company, wasn't it?"

"Yes. In St. Louis."

"Didn't he get away with millions of dollars?" Rosey asked.

"Yes, and it was never found."

Mary's eyes gleamed with excitement. "Wouldn't it be great if it was hidden somewhere in Sanctuary? If we found it, maybe the town would get a reward."

"That would be nice. But don't go tearing up Sanctuary looking for it. I've come to the conclusion it's unlikely Chase was ever here."

"But if he was," Evan interjected, "where would he hide millions of dollars?"

I shook my head. "I actually had an idea about that, but after all the trouble I've caused so far, I have no intention of following up on it."

Mary patted my arm. "We understand, and I'm sorry things didn't turn out the way you'd hoped. Again, we're all glad you're okay. Hope you stick around our town for a while. You fit in nicely."

I was touched by her kind words. "I'm not sure anyone else feels that way, but it means a lot to me that you do."

"You'd be surprised, Emily," Evan said. "This town is very special. As are the people. Don't underestimate us, okay?"

"I'll try not to. It really is a special place, isn't it?"

Rosey slid her arm around my waist for a quick hug. "Yes, it is." She looked at me carefully as she stepped away. "You look tired. Hope you get some rest this afternoon."

"Actually, I'm headed back to Esther's right now. Then I think I'll take a nap. Not something I usually do. Tonight, Jonathon's taking me to some restaurant in Fredericktown. I guess they have good Mexican food."

Mary clapped her hands together. "Oh, they do. You'll love it. I'm so glad you're getting a night out. I hope you have a wonderful time."

"Thank you. I plan to." I said good-bye to them and walked over to where Zac waited for me.

"Have any other plans for today?" he asked, a smirk on his face. "You could blow up something. I know where there's some dynamite."

"I think I've done enough for one day." I leaned against his car, right next to him. "And it worries me that you know where dynamite is."

He cocked his head to the side. "They're dynamiting that old mine tomorrow."

I straightened. "Really? In the morning? I need to talk to Reuben. Do you know where he is?"

"He went home. Esther's over there visiting with Wynter. You can see him when he brings her home."

"Yeah. Maybe."

He put his hand up, shielding his eyes from the sun that was glaring down on us. "Reuben let me in on some of what happened. Is there something else going on?"

"Maybe. Probably not."

"Well . . . okay. You sound very positive about it."

I laughed. "I'm not. That's why I'm hesitating." I took a deep breath. "Okay, don't call me crazy, but remember what Esther said about the mine at lunch? That it was originally called the Gabriel Mine?"

"Yeah, so?"

"A source once told me he overheard a guy he thought was Terrance Chase talking on the phone, he mentioned coming to a town called Sanctuary. Then he said something about it being protected by an angel. I know it's a reach, but could he have been talking about the money? Is it possible he hid the money in the Gabriel Mine?"

"Oh, Sophie. I don't think so. People have been in and out of that mine. Kids and . . . well, other people. Surely the money would have been found by now. I mean, officials from the state have been in there, too."

"But aren't there a lot of tunnels? Even some that have already collapsed?"

"Yeah. I mean, it's not impossible. But you're still assuming Chase was ever in Sanctuary. Do you still believe that?"

I shrugged. "I'm not sure. I spent hours looking through records at the Mennonite church. Records that track the residents of Sanctuary. After all that work, I ended up with only two possibilities, and neither one of them turned out to be Chase."

"Wait a minute. What records are you talking about?"

I quickly explained what I'd been doing at the church.

"Okay, well, shouldn't you finish going through them?"

I shook my head. "I can't. Someone burned them. It's hard to believe all those details from Sanctuary's history are gone. I feel awful about it."

His eyes widened. "I heard about the fire at the Mennonite church, but I had no idea what was burned." He peered into the distance as he considered what I'd told him. "Who would have done that?"

"Nate. He was behind all of the weird stuff going on."

Zac was quiet for a moment. "I don't get it. Reuben didn't have time to explain everything."

"One of the guards shot in the robbery of that armored car company was his brother. He wanted to find Chase on his own. He already had my list of names. He took that from me earlier. Then I guess he wanted to keep me from finding any more information. I had almost everything on my laptop, though. I guess he didn't think about that."

Zac pushed himself away from the car. "Well, if that money is in the mine, six million dollars is going up in smoke tomorrow."

"Frankly, I don't care anymore." I kicked at a rock with the toe of my shoe. "I'm giving everything I have to Paul. Who knows? Maybe he can use it to find Chase. That would be awesome, wouldn't it? I'd really like to see the families of those guards get some justice."

"Yes, that would be awesome." Zac casually put his arm around me and gave me a quick hug. "You can only do what you can do. Then you've gotta let it go. Something I'm learning." He tilted his head toward his car. "Can I give you a ride back to Esther's?"

"No, thanks. I think I'll walk. Clear my head. But thanks, Zac. For everything."

He grinned. "Not sure what I did. Keeping your secret didn't last long. Seems the cat's outta the bag now."

"That's for sure. I'll give you a call and let you know when I'm back in town. We can set up that dinner. Oh, and if you'd drop that glass off at the restaurant on your way out of town, I'd appreciate it."

He waved. "Will do. Not sure how I'm going to explain that to Randi, but I'll try." He got into his car and drove away.

I started down the road. It was a little chilly, and I wished I'd brought my coat. But it didn't take long to get to Esther's. The house seemed empty with everyone gone.

By the time I got upstairs, I'd started feeling really sleepy. I was certain it was from all the stress. I set the alarm on my phone to wake me up after two hours, but when I climbed up on the bed, all I could do was lie there and stare at the ceiling. Clyde and Maizie joined me, cuddling up next to my legs. Even their gentle purring didn't lull me to sleep. I couldn't stop thinking about what Jonathon had said. What *did* I really want? I didn't know how to answer that question. I wanted to be an investigative reporter, but for some reason the desire wasn't as strong now. I was beginning to see that a job wasn't enough to make me feel like a success. My real value was in God, and in the people He put in my life. People I cared about.

"What about Jonathon, Lord?" I said aloud. "I love him so much that I want the best for him. And I'm not sure that's me. He needs some woman who can play the piano, bake cookies, and lead the women's Bible study. And that's definitely not me. How can I be selfish and ruin his life?"

The room was silent. I sighed so loudly that Maizie raised her head and stared at me.

"Sorry," I said to her. As if satisfied, she put her head down again.

It would be nice if Jesus would just walk into the room, sit down, and have a conversation with me. "I can keep it brief," I whispered. "Just a few minutes."

I was answered with silence. I hadn't really expected to hear an audible voice, but it was worth a try. "I'm not sure what to do, Lord. All I can do is count on You to lead me. I don't have the answers, so I'm just going to try to trust You to show me what to do at the right time. Thanks."

A scripture I'd heard at church once drifted into my mind. *Commit thy way unto the Lord, trust also in Him, and He shall bring it to pass.* "I guess that's what I'm doing, God. I'm committing this to You and trusting in You to work it out." As soon as I said the words, I began to feel more relaxed. When my alarm went off, I didn't even remember falling asleep.

I sat up in the bed, gently moved my feline sleeping buddies, and turned off the alarm. I went to the bathroom, refreshed my makeup, and brushed out my hair. Then I hurried back to my room and changed clothes. I picked black wool leggings, a black skirt, and a soft turquoise sweater. My dangly silver earrings and matching bracelet set off the outfit. As I pulled on my black leather boots, I thought I heard someone knock on the front door. A quick look out the window revealed Jonathon's truck out front. I quickly scribbled a note to Esther so she'd know where we were, and then I grabbed my leather jacket out of the closet and ran down the stairs.

After putting the note on the kitchen table, I flung the door open and found Jonathon standing there, a strange look on his face. Evan Bakker stood behind him. It wasn't until Jonathon stepped inside the house that I saw the gun.

CHAPTER TWENTY-FOUR

Shocked, all I could do was step back as Evan pushed Jonathon through the front door.

"Get over there and sit down," Evan barked out.

Jonathon and I obeyed, walking quickly over to the couch.

"I don't understand," I hissed. "What's happening?"

"I don't know," Jonathon said. "He met me at the door." He glared at Evan. "I don't suppose you plan to explain yourself?"

"Shut up!" Evan yelled.

"Esther could be back any minute," I said, my voice shaking. "I don't want her to walk in on this."

"Esther goes to Reuben's house every other Sunday," Evan fired back. "It's her routine. She doesn't come home until after dinner. We're not going to be here that long. Unless you force it. Then I'll have to take care of her, too. It's your choice."

I thought about the note on the kitchen table. When she read that, she wouldn't wonder about me at all. She wouldn't realize I was missing until tomorrow morning.

"Why are you doing this, Evan?" Jonathon asked. "I've known you for a long time. This doesn't make any sense."

Evan sat down in the chair across from us, his gun leveled straight at me. This was the second time I'd had to face a gun today, and I was getting tired of it.

"Surely this has nothing to do with Terrance Chase," I said. "You're not him."

"You're right," he said slowly. "I'm not him. You were so close to the truth, but you missed the most important part of the story."

"Then explain it to me."

"You were right when you guessed he came to Sanctuary. It was in 2009. After the robbery, he hid out with some friends near Kansas City for a while. Then someone told him about Sanctuary. Someone who used to live here. Sounded like the perfect place to hide, so he came here. He used the name Peter Bakker."

"Your brother?" Jonathon said, surprise written on his face.

Evan made a sound that could have been interpreted as laughter, but there was an edge of anger to it that made it unpleasant and disturbing. "Not even close. Terry used the name Bakker because of some old family friend." Evan pulled off his jacket and rolled up his sleeve. On his upper arm was a frightening tattoo. Of a snake.

"You're . . . you're Richard Osborne. The partner. The man nicknamed Snake. But I thought you were dead."

"You and everyone else. Including my so-called partner. He left me with a doctor who nursed me back from the brink. But by then, Chase was gone. He didn't bother to leave a forwarding address."

"But you found him?"

Osborne crossed his legs, still keeping the gun trained on me. "Yeah. Chase's friend in Kansas City knows my sister. After I recovered, I hid out for a while, living in two-bit dumps where no one cared who I was. When the heat died down, I went to stay with my sister in Washington, Kansas. She contacted Chase's friend, and he told Chase I was alive."

"So Chase went to Washington to see you." I couldn't believe I was finally hearing the whole story. "That's where he met Tom."

"Tom? Oh, you mean the kid who sold license tags? Yeah, that's when they got together."

"Why did you come here?" Jonathon asked.

"Chase said it was a good place to hide. And the money was here. He said he felt bad about leaving me behind and wanted to make it up to me. I think he meant it."

His innocent, geeky persona had disappeared, and I could see the hardened criminal he actually was.

"When I got here, Chase told me he'd give me half, but I told him no. I'd spent years living like a dog, hiding from the cops. I deserved a lot more. But he refused. We got in a fight, and I killed him. Didn't mean to. Not before I got my money, anyway. I just made up a story about him going back home to care for our poor old mama. My mistake was in not letting him live long enough to tell me exactly where the money was."

"You . . . you killed him?" I was horrified. "Chase is dead?"

"Well, I hope so. I threw his body down a deep shaft in that old mine outside of town. If he wasn't dead then, he certainly was after that. And then I went looking for the money. I figured it would be easy to find. But Chase messed me around again. I've never found it. The joke's on me, huh?" His toothy grin couldn't hide the cruelty in his eyes.

"If you'd gotten the money, you would have left town," Jonathon said matter-of-factly.

"Obviously. I've been stuck in this stupid, one-horse town ever since. But I'm going to get what I deserve now, aren't I, Sophie? You're going to tell me where it is."

I stared at him with my mouth open. "Is that what this is about? You've done this for nothing. I don't know where Chase hid the money."

He stood up, his face twisted into a snarl. "I was ready to walk away. After your comical attempt to find Chase ended in the church, I thought I was through with you. But then you said you had an idea where the money might be."

"Oh my goodness. An idea doesn't mean I know anything for certain."

He advanced on me with the gun. "You're going to tell me where you think it is. And if you don't"—he swung the gun toward Jonathon—"I'm going to shoot your boyfriend. You hear me?"

Fear coursed over me like a cold shower, driving all the feeling from my body. Even my lips felt numb. I tried to form words, but terror made me mumble and make noises that couldn't be understood.

"Put the gun down," Jonathon ordered. "You're scaring her. If you don't stop, you'll never find out what you want to know."

Osborne slowly lowered the gun. "Okay. Now spill it. Where is it?"

"That was you in the basement, wasn't it?" I asked. "You hit me on the head and took my notes. I thought it was Donnie."

"Yeah, it was me," he snarled. "I knew what you were up to when I saw that picture in the post office. I kept hoping you'd give up. When Pastor Troyer told me you were going through those church records, I figured out what you were looking for. I even burned the books so you wouldn't be able to find anything that pointed to me. But you still wouldn't take the hint."

I took a deep breath and tried to slow down my breathing. My heart pounded so hard it felt as if it would jump out of my chest. "I—I only thought . . . I mean, Tom said he heard Chase on the phone, talking to someone. He . . . he mentioned Sanctuary, and he said . . ."

"It was protected by an angel."

I gulped in surprise. "Yes. That's it."

"That was me on the phone. But I couldn't ever figure out what he was talking about. I figured he got religion."

I shook my head. "Look, today at the restaurant, we were talking about the mine outside of town. Someone mentioned the original name of the mine. It was called the Gabriel Mine. See what I mean? I just wondered if he might have been referring to the mine. Maybe he hid the money somewhere in the mine."

Osborne's jaw dropped. "I've been in that mine several times. I never saw any money."

"There are a lot of tunnels inside," Jonathon interjected. "I doubt seriously that you searched them all."

Osborne nodded, as if coming to some conclusion. "You're right. The money's probably been there all this time. I've been tearing Chase's house and yard apart. And checking every spot I could think of in the post office. I—I never thought about the mine. It's so public."

"But it's not," Jonathon said. "We do everything we can to keep it closed because it's unsafe. Actually, it's the perfect place to hide something." His eyes widened. "Look, if you're thinking about searching that mine before they blow it up tomorrow morning, forget it. There are spots inside already collapsing. And most of the supports have been removed. It's way too dangerous. You could die. Is it really worth it?"

"Is it worth six million dollars?" Osborne laughed maniacally. "Yes, it's worth it." He backed up a bit, the gun still pointed at us. "I've been stuck in this town all these years because I was determined to get what I'm owed. I'm not giving up now."

"You accidentally killed Terrance Chase, a notorious thief and murderer," Jonathon said. "There's still hope for you. Why don't you give yourself up? You've been a model citizen in Sanctuary for several years. You might be surprised by the light sentence you could get."

Osborne's expression tightened. "You don't get out of prison for killing three people."

"Th-three people?" I stammered. "*You* killed the guards?"

"While Terry went to get the money, I shot them. First up was the one who was supposed to let us in. He wimped out and tried to call for help. When I shot him, the other guard shot me. Almost killed me. I shot him just as Terry came back. That guard just wouldn't give up. He fired off one more shot before he kicked the bucket. Hit Terry in the arm. Boy, Terry was mad. He didn't want anyone to die. He was weak, but I'm not. I went in there knowing we had to clean house. Especially the guy who wanted out. He knew our names. He would have turned us in."

I didn't know what to say. I realized in that moment that Osborne planned to kill Jonathon and me.

Osborne looked at his watch. "We need to get going."

"Get going?" I said. "Where?"

He pointed the gun at Jonathon. "You're going to drive your truck to the mine. I'll be right behind you. With her. If you do anything funny, I'll kill her. Then I'll come after you. You understand?"

"You're going to kill us anyway," I said. I sounded calm, but I didn't feel that way inside. I'd just begun to find something in my life. Something wonderful. And this criminal was about to take it away.

"I'm not going to kill you," he said. "I'll leave you tied up inside the mine. When I have the money, and I'm far enough away, I'll call and tell someone where you are."

I knew he was lying, and from the look on Jonathon's face, he knew it, too.

"Now get up."

It was clear to me that if we got in those cars, we wouldn't be coming back. In my mind, I cried out to God for help. Jonathon and I were walking toward the front door when I suddenly heard a screech that sounded like something from another world. I turned to see Clyde streak out of the room as if he were being chased by demons. Obviously, he'd gotten under Osborne's feet, and Osborne had stepped on Clyde's tail.

I took that moment of distraction to fling myself at the gun, trying to grab it out of Osborne's hand. As I yanked it away, Jonathon tackled him, throwing him to the floor. Osborne began to fight back, striking Jonathon in the face. I began to pray. If I had to shoot Osborne to save Jonathon,

I would. But I knew it would haunt Jonathon forever, so I decided to give him every chance to subdue Osborne without me pulling the trigger. Finally, after Jonathon landed a few good punches, Osborne was unconscious.

"Get something to tie him up with, Sophie!" Jonathon yelled. "And give me that stupid gun!"

I handed him the weapon, glad to get rid of it. Then I ran upstairs and grabbed some scarves and a couple of belts out of my luggage. I hurried back down the stairs, taking two steps at a time until I reached Jonathon. Together, we trussed up Osborne so tightly, there was no way he could get loose.

"Call Paul," Jonathon instructed me, still training the gun on the hog-tied criminal. He rattled off the number while I dialed. When Paul answered, I tried to explain the situation to him without sounding insane. I must have done a reasonable job because he promised to be right over. When I disconnected, I slumped down on the couch and cried, waiting for Paul to arrive. My tears were tears of relief and thanksgiving to God for hearing my prayers. Who knew He would use a cat named Clyde to save our lives?

CHAPTER TWENTY-FIVE

A week later, Jonathon and I sat at a table in The Oil Lamp, having breakfast. The authorities had recovered Terrance Chase's body from the mine. They'd searched as much as they could for the money, but it wasn't found. There were smaller tunnels that had already caved in. It was highly likely the money was in one of them. But trying to recover it was just too dangerous.

There weren't many people in the restaurant this morning. Most of them were out near the site of the old mine, moved back to a safe distance, while they waited for the mine to be blown up. I was certain Sarah Miller and Paul were there. Esther had told me about Sarah almost losing her life inside that mine. Seeing it destroyed would be cathartic for both of them. But I just wanted to move on. The mine didn't mean anything to me. Frankly, I was grateful for the quiet this morning. I'd said good-bye to almost everyone and planned to slip out of town unnoticed. Leaving Esther had been really difficult. Her prediction had been right. I believed with all my heart that God had sent me to Sanctuary. I was leaving with much more than I'd planned on. My article had been written and turned in. It didn't work out quite the way I thought it would, but in the end, I had found Terrance Chase. My story was on the front page, and my editor had told me when I got back, we needed to talk. I was pretty sure an offer would come. One that would give me everything I'd wanted. Oddly, in the end, that thought didn't make me as happy as I'd once believed it would.

My editor agreed to contact the authorities in Kansas to see what could be done to help Tom. I couldn't be sure it would do any good, but at least I was able to keep my promise to him. I'd talked to him on the phone. He was fine, although finding out his friend Donnie had arranged for him to be beaten up was hard on him. The sharp-faced guard who'd helped Donnie carry out his plan had been fired. Of course, Donnie had lost his job, as well, but other than that, he would probably get off lightly due to the circumstances. I really hoped so.

Most importantly, I was happy that Donnie and his family could get some satisfaction knowing that the man who killed their brother and son was going to prison. And I prayed that finding out that, at the end, their loved one had tried to do the right thing would give them some comfort, too. Of course, the family of the other guard would have closure now, as well. Those outcomes made everything worth it.

I'd just taken a sip of coffee when the ground shook slightly.

"There it goes," Jonathon said. "That ends it, I hope."

"Unless the story gets out that there might be six million dollars buried underground."

"I think we'll keep that to ourselves. I'm glad you didn't say anything about it in your story."

"I think Sanctuary has had enough attention lately. Having a bunch of people digging holes around the mine isn't something you need. Besides, I'm still not sure the money was in there. Chase could have done anything with it. We may never know."

"You're right about that."

Another small shaking signaled the second blast. There were supposed to be three. I downed the rest of my coffee. I wanted to be gone before everyone headed back.

"I'm going to miss you." Jonathon fastened his incredible blue eyes on me.

"I'm going to miss you, too, but I'll be back soon. My editor is giving me an extra two weeks of vacation since I worked during this one. I'll be here in May. We'll have lots of time together. We can sort out everything then."

He leaned toward me. "Unless you get so enamored with your new job you decide you're too important to spend any time in a small hick town."

"Sanctuary isn't a hick town," I shot back. "I love it here. This place—and you—changed me."

He smiled. "I'd rather think that we helped you to become the person you were always meant to be."

I stared down at my coffee cup. Was he right? More than anything, I'd wanted to become an important person. Someone people looked up to. I'd worked hard to get rid of the dirty, ignorant girl from Kingdom. But instead of banishing her, I'd begun to care about her. To have compassion for her. As ashamed as I'd been about my past, I was beginning to embrace it. That girl was part of me. Someone Jonathon had cared about. Someone God had loved. Although I still had a lot of healing to do, I knew God and I would get through it together.

"I should get going. They'll all be back soon."

He reached over and took my hand. "I'll miss you."

I smiled. "You already said that."

"I know."

As prepared as I was to leave, I realized it would be harder than I'd anticipated. "Everything will work out. You'll see."

"If you say so."

"You really think I'm going to fall in love with my new job and forget about you?"

He didn't say anything, just looked at me.

"I won't. You'll just have to trust me."

"Okay."

I pulled my hand away. "Walk me to my car?"

"Sure."

He picked up our ticket, and we went up to the cash register by the door. Maxie met us there. She took the ticket and stuck it on a metal spike sitting on the counter.

"It's on us. Randi said not to charge you. It's our going-away present."

"But I'm not going," Jonathon said. "Let me pay for mine."

Maxie shook her head. "Nope. Randi would chew me out royally if you paid a penny. What Randi says goes around here."

Jonathon chuckled. "I can believe that."

"Thank you, Maxie," I said. "I'm going to miss the good food here—and the good company. Would you say good-bye to Mary and Rosey when you see them?"

She nodded. "They closed up so they could see the mine blow up. Randi considered it, but she and I didn't care about it much. Figured we'd stay here and serve the customers who don't like explosions."

"I'm glad you did. Great breakfast."

"I'm happy you liked it. You take care, honey. And come back soon, okay? I know this man will miss you a great deal."

I waved and walked out the door into a clear, crisp March morning. Had it really only been two weeks since I'd driven into this town? In that short amount of time, everything in my life had been turned upside down.

I opened the car door and swung around to gaze up at Jonathon. The look on his face made my chest hurt. I reached up and stroked his cheek.

"I want to kiss you, but I won't," he said, his voice breaking. "Someday, I hope you'll ask me to."

I stood on my tiptoes and kissed him softly. This time there was no fear. All I felt was love. The ground shook one more time. "Either that was one great kiss, or they just set off the last blast," I said with a smile.

Jonathon laughed. "Both, I think."

"Who knew that one day Jonathon Wiese and Sophie Wittenbauer from Kingdom, Kansas, would fall in love?"

The corners of Jonathon's lips curved upward. "God knew."

People would be heading back to town any minute. I turned away and got into my car, closing the door. "I'll call you when I get home," I said through the open window.

"I'll be waiting."

It took almost everything inside me to put the car in gear

and drive away. When I reached the main road outside of town, I could see cars coming from the other direction. I turned and drove down the road leading to St. Louis, glad I wouldn't have to say good-bye to anyone else.

Wanting some music, I turned on the stereo. Immediately, my positive affirmations began to play. I hit the button to eject the CD. The system made a whirring noise, and the CD popped out. I picked it up and flung it out the window. I didn't have any further use for it.

I turned on the radio, and a song I knew came on. John Denver. He began to sing about country roads taking him home. When he reached the part about the radio reminding him of a home he should have reached yesterday, I pulled over and stopped the car.

Then with a smile, I turned around and headed home.

ACKNOWLEDGMENTS

My thanks to my Inner Circle for their support and encouragement: Mary Gessner, Tammy Pendergast-Lagoski, Lynne Young, Zac Weikel, Michelle Durben, Michell Prince Morgan, Karla Hanns, Shirley Blanchard, Elizabeth "Liz" Dent, Tara Jo Banks, Bonnie Traher, Mary Shipman, Rhonda Nash-Hall, Cheryl Baranski, and JoJo Sutis. God bless you all for your support and prayers.

As always, thank you to my friends and editors at Bethany House. Working with you is a privilege.

ABOUT THE AUTHOR

Nancy Mehl is the author of twenty-one books, including the ROAD TO KINGDOM and FINDING SANCTUARY series. She received the ACFW Mystery Book of the Year Award in 2009. She has a background in social work and is a member of ACFW and RWA. Nancy writes from her home in Missouri, where she lives with her husband, Norman, and their Puggle, Watson. Visit www.nancymehl.com to learn more.

More From Nancy Mehl

Visit nancymehl.com for a full list of Nancy's books.

Don't miss Wynter's and Sarah's stories!
The small, primarily Mennonite town of Sanctuary, Missouri, is something of a refuge. In this private community, many secrets dwell undetected. As three young women investigate mysteries centered here, each will unknowingly put her life—and her heart—in jeopardy.

FINDING SANCTUARY: *Gathering Shadows, Deadly Echoes, Rising Darkness*

As the Mennonite town of Kingdom, Kansas, is plagued by strange incidents and attacks, three young women have their community and their faith in God tested to the limits. Will they all survive the dangerous road ahead?

ROAD TO KINGDOM: *Inescapable, Unbreakable, Unforeseeable*

BETHANYHOUSE

Stay up-to-date on your favorite books and authors with our free e-newsletters. Sign up today at bethanyhouse.com.

Find us on Facebook. facebook.com/bethanyhousepublishers

Free exclusive resources for your book group! bethanyhouse.com/anopenbook